Louise Harwood is the bestselling author of *Lucy Blue, Where Are You?* and *Calling on Lily*. She is a full-time writer, and lives in Oxfordshire with her husband and two sons.

HIPPY CHICK

Ibiza: paradise for the clubbers, hedonists and sun-seekers, but for Honey Ballantyne it is the only home she has ever known. With the responsibility of running a hotel on her shoulders, and two hippy-dippy parents whose idea of a hard day's work is a yoga class without their clothes on, Honey feels trapped. When her first love, Edouard, returns to the island from London and truths about her parents start to unravel, Honey is forced to realize that before she can make decisions about her future she must reconcile herself with the past . . .

Books by Louise Harwood
Published by The House of Ulverscroft:

CALLING ON LILY
LUCY BLUE, WHERE ARE YOU?

LOUISE HARWOOD

HIPPY CHICK

Complete and Unabridged

ULVERSCROFT
Leicester

First published in Great Britain in 2007 by
Pan Books
an imprint of Pan Macmillan Ltd
London

First Large Print Edition
published 2008
by arrangement with
Pan Macmillan Ltd
London

British Library CIP Data

Harwood, Louise
Hippy chick.—Large print ed.—
Ulverscroft large print series: general fiction
1. Ibiza Island (Spain)—Fiction
2. Large type books
I. Title
823.9'2 [F]

ISBN 978–1–84782–326–7

Published by
F. A. Thorpe (Publishing)
Anstey, Leicestershire
Set by Words & Graphics Ltd.
Anstey, Leicestershire
Printed and bound in Great Britain by
T. J. International Ltd., Padstow, Cornwall

This book is printed on acid-free paper

This is a work of fiction and is the production of the author's imagination.
Any relationship with real events, places or people is entirely coincidental. That said, most of the places referred to in the book do exist, although Santa Medea does not and I have taken liberties with the layout of the beach at Cala Mastella too.
Throughout I have chosen to use the Spanish names rather than the Catalan, although both are used on the island.

For my brother, Charlie

Acknowledgements

Not surprisingly, Ibiza was a magical place to research, made all the better by beautiful Can Marias, my brother's house on the island (thank you, Charlie). But better still by the many friends I have made there who helped me so much with this book. Most of all I would like to thank Clare Bloomer and Toni Guasch, Victoria Durrer-Gasse and Hilly Shields, for all their advice and insights, and without whom Ibiza would be nowhere near such fun. And many thanks too to Kristiina and Jaume Guasch at the incomparable Atzarõ, and to Tina Cutler, whose vivid and wonderful memories of growing up on the island proved invaluable.

Back in England I was comforted and tied down to my desk by my always perfect husband Ant, and by Tom and Jack too. Thanks as always to you. And thanks too to my many friends who tramped Ditch Edge Lane and Brancaster beach with me, especially Karen Heron, Caroline Seely, Sarah Walker, Candida Crewe, J. B. Miller and Victoria Pougatch, all of whom valiantly kept on listening at the early stages of the book and helped me through to the point where at least I knew what I wanted to write.

And huge thanks, as always, to the sales, marketing and publishing team at Pan Macmillan, especially to Trisha Jackson, Steph Sweeney, Liz Cowen and of course to my wonderful editor, Imogen Taylor. And finally thank you to my agent, Araminta Whitley, who always knows exactly when to prod, reassure, inspire or calm me down. I'm very lucky to have her.

1

Ibiza

Hughie Ballantyne took a quick sharp breath and raised his arms out wide. At the other end of the pool the woman was lying on her sunbed, one tanned leg bent at the knee, a lazy finger now running tantalizingly along the elastic edge of her bikini bottoms. Then, as if she'd heard him, she lifted her sunglasses high off her nose and smiled at him and he knew he'd got her. He looked up at the sky and rose to her challenge, clasping the edge of the pool with his toes, swaying slightly on the balls of his feet.

Skirting the olive trees on her way to the pool, Honey froze as she saw what he was about to do, and then she could only watch as her father launched himself into his swallow dive, his pigeon chest straining forwards so that for long seconds he hung suspended, motionless against the empty blue sky. It was only when he smacked into the water that she finally started to run, wine leaping free from the open bottle in her hand, marking her

1

passage in spreading splashes across the limestone tiles. '*Dad*,' she yelled, her voice cutting through the gentle chatter of the hotel guests. '*Dad!*' And she ran to the edge of the pool, kicking off her flip-flops, leaped into the water and swam towards where her father had disappeared, grabbed a breath and ducked under, reaching forwards through the sudden silence with her hands. Then, within a few seconds, she was wrapping her arms around his waist, kicking them both back to the surface, bursting through the water into the brilliant sunshine with his enormous weight in her arms.

'Sweetheart, what has he done?'

'Is he dead?'

'Oh, Jesus, look at the blood.'

'Stupid fucker. How much has he had to drink?'

She started to drag him towards the voices gathered at the edge of the pool, but suddenly his bulk burst back into life and he pushed himself to his feet, then stood waist deep, swaying in the water, staring at the line of people watching him.

But now that they could see he was all right, that this dive into the Can Falco swimming pool was just another Hughie-mishap to be logged alongside the many, many others, people were even starting to laugh.

'Nul point,' she heard someone chuckle.

'Oh, much too harsh! I thought he was rather good.'

'Come on, Hugh-boy, let's help you out.'

He staggered silently on towards the steps while Honey followed a few paces behind, watching as he tripped up the first one and then allowed himself to be hoisted from the water by his friends.

She climbed out after him, wringing out her skirt, wiping her face with her hand.

'Dad?'

He turned at her touch, water streaming off him, blood dripping freely from his nose.

'Deep end good, shallow end bad.' She smiled at him, wiping the water from his face and gently smoothing back his hair. He was shuddering with shock. 'OK?' She peered closer at the shape of his nose and the smile turned to a wince. 'Are you? Can you tell if you've broken it?' He stared back at her with wild unfocused eyes. 'You know what? We might have to take you to hospital.'

Someone came forwards and dropped a heavy towel around his shoulders. A clean white *bath* towel, she couldn't help noticing, hoping he wouldn't get blood all over it.

'Let's go inside.'

She reached forwards and gently took his hand, but at her touch he suddenly cried out.

'Rachel!'

She was aware how everyone around them fell silent at the same time.

'No, Honey.' She said it quietly, trying to coax him away. 'Please, come and get dry.'

'Rachel!' This time it came out softly, full of wonder. 'Rachel! You can't be here.'

'Oh, Dad, for God's sake shut up.'

'Has Tora seen you?' He turned guiltily. 'Where's Tora?'

'She's got a class. Come on, beer-for-brains, you've hit your head. You've got concussion. You need to lie down.'

He looked back at the pool, then down at the blood-spattered stone at his feet. 'I'm sorry.'

'Don't worry about it. It was an accident. Claudio will clear it up. Come on, nobody minds.'

'You look beautiful.'

Behind her she heard someone laugh. Hughie heard it too and in answer he took a deep sobbing breath and fell dramatically to his knees, wrapping his arms around her legs.

'Let me go,' she whispered, patting his wet head.

'But I've been waiting to tell you.'

'Shut up, Dad. Stand up.'

Concern at what he might say next made it difficult to speak gently. Who was she, this

Rachel? Ex-girlfriend, or a current one? She'd never heard any mention of her, this Rachel . . .

Her father looked up at her pleadingly, still hanging on to her soaking wet skirt. 'Don't be angry. Oh yes, be angry. But hear me now, for God's sake, please, listen to me now. I'm saying sorry, Rachel, please.'

She glanced around at the captivated faces of his friends. They were used to devil-may-care Hughie, mad and bad and sometimes even dangerous to know, exuberant and noisy, as quick to cry as he was to laugh, but this was different and they knew it. And Honey did not want to share any more of it with them.

She bent her head to his ear and said in a whisper that only he could hear, 'Come inside with me now, without saying another word, and then I'll tell you why I'm here.'

'I'm taking him in.' She stood back up. 'Find him some dry clothes and a bandage . . . and a hospital.' She touched his shoulder. 'We'll go inside. You do know where we are, Can Falco? Home, yes?' Wide-eyed incomprehension stared back at her.

She picked a towel for herself off an empty sunbed and slung it over her shoulders, then walked him carefully away. He came with her docilely, allowing himself to be threaded between the wooden sunbeds that had been turned haphazardly by guests following the afternoon sun, muttering to himself as they moved up the gentle flights of stone steps and pathways that took them away from the pool and through the terraces, winding them on between the almond and orange trees, past his own cottage and hers too, and finally on to the main house itself.

As they arrived she saw with relief that Claudio was there ahead of them, halfway up a ladder, pinning a huge branch of purple bougainvillea back to the sugar-white wall. Twenty years old and with them at the hotel on a placement from the University of Palma, he was trustworthy, completely unflappable and right now exactly the person she needed. He turned as she came nearer and she caught his eye and went straight on, not wanting her father to break the momentum of walking, and immediately she heard Claudio rattling down the ladder behind them. She propelled her father towards the last flight of steps and then took him through a stone archway and out of the heat of the sun into a cool and shady courtyard that led them through the front door of the hotel — an arched and ancient studded door, wide open now — and then on into the front hall. She was taking a chance bringing him in here — regular guests would most likely take the sight of a raving and bloody-nosed Hughie in their stride, but new arrivals might not . . .

'You are taking your father to the hospital?' Claudio asked as he moved smoothly on to the reception desk at the far end.

She nodded. 'But I think I should find Tora first.' She said it quietly, not wanting to upset her father. 'Keep an eye on him while I look for her?'

'Your mother has a class in the Garden of Serenity.' He was rapidly opening and shutting drawers as he spoke, pulling out bottles, boxes of plasters and mosquito repellent, until he found what he wanted.

'Now then,' he said, coming around to Hughie with a large wad of cotton wool in his hand and placing it firmly on the bridge of Hughie's nose, 'Hold on to that.' He led Hughie over to a window seat and pushed him gently down, then squatted beside him, looking relaxed and in control in his immaculate white T-shirt and baggy brown shorts, leather flip-flops on his long brown feet. 'Are you OK? You'll feel better soon, I'm sure.'

Hughie shook his head but then his familiar wide-mouthed grin slowly broke across his face.

'Never felt better than Tora.'

7

Claudio nodded back benignly, misunderstanding or not quite hearing what Hughie had said.

'Sixty-nine and ninety-six, on the beach, in the sea, upside down, back to front. You name it, we did it.' Hughie produced such a brilliantly shocked look on Claudio's face that Honey couldn't help herself letting out a great snort of laughter, but then her father turned at the sound and again started in surprise at the sight of her.

'Rachel? Christ alive, it can't be you!'

This time she decided to ignore him. She put out a hand and helped Claudio to his feet. 'Don't worry. He hit his head on the bottom of the pool. He's concussed.'

Claudio smiled with obvious relief. 'Of course.'

'So don't expect him to talk any sense.'

'The doctors will bring the old Mr Ballantyne back, I'm sure.'

'I don't think I'll ever be so pleased to see him.'

She went and crouched at his side and took his shaking hand in hers.

'Honeybee, that's the name you gave me, you and your equally mad wife. It's Honeybee, look at me!' She came closer, aware of the plea in her voice. 'Do you still not know me at all?'

He shook his head, retreating into his chair, then pulled his hands free and covered his face and she found she could no longer look at him either. She was used to seeing him weepy and sentimental. She'd seen him distraught when he'd accidentally shot Bugger, his dog, and sufficiently off his face to walk naked through a packed restaurant in Ibiza town, but even then he'd somehow retained a degree of style and self-control, had never been as hopeless as he was now.

She pushed herself back to her feet. 'It's every time he looks at me . . . I don't know what to do with him.'

Claudio nodded, then touched her shoulder sympathetically. 'We will fetch him some dry clothes and I will just pick up my car keys . . . ' — he returned swiftly to the desk, opened another drawer — 'And my wallet . . . ' He closed the drawer again. 'And I will take him to the hospital and you will wait for your mother to finish her class. Yes? And then you can come to the hospital later and I will be here to check in our guests. And you needn't worry, not about anything at all. And tonight, you must take time with your daddy, yes? For once you take the evening off. You must stay with your daddy if you need to.'

'Thank you,' she agreed with relief, 'that would make all the difference in the world.'

She touched her father's bent head. 'I'll follow as soon as I can. I promise. Will you go with Claudio now?'

Claudio put a hand under her father's elbow and half coaxed, half pulled him to his feet and Hughie allowed himself to be turned and then led away, only stopping once in the doorway irritably to shake himself free of Claudio's arm.

As they made their way through the hotel towards the door that led out to the car park she found herself walking slowly along behind, keeping far enough back for them not to be aware she was there. And eventually the tall rangy figure of Claudio and her grey-haired, shuffling father reached the doors and then walked back into the hot dry sunshine of a late-August afternoon, Claudio keeping his hand beneath her father's elbow to support and gently guide him forwards. And then, finally, the two of them turned a corner and disappeared from sight.

Honey came back into the hall, held her head in frustration, thought about banging it against the wall, and instead went to straighten the cushions on the window seat where her father had been sitting. Then she moved on to her desk and her chair and sat down, as if by tapping at her computer she could somehow take control of everything that had happened. Perhaps she should go back to the pool and reassure everybody, tell them how Hughie had forgotten 'Rachel' as fast as he'd conjured her up? She could laugh it all off — of course her father's hallucination would be a beautiful woman, what else? But she didn't want to go back down there, to face the laughter or, even worse, the silence of a gang closing ranks, a gang who probably knew exactly who Rachel was but weren't going to tell her.

With her chin in her hands she watched the fine cotton curtains billow in and out, in and out, at the four-hundred-year-old windows, making dancing shadows on the polished stone floor. Out there, in the Garden of Serenity, her mother's class would be nearing its end. In her sexy rasping voice that six years of relatively clean living hadn't softened at all, Tora would be preparing her little flock to face the world once more. *Breathe in and breathe out again. Feel the joy in your veins, hear the laughter in your ears.*

But clearly there were to be no joy and laughter winging their way towards Tora. Whoever Rachel was she clearly mattered to her father and somehow Honey knew that all the undoubtedly messy, sad, private details were going to come out now. Honey remembered how everybody had drawn back

11

when her father had shouted Rachel's name, embarrassed by the desperation in his voice. *Had* they realized who he was talking about? Did they know all those messy details? She pictured them, her father's friends, his motley crew, crumpled and creased from decades of too much sun and wild living. With insouciant style the men would sit together on the edge of the pool at tea-time, mingling with the other guests yet completely apart, feet dangling in the water, knobbly nut-brown knees all in a line as they ate their little lemon meringue pies and ordered endless rounds of tea that they'd never dream of paying for, talking their way through the sunny after-noons. This lot shared her parents' history. They'd been in Ibiza for over thirty years. They surely knew everything about Hughie. So what was it that they'd be saying about Rachel now? Were they talking about how much he loved her? The thought sent a shaft of sadness running through her because that was perhaps the worst of it — not that there was another woman, but that she had the power to make him cry.

And, at least as powerful as the sadness, there was irritation too. No, more than irritation, a real red-blooded anger that had burst into life as she'd watched his typically flashy, typically irresponsible dive. Of course he'd choose the shallow end. Of course she'd be on hand to jump in afterwards, to fish him out and patch him up. And now he'd presented her with 'Rachel' to contend with too, and that made her angrier still, not just with Hughie but also with her mother, Tora, for letting it happen, for being so away with the fairies that reality barely figured at all. Because if Tora had not been quite so self-obsessed, Rachel — whoever she was — would surely not have got a look-in.

So, at that moment, Honey wanted to tell her mother everything that had happened. She wanted to see the news of Rachel slap the rapt smile off Tora's face. She wanted a reaction, wanted to see her mother hurting and remorseful. Even better, she wanted to see her jealous. She wanted her taking control for once, driving to that hospital in a cloud of dust and fury, ready to fight for Hughie and prove after all these years that she did still care for her family and husband after all.

And then, perhaps, Honey would be free. Not completely, not forever, but just enough to walk out of the hotel without always having to call in someone to cover for her. Free to jump into her car on the spur of the moment, perhaps drive to a beach, somewhere small and unknown where she would strip off and spend the whole day sunbathing and swimming and rediscovering Ibiza, the island of freedom and love that for her had become an island of bills and broken boilers, bounced cheques and demanding guests, power surges that blew the electrics, water shortages, stroppy chefs and nymphomaniac waitresses. An island where, centre stage, stood her feckless, unfaithful father and her beautiful butterfly of a mother, who had left their daughter to shoulder Can Falco all on her own while they drifted through their days on a sweet-scented breeze of marijuana and patchouli oil, just as they always had, just as they always would do, with no sense of her increasing loneliness, and absolutely no understanding of how relentless running Can Falco could be.

Honey pictured her mother as she would be now, sitting in the Garden of Serenity — her perfect rectangular garden carpeted with the softest, greenest grass, protected by high hedges of jasmine and lavender, at the far end a massive stone fountain carved in the shape of a pair of cupped hands, gently spilling water. The hands were so huge it was possible to climb up and lie back inside them, and listen to music through speakers bored into their fingertips. Her mother could spend hours lying there contemplating the world. But now, nearing the end of her class, she would be sitting crosslegged on the grass, facing her pupils, palms turned upwards as she cast a last, loving look around their rapt faces.

And standing wearily up to go and find her, Honey knew that she had been conditioned by too many years of calming and reassuring to hurt her mother now. Her role was to act as a buffer between Tora and the nasty world outside, it wasn't to make things worse. She would go and find her and she would tell her about the accident and perhaps even mention Rachel's name, just to prepare the way in case it came up later, but in a breezy, light-hearted kind of a way so that her mother would instantly forget it. And then she would drive to the hospital and see her father and find out exactly what he'd been up to.

2
A Week Earlier

'You know you want to.'

Edouard Bonnier was on the other side of Honey's desk, leaning in towards her on the flats of his hands, messing up all the invoices and letters that lay in orderly piles in front of her, certain he was going to get what he wanted, eventually.

'Let Claudio run things. Tell him you're having some time off.'

'I do take time off. It's just I don't like spending it with you.'

Edouard didn't flinch and she looked back at him steadily, her own hands folded neatly in her lap. 'OK, not you, your noisy, ugly, loud-mouthed friends.'

'Honeybee, I'm hurt.'

'But they were a bunch of wankers weren't they?'

'It's bankers, Bee, bankers.' He was still smiling but she knew that she'd rattled him. 'And you didn't give them a chance. They weren't so bad. They hadn't left work behind,

16

that's all.' He pushed himself away from her desk. 'And I've already said I'm sorry that they danced on the table.'

'And poured hundreds of pounds' worth of wine in each other's hair?'

'Yes, and paid for it too. We went through all this last weekend. Do we have to do it again now?'

She shook her head.

'You know the strangest thing is they loved you. Took one look at your dirty feet and your toe rings and thought they'd found themselves their very own hippy. Obviously they hadn't expected you to be so bad-tempered but they still loved you.'

He went over to the window, looking out at the early-evening sun, and she stared at his broad pinstriped shoulders, his flight bag at his feet, and wondered why it was that she always had to try to knock him down.

'So,' she went on. 'Here we are on a Friday night again. Have you brought some more? Are they up at El Figo right now, waiting for you to take them out on the town? We can't look after them here tonight, we don't like plate smashing at Can Falco.'

She imagined him driving up to his beautiful house, stripping off his stripy shirt and diving into his spectacular navy blue swimming pool, joining his horrible friends, who turned him into one of them.

'That's why I want *you* to come to El Figo.'

'You'd like me to entertain them?'

'Yes.' He didn't turn back from the window. 'So put some flowers in your hair and bring your guitar.'

She laughed. 'That's what they'd expect, after all. And you know I haven't got a guitar.'

He came back to her desk, leaned in on her once more. 'So borrow one.' And she was glad to see that he hadn't minded what she'd said after all, that his eyes were warm and full of fun, so much the old Edouard that she nearly held out her hands for him to pull her to her feet.

But he kissed her briefly on the cheek, then stepped back, picked up his bag and hitched it over his shoulder.

'Imagine how impressed they'd be, the most beautiful girl in Ibiza turning up at my little party. If you change your mind, you know I'll be there. And you should give them a chance because this time I think you'd like them . . . I think you'd be pleased you came.' He paused, frowned, thought about it, 'Or perhaps, maybe not.'

And he was out of the door before she'd decided how to respond.

She didn't watch him go. Instead she spun on her chair and went back to her computer, forgetting about him as she checked emails and worked her way through the staff lists for the weekend, then moved on to the details of guests arriving that evening, double-checking them against the rooms that had been booked for them. Friday night, end of August. They'd been full almost every night since May and she could still see no sign of demand slacking off, even now, nearing autumn. The emails requesting rooms were flooding in every day. She sent off her regretful replies, thinking how the hotel could double, treble in size and she'd still fill every room. For a season at least, or perhaps even two, until she finally died of exhaustion, keeling over in the middle of the hall as she welcomed her ten thousandth guest through the door.

When she made her routine call to Ibiza airport she heard there'd been a six-hour delay on the flight from Gatwick, which meant she'd be staying up until three or four in order to check in the last guests. She ran her finger down the arrivals list and saw it was a family, chasing the late rays of sunshine before the start of the new school year and long winter back in England. Not the best of starts then, for them. Altogether there were fourteen guests arriving that evening: two families of four, a honeymoon couple booked in for a fortnight, and two couples out for the week.

At about six her mother appeared, floating down the hallway in a gauzy see-through kaftan and bikini bottoms. She put her finger to her lips and gave Honey a wide berth, sending her a beam of a smile but not pausing and certainly not speaking because, for Tora, the first Friday of every month was always a silent day.

For her father, on the other hand, Fridays were always extremely noisy days, days to be exuberantly celebrated as the end of the working week — by Hughie, who had hardly done a full day's work in his life. Honey could hear the boom of his laughter from the bar.

And yet, without lifting more than an occasional finger to summon a bottle of wine, a great deal of the success of Can Falco was down to them. Honey had lost count of the times she had been told by enthusiastic and well-meaning guests how her priceless parents had made their holiday. Invariably they would go on to tell Honey in confiding whispers how special it was, in a world so tainted by greed and commercialism, to find somewhere like Can Falco; what a joy to be able to recapture something of their own hippy pasts. It was then that Honey wished she could check them into just that, an un-modernized bedroom, in a hippy chic Can Falco from the seventies — the derelict finca she'd been born in — complete with rats, no running water and no electricity, at the end of a two-mile dirt track that wound so steeply up into the hills that even a donkey and cart struggled to manage the climb.

Of course the truth was that these guests liked goose-down pillows and crisp cotton sheets, air-conditioning, power showers, imaginative and beautifully cooked food, carefully polished terracotta floors, colourful drapes and ancient furniture, but they would only have mentioned them if they hadn't been there. What guests remembered when they got back home afterwards, what they wanted to tell their friends about, was the delight of having Hughie and Tora as hosts because, although they'd never acknowledge it, even to themselves, Hughie and Tora made them feel rather raffish and fun. Through Hughie and Tora they could recapture a youth they'd never really known in the first place. And for all his noisy ineptitude Hughie had a gentleness and rare kindness about him that nurtured them and made them blossom; while Tora, for all her earnest chatter about Zoroastrianism and atomic essences, did indeed seem lit from the inside with a kind of radiance. And so, between the two of them, without trying at all, they gave people exactly what they were looking for and just what they'd hoped to find.

Then there were the other, mostly younger, guests who smiled politely at the way Tora and Hughie treated Can Falco as their own private hotel — which, of course, it was — but were much more interested in Honey. She knew what they saw because they told her all the time. To them she was the smiling, sun-kissed Ibiza girl, free from the cares of the world, gold from the sun, glowing with the good life, the spirit of Can Falco. And they came back to see her time and time again, hypnotized by the near-perfect escapism of what she'd created there. After city fumes and skyscrapers, here they opened their windows in the morning and breathed in the scent of the pine forests, looked out over the spectacular view of the sea, or up into the flawless sky to watch the eagles that gave Can Falco its Catalan name circling lazily above their heads. They came for nights at Pacha and Privilege and Bambuddha Grove, to watch the sunset on Benirras beach, have dinner at La Paloma, sunbathe with the supermodels on Aguas Blancas, or simply to stay put and sleep and swim or wander lazily through the forests around Can Falco. And, refreshingly for Honey, they loved

Ibiza for what it was now rather than for what it had once been and, in return, she loved having them to stay, basked in their enthusiasm, made friends with many of them, even if each time they left she had to cope with the fact that they made her feel just that little more restless — each one, in their leaving, emphasizing the big wide life beyond the shore.

At seven she heard a taxi pulling to a halt at the front of the hotel, the sound of slamming doors and raised voices. And then through the doors came Claudio carrying cases and with him a tall blond man, a sleeping child in one arm and a suitcase in the other, his wallet and passport clenched between his teeth. He made his way across the hall towards Honey and she came from behind the desk to meet him and carefully tugged the wallet and passport free.

'Thanks,' he grinned, 'Steve Kelly.' He unceremoniously dumped the child straight into her arms. 'And this is Joe.' Then he turned back to help his wife, who was now making her way through the door, gamely dragging with her another small, blond-haired boy, who was sitting on her foot and gripping tightly to one of her bare brown legs like a monkey around a tree. 'Charlie.' The woman grinned at Honey, tucking a long dark curl behind her ear, then gritted her teeth as her husband wrenched their son free of her leg 'And Freddie.' She reached forwards to take the sleeping Joe from Honey's arms.

Truth be told, Honey quite liked her guests arriving completely frazzled and therefore primed to appreciate the beauty and calm efficiency of Can Falco. With guests like these she could fly into action, whisk away their luggage, order them a herbal tea or a cold beer, listen to their horror stories of delays and lost luggage, calm their shattered nerves and distract their kids. It wasn't nearly so satisfying to play host to people who behaved as if they spent their entire lives on holiday.

Immediately after the Kellys had been taken upstairs two couples arrived at the same time. But of course this was as Honey liked it best: the hotel full, running smoothly, seemingly effortlessly, laughter carrying down the hallways, footsteps clattering on the stone steps. She sat at her desk, swiftly checked in the four new guests and drove Can Falco seamlessly on towards the evening.

The desk had been her father's but she'd always thought of it as hers. It had been one of the few items to join her father at the start of his life in Ibiza, making the journey from Wiltshire to Can Falco in the back of a lorry driven by a friend of Hughie's. As with so many who made the journey over to Ibiza in the sixties and seventies, the lorry and the friend both ended up staying for good. And with the desk, carefully wrapped in cotton sheets, had come an eccentric collection of other things Hughie's parents knew their son couldn't do without. First and most importantly there'd been an envelope with details of the modest monthly payment that would be wired straight into his bank account. Then there was his bed, but no mattress, a watering can, a packet of pea seeds, a prawning net and a wind-up gramophone. Griffon and Meriel Ballantyne, frugal and hard-working, had taken a very dim view of their only son's decision to move to Ibiza, realizing quite rightly that it would herald a lifetime of lethargy and wanton indulgence. And yet, even so, they'd carefully discussed what to send him and they'd got him spot on, shipping over the only things he'd ever have missed, apart from themselves, of course, whom he missed most of all. In all the years since Hughie had moved to Ibiza they hadn't yet made it out. Honey knew that he still hadn't quite given up hope that they would.

To Honey, the desk had stood out like a jewel. She had found it on an April day in 1999, the same day that she'd returned from her first year at university in Barcelona to pay her parents a surprise visit . . . and had never left again.

What was it that had made her return to them that day? Not the disconnected phone line because that had happened so often it was almost more of a shock when she found it working. And it wasn't even the news, second hand and a couple of weeks late, that Hughie had spent a night in a police cell (on suspicion of stealing and eating a neighbour's goat) because that too had happened before and skirmishes with the neighbour (who lived half a mile down the valley and was, to use Hughie's phrase, 'a little Brit shit') took place almost every month. Instead it had been her parents' oldest and dearest friends, Maggie and Troy, who had brought her back. Maggie and Troy Ripley, who of everybody had been most determined that she should leave Ibiza, who'd badgered and insisted and persuaded through all the months when Honey had agonized; who'd searched through the various courses on offer at the university in Barcelona, and had even paid the fees for her first year, had then ruined everything by sending her a postcard, mentioning, among other things, how her father had asked to borrow their fishing lines. They weren't to know what alarm bells they'd sent ringing with that one innocent remark. Honey had returned the next morning, suspicious of what she might discover, but at that stage full of hope that she'd prove herself wrong.

But she'd been right. Honey had arrived home to find Tora in the garden. As Honey had quietly come up behind her, Tora had carried on what she was doing, unaware. She was bending over, tugging at a sprig of rosemary, but without quite enough strength to snap it free, and each knuckle of her spine was fascinating in its knobbly awfulness. Honey had been gone just six weeks and Tora looked as emaciated as if she'd been on hunger strike the whole time. In a way, perhaps she had: present Honey with her starved, pathetic body and she didn't need to say the words aloud, *look what happens when you leave me*.

At the sound of Honey's footsteps, Tora had turned slowly. She'd been collecting herbs for an omelette, she'd explained defensively. Back in the house the fridge was empty but for a bottle of cava and a paper bag full of stinking prawns. And then Tora had admitted of course there were no eggs for the omelette, no milk either, but it didn't matter because she wasn't hungry anyway.

At that Honey had exploded at her, demanding to know where Hughie was, and in answer Tora had collapsed weakly back into a kitchen chair but had still refused to wilt in the face of her daughter's fury. She explained that Hughie had walked to town the day before and now she didn't have any idea where he was. And yes, they'd run out of money. And what the hell, yes, as soon as Honey had gone they'd had a party, several joyful parties. And when next month's money came through they'd have some more because at least with boring Honeybee out of the house, finally they were having *fun*.

But what about surviving, Honey had pleaded, and Tora had looked back at her, infuriatingly calm. What could Honey mean, when they lived among so much plenty? They ate from the fruits of the land and the sea: there was fresh fish to be caught, wild asparagus to be picked, olives, there were figs from the garden, nuts and oranges, melons . . .

It was such a ridiculous fantasy that Honey had had to walk away, tears smarting at her eyes, because at that stage the land around Can Falco was completely barren. There were no orange groves, no fig trees, and as for the wild asparagus, Tora had eaten it once and had never forgotten it, because of how *romantic* it had sounded, *wild asparagus*, how perfectly it had conformed to her absurd view of her life. Left high in the hills, unwilling to drive and with only Hughie to look after her, Tora was as helpless and as irresponsible as a young child.

But that was OK, because instead of food they'd had *fun*!

Honey had stormed from room to room, opening windows, kicking over the discarded wine bottles, holding her breath at the old familiar stench of her childhood: blocked drains mixed with marijuana and damp, rotting rubbish and squalor. *The parties had been worth it, had they? Worth starving for were they? They thought this was fun, did they?* And alongside the rage at her parents' irresponsibility, at the way she was being given no choice but to take on the role of nanny and nag once more, there was also the hurt that they only saw her as a killjoy, not the saviour at all.

And then she'd returned to the kitchen and Tora had fallen into her arms because of course it wasn't true, of course Tora didn't really mean it, didn't truly want to live this way, of course she wanted Honey home: without Honey there, she hardly knew how to exist on her own.

And so Honey's choice had been a simple one: break away from them, grit her teeth and turn her back, this time knowing exactly what she was leaving behind; or stay and

29

acknowledge that, for all her hopes for the future, her place for now was with her parents, her world was Ibiza and no further.

Some tiny part of her was even relieved that the decision was so clear-cut. That same day she'd scootered down to Santa Gertrudis to make calls to her tutor and university friends, and to pay the telephone bill and get the phone reconnected. And afterwards, when she'd returned, she had found the beautiful oak desk sitting on top of the logs in the wood shed and had brought it inside, wiped it clean and had sat down behind it, almost immediately feeling surprisingly enthusiastic and hopeful. And when Hughie had reappeared the next day and found her there, writing the first of many letters to the bank, he had expressed more surprise at seeing his old desk again than at seeing her. And the strange thing was that, from that day on, neither he nor Tora ever really acknowledged her decision to come home. Perhaps they were embarrassed by it, or perhaps it simply didn't occur to them that she'd sacrificed anything at all, because what, after all, could be better than a life at Can Falco?

But still, there was no doubt they'd changed as a consequence of her return, Tora particularly. Always the free spirit, childish and beautiful with it, with her blonde hair and huge blue eyes, Honey's return had signalled the moment Tora turned away from her old life and zoned in on the new. She started yoga classes, began to read books with titles like *Give Me Joy in My Heart* and *Here Comes the Sun*, and to talk of tasting the bliss and thinking outside her shell of mud, and within just a few months had embraced her new spiritual world with a speed and passion that Honey found both sweet and deeply infuriating.

Six years later Can Falco had, according to Condé Nast *Traveller* magazine, become a hotel worth crossing continents to visit and Honey had managed only two two-week trips off the island, once to Bali to stay with an Ibiza-born girlfriend and buy a ship's container worth of outdoor furniture for Can Falco while she was there, and once to England, to combine a friend's wedding with a visit to the land of her father. But even with two weeks and the freedom to go wherever she liked, she hadn't gone to see her grandparents — Hughie hadn't wanted her to.

The trip to England had been the winter before last, now over eighteen months ago, and since then she had not left the island again. Only in the past few months had she started to think about it, not least because of

Claudio questioning her in the same way Maggie and Troy had done before, disbelieving when she denied she was bored, occasionally teasing her, forcing her to defend herself against the charges of all work and no play. Because there *was* play, of course, how could there not be, living in the party capital of Europe. But even so, she was light years older than the mad sixteen-year-old who'd loved her forty-eight-hour house parties, who'd bicycled to Marrakech and trekked across India, a different person to the Honey she'd been before the weight of Can Falco and her parents had fallen upon her shoulders.

At eight o'clock, the second to last of that evening's arrivals were shepherded gently towards her by Claudio, a honeymoon couple who'd got married in Barcelona that day, the girl, still in her wedding dress, carried through the door high in her husband's arms, a laughing, shrieking bundle of net and white silk, long dark hair cascading down her back.

Looking up from her desk, for once Honey had to force the smile of welcome. The girl was too noisy, too triumphant, too keen to sweep everyone else into her celebration. Fleetingly, Honey wondered about losing their reservation, then pulled herself together, welcomed them in perfect Spanish and waited patiently while they kissed and kissed some more.

'We want our bed,' the woman dragged her lips free just long enough to say.

Honey handed her their key.

'It's a big bed, yes?'

Honey nodded. And knew that it was only her own bad mood, and a healthy dose of jealousy, that was making her feel so irritable.

How had they made it as far as the hotel, she asked Claudio as they sat together afterwards, Honey with her bare feet up on the desk, a glass of wine in her hand. How had they negotiated customs, baggage reclaim and found their Can Falco taxi?

And Claudio looked at her with a big smile on his face and suggested she needed some fun herself, and why didn't she finish early and let him take over?

After Claudio had gone she'd left her desk and walked noiselessly through the gardens, right out to the boundary, to where the vibrant green Can Falco lawn ran abruptly into red Ibiza dust, where guests would say the fairytale ended and real life began, but where Honey would say the opposite. She stood for a moment, staring at the gigantic flaming sun as it slipped towards the horizon, then sat down on the grass to watch it go, still startled by how fast it moved, exploding across the sky in a way that took hold of her breath and her thoughts and forced her simply to sit and behold. And then, afterwards, she sat on, as every last fire died down and the embers disappeared, her bare brown legs and bare feet stretched out in front of her, feeling lonely and left behind, in her skinny white vest and long silk skirt, as the darkness of the evening immediately began to settle all around her.

She let herself fall back slowly until she was lying flat on the ground and she looked up at the midnight-blue sky and said in a low voice, each word clearly enunciated, '*Now I am sad.*'

And as she heard herself say it out loud she immediately sat back up again, then jumped to her feet and looked self-consciously around though she knew there'd been nobody there to see or hear her.

The garden lights were all on now, little red raffia lanterns strung out across the gardens, dimpling and twinkling in the trees, marking out the pathways back towards the restaurant. With someone to walk with her, the garden at night-time was the most magical place to be, yet for so long there'd been no one and to be walking back alone now — with nothing but her work and her desk and another evening stretching ahead of her — it felt as if there was no more lonely place on earth.

She passed her cottage. Just two white-washed bedrooms and a tiny garden of its own, shaded from the harshness of the sun by olive trees. It had once been a pigsty, and from the age of fourteen, when Honey had first imagined converting Can Falco into a hotel, she had eyed it up for herself, had run through the darkness to reach it, had camped out in it night after night with her friends. Then it had seemed the perfect hideaway, a den supreme. She'd moved in permanently when she was sixteen, years before she'd been able even to connect the water, and in time she'd made it exactly as she'd always imagined it could be, far more girly and pretty than Can Falco, with floating white lace at the windows and gossamer-thin mosquito nets around her bed, pale blue shutters and red geraniums growing in terracotta pots outside. But now in the darkness with no lights on to welcome her in, it looked cold and uninviting.

By contrast and just a few hundred yards further on, and far enough away not to disturb the hotel guests — it had been a strategic decision to site their cottage there — the lights were on in Angel's Wings, her parents' home. Honey took a few steps towards it, careful not to bump into the

Portland stone bird bath, ghost-white in the darkness, and then she stopped abruptly as Mozart's exuberant Horn Concerto came bursting through the open windows towards her.

At this time of evening Hughie and Tora were always there and if Honey walked in now she knew exactly how she would find them. Her father would be in the bath, a large gin and tonic balanced beside him, soaking in his favourite Hermès bath oil, contemplating the evening ahead and conducting a random and at times incoherent conversation with her mother, who would be on her yoga mat, destressing at the end of what Honey presumed had been another completely stress-free day. Both of them would be surprised and delighted to see her, both of them would immediately arrive (naked) at her side, would hold her hands and ply her with drink. Then they would sit her down and her father would chat, chat, chat, twitter, twitter, twitter, bombarding her with that day's thoughts and observations. He would have met a beautiful new guest, her mother had a new and wonderful idea for a yoga class, he would relish the opportunity of telling Honey all about them.

But she couldn't face either of them, not tonight, and she slipped away again quickly before they saw her.

She sat alone, tucked away in the corner of the restaurant, eating a plate of prawns and potato salad and realizing with every delicious mouthful how hungry she'd been. And by nine thirty she'd been back at her desk for an hour and had checked everybody in apart from the guests arriving on the delayed flight from Gatwick, who wouldn't be getting to the hotel for another six or seven hours; she'd played several games of Solitaire on her computer and had ordered eleven hammocks for Can Falco from a new shop in Formentera and slowly her mood had improved again. And so when Claudio came in to find her and opened his mouth once more to persuade her to take the rest of the evening off, to let him stay up for the very last guests, she astounded him by smiling up at him and for once agreeing.

She left him while she went back to her cottage, stripped off her clothes and jumped into the shower and then changed into a dark green, thigh-skimming, daisy-printed dress and crocheted white sandals. Then, with her thick blonde hair hanging wet and heavy down her back and almost before she'd known she was going to do it, she walked through the ink-dark night to her car and climbed in.

3

Edouard might have known she'd come but, until the moment Honey turned left onto the San Miguel road rather than right towards the village of San Carlos, she hadn't acknowledged to herself where she was heading. She drove fast through the hills, roof down, the wind in her hair, and with every mile her mood improved further. She remembered making her way to Edouard's on the night of her thirteenth birthday on an old scooter her parents had just bought her — concluding she was better off driving herself than relying on lifts from other inebriates, themselves included. She remembered how she had wobbled her way up in the darkness to find Edouard and ask him to ride out with her to celebrate. She'd been met at the door by his mother, who'd looked at the rackety scooter and at skinny, defenceless little Honey and had promptly burst into tears at the thought of Tora and Hughie's irresponsibility. She'd fetched Honey a helmet, telling her sternly that Edouard had worn it for his first six months and she was going to do the same. Honey had nodded eagerly, thanked her enthusiastically and had thrown it into the first field they'd passed.

And she'd known even as it unfolded that this night was an important one, the night when all the fun began, the first night of being a teenager. As she'd raced Edouard along the narrow roads down to the coast to meet their friends, feeling the warm night air on her skin, she'd believed and she'd been right to believe that this night would mark the beginning of the best four years of her life.

They'd moved within a great group of friends, some Ibicencos, others ex-pat off-spring like her and Edouard, the children of her parents' friends, mainly British, German or Dutch, who'd been part of the first wave of hippies coming out, like Tora and Hughie, in the late sixties and early seventies.

As they'd got older they'd followed in their parents' footsteps, making their own fires on the beaches, camping in the sand dunes or in the untamed gardens of Can Falco and El Figo. Like them, they'd drummed out the sunsets, slept out on the beaches and gone clubbing together, starting at Pacha and moving on to Ku, then the most famous, spectacular nightclub in the world. Edouard had had a succession of flings, usually with British girls who lived on Ibiza, and Honey just one big love affair with a Spanish DJ working at the Café del Mar. They'd split up after the summer of her seventeenth year and the end of their relationship had marked the end of her four-year idyll, the end of a carefree and easy way of life, the last summer before she grew up and left Ibiza for university. The last summer she spent with Edouard and their gang of friends before they all went their separate ways.

The following year, when Honey had been forced to abandon her degree and return to Ibiza full-time, she'd been disappointed to find he could hardly make it out to the island at all. And from then on, as he emerged from university and began work in London, she saw him less and less, until it was barely more than the odd weekend, occasionally a full week, but never long enough to gather up with the others again and re-create the wonderful laziness of that one glorious summer. In any case the reality was that most of the others had gone too, leaving Honey almost alone as she embarked on the huge project of turning Can Falco around.

So over the next few years, El Figo stood mainly empty, Edouard's parents finally admitting that, hard as they'd tried, they'd never truly enjoyed the hippy lifestyle after all, preferring now to live in Geneva instead. Then when Edouard was twenty-five, they formally passed the house on to him, shrewdly absolving themselves of the bills whilst still retaining a place to stay. And because Edouard had become rich by then and had no one other than the occasional high-maintenance girlfriend to spend his money on, the house had been swiftly upgraded. Overseen by Honey, landscapers got to grips with the gardens, planted olive groves and lavender walks, added a pool and a tennis court, and so his parents' foothold on the island had become unexpectedly luxurious.

And with El Figo his own place, in the last year Edouard had finally begun to return. But now he filled the place with his London friends, work colleagues, clients and hangers-on and juggled his three mobile phones and was frequently so distracted she knew better than to ask if he wanted to re-create a sleep-over on Es Palmador or an evening sail to Es Vedra.

El Figo was on the range of hills next to Can Falco, built high on a cliff and facing out towards the sea, and was only five or six miles away as the crow flies. People joke that every journey in Ibiza takes twenty minutes, but it was at least that before her car turned off the main road and began to bump and bounce its way up the steep rutted track, dust billowing out behind her. She eventually turned the final corner, shot through the olive-green painted gates, and came up against a great jam of tightly parked cars. She slipped in between a dusty jeep and an immaculate 4×4 and then sat in the car for a moment, listening to the sounds of the party in the gardens below her. She tried to run her fingers through her hair and found that the journey there had blown it dry too thoroughly. She imagined she looked rather wild — presumably just what his guests were expecting.

She left her car and walked between banks of lavender, the scent heady on the warm night air, the lights from El Figo twinkling in the dark and the steady beat of music and ripples of noisy laughter guiding her towards the house, white and stark and beautiful, three perfect sugar cubes shining in the light of the moon. She felt at home here as ever, even now that it was landscaped, smoothed over and upgraded to Xanadu. For so many years it had been just as untamed and tumble-down as Can Falco, both of them ancient fincas with the same whitewashed, metre-thick walls. Honey and Edouard's parents had moved in at the same time, had both been enchanted with what they'd found and completely disinclined to do anything to change them. Edouard's parents had built a mud bath, but for years that was as far as the home improvements had got.

And now here she was again, she who had never left, standing outside El Figo once more. And for a moment, as she stood at the top of the steps that led down to the beautiful white house, she could believe that time had stood still after all. Now another party was beginning, another group of people was there below her, sitting in candlelight, spread out around the house, listening to music, dancing under the trees, unwittingly re-enacting all those parties of the past. And despite her reservations about Edouard's guests, she found herself smiling down at it all because this was just as it should be, it was what El Figo was best for — providing a beautiful setting for a party.

She walked to the edge of the steps and looked down, and saw that there was a man, spotlit just below her, at the edge of the pool. He had a cigar in his mouth and was wrestling with a girl who was doing a good job of not falling in. He was wearing pinstriped trousers, a pink shirt and red braces and his bleached white feet were planted firmly on the ground. She was slight and blonde, wearing a short flouncy skirt and a shocking-pink T-shirt that said Gold Digger across the front. And there was something so determined, almost ferocious, about their battle, a complete absence of any shrieks or laughter, no cheers or clapping from the other guests, no noise from either of them save the odd grunt, that Honey hesitated for a moment, wondering what on earth she was walking into.

Seconds later the man's brute strength finally overwhelmed the girl and with a final shove she was shot backwards into the water with a high-pitched squeal and an almighty splash. Without waiting for her to return to the surface the man rubbed his hands on his trousers, turned his back on the pool and strolled to a nearby sun lounger and sat down. Beside him Honey could see there was another man lying flat out, also smoking and dressed incongruously in a suit. She imagined they'd caught the late plane over and had probably only just arrived, but still it seemed odd that they hadn't immediately wanted to change.

But she was transfixed by the surface of the rippling spotlit water, waiting, waiting, until finally the girl burst back into the air. Honey watched as she trod water for a few seconds, taking several deep breaths and wiping her eyes, then swam to the edge and gracefully lifted herself out. Honey couldn't see her face. Had it all been one big game, she wondered, or was she really pissed off?

Once out of the pool the girl walked stiffly towards where the man was lying. Soaking wet, she looked even smaller, her pink T-shirt stuck to her skin, running mascara giving her panda eyes. And as she got closer to the man, Honey could see she hadn't found it funny at all. The man, with his back to her still and now engrossed in conversation with his friend, didn't first realize she was there.

'You trod on my toes,' she told him in a high, shaking voice.

He held up his hand to her, still talking to his friend and didn't even turn around.

'Paul, look at me. You ruined my clothes.' She stood her ground and waited but he still didn't react. 'What's the matter with you, fucking bastard?' She walked around his sun lounger so that she could look at him and at the sight of her he slowly dropped his arm, placed his cigar carefully between the other man's fingers and got to his feet. 'The least you could do is apologize.'

And then, so fast that neither Honey nor the girl herself had time to register what he was about to do, the man had caught her wrists and manhandled her to the edge of the pool and pushed her hard. This time it was a nasty, shut-up-bitch-don't-hassle-me push and she went backwards into the water with such momentum that waves rocked angrily over the edges of the pool.

'Watch her,' he said to his friend, as he sauntered back to his chair for the second time. 'Two hundred pounds says she bursts into tears.'

'Three hundred pounds says you get a well-deserved slap across the face.'

'I don't think so.' He sat back down, then swung his legs up and grinned. 'Five hundred pounds I'll still get a blow job tonight.'

Behind him the girl again broke back to the surface but this time made her way slowly over towards the shallow end and the steps, where another girl was silently waiting to help her out.

Honey found she couldn't step forwards. Uncertain if she still wanted to join the party, she stood wavering at the top of the steps and then the second man sat up to hand back the cigar, and as he did so, looked up and suddenly caught her eye. He immediately got to his feet.

'Well, hello, eavesdropper,' he said, walking over and looking up at her. 'Enjoying the show?' He moved forwards as if he was about to come up the steps to join her but then, quick as a flash, the other man, Paul, appeared at his side.

'Do we know you?' he barked up at Honey. 'No.'

She made her way slowly down the steps and once on the ground gave them the briefest nod of acknowledgement and then made to walk away, scanning the area around the pool to see if Edouard was there.

'You realize this is a private party?' Paul stepped forward and effectively blocked her route.

She gave him a quick glance. Close up, he was good-looking in a swarthy, heavy, bully-boy kind of way, with big dark eyes and a large well-shaped head, thick hair cut close to his scalp, high cheekbones jutting out from the flesh that had settled on his cheeks and around his neck.

'So are you going to throw me out, or throw me in too?'

He laughed at that and suddenly there was interest in his eyes.

'It depends who you are. Looking at you, I can't believe you're the entertainment.'

'Oh, Paul, don't be so damned rude,' said his friend.

'I'm saying she doesn't look like a fucking tart. She should take it as a compliment.' He folded his arms, enjoying himself. 'So what were you doing up there?'

Honey felt the heat of battle flaring inside

her. 'As your friend says, I was eavesdropping. And I was watching you too, having such fun with that girl. I'm sure you wouldn't have wanted anyone interrupting. How do you know she didn't want another go?'

For a few moments he looked stunned but then he recovered and smiled as if, perhaps, he'd misheard the contempt in her voice.

'Are you saying you'd like a turn?'

'No, thank you.'

'Then don't tempt me.'

'You don't tempt me either.'

She said it recklessly, daring him on, and as if he knew she was in mortal danger, his friend let out a great burst of desperate laughter. 'Edouard,' he cried, directing his call to the far side of the pool. 'For fuck's sake, get over here.' He turned to Honey. 'Quick, what's your name?'

'Honey Ballantyne,' she told them both. 'I'm a friend of Edouard's.'

'Honey's here,' called the friend while Paul let out a great hiss of shock and clutched dramatically at his face. 'You're not? Honey-bee Ballantyne? Oh Jesus-Fucking Christ!'

'Paul!' his friend laughed, staring at him in surprise. He grabbed Paul's hand and prised his fingers off his face. 'What's wrong?' Then he swung back to Honey. 'Who *are* you?'

'I'm so sorry,' Paul groaned. He let his

hands slide slowly down his face and stared back at Honey. 'What the fuck was I thinking? Who else could you be? Was I very rude? Please don't say yes or Edouard will crucify me.'

'Who is she?' the friend insisted again.

'It's not a problem.' Honey gave them both a brief dismissive smile. 'Excuse me now, there's Edouard . . . ' She made to walk away and immediately Paul held out his hands to her.

'Of course you're her, look at you. Friends? Please? Forgive me before you go?'

'Why does it matter to you?' she couldn't resist asking.

'Because, Honeybee Ballantyne, you're only the one person Edouard hasn't stopped talking about. Only the one person I've spent the whole evening waiting to meet.' He turned to his friend. 'This is the smartest, most talented, coolest woman on the island, that's who she is.'

The friend looked decidedly unconvinced.

'Shit I've practically flown over here to meet you. Tell me I've not blown it.'

'What?' asked Honey.

'Come on and I'll tell you. Let's grab Edouard and find you a drink.'

'But what about your friend?' Honey stayed where she was.

Paul laughed. 'You mean this one?' He nodded at his companion. 'He's not a friend he's a hanger-on.' Then he grinned. 'Meet Carl.'

'No, I'm talking about that girl. You should be worried about her not me.'

For a moment it was clear that Paul had no idea what she was talking about. He paused, looking at her in genuine surprise.

'The poor girl you threw into the pool,' Honey reminded him. The girl you wanted to drown, she thought.

At that, Paul sighed a long sigh and sadly shook his head. 'Oh, you mean Nancy. The thing is, Honeybee, Nancy had been a very naughty girl and I had to teach her a lesson . . . ' He saw the distaste in her face and stopped abruptly. 'I threw her in a swimming pool not a vat of hot oil! We were having a laugh that's all.'

She shook her head. 'It looked very cruel to me.'

'I promise you Nancy is fine. You'll meet her in a moment and you'll see. It must have looked horrible to you but honestly it's what we *do*. Get to know us better and you'll see. I don't know, she must have thrown me in *fifteen times* since I got here. I *had* to do it.' Honey shook her head again refusing to believe it. 'But it's true,' Paul insisted. 'It was my revenge, that's all, Nancy loves it. It's how we are. I promise you. We've stuck around together so long we have to find new ways to keep each other on our toes — off our toes even. It's how we are, I promise,' he repeated. 'Edouard will tell you it's true.' He grinned at her again, all charm and innocence now, twinkling and laughing at her mistake, enjoying it even, so that she couldn't help but doubt what she'd seen, wonder if it had, after all, simply been a light-hearted tip into the pool and not a modern-day Nancy facing up to her own Bill Sykes.

Meanwhile Edouard had still not materialized but now Honey saw lights and a cluster of people sitting close together under a thatched gazebo and as she and Paul and Carl drew nearer suddenly he stood up among them, and she guessed it wasn't just pleasure at seeing her again that got him striding towards her in such record speed.

'Bee, you came! And you've met these two?' He kissed her cheek and gave her a quick concerned glance. 'Are they behaving?' He immediately started to steer her away from Paul and towards the house. 'They're not, are they? Come with me now, out of danger. How did I miss you?' He turned back to Paul and Carl. 'Wait for us. I'll bring some drinks out.'

'Hope they wait all night,' she whispered quietly, as she slid her arm around him.

'You're serious? Why what's wrong? What's he done?' Edouard looked down at her full of concern.

'Nothing,' she muttered, 'apart from behaving like a stupid bastard, a pinstriped arse. Why do you bring them here?'

He stopped in his tracks and turned to face her. 'Please don't say that.'

'Edouard! Come on. It's exactly what he was.'

'The pinstripes are a problem?'

'No! He's a bully, a thug. You surely see that? And I don't understand why you let people like him stay here.'

'People like him?'

'Yes,' she retorted, 'people like him.'

'City wankers in their pinstriped suits? Honey you're such an Ibiza snob. He's only just left work, he's had no time to change. What would you like him to wear, a sarong?'

'You know his clothes have nothing to do with it, for God's sake.' She glanced quickly around. They were so close to the house, to all his friends, she couldn't believe he'd be so loud. She could see Paul disappearing through the doorway into the house and Carl settling down on the huge wide sofa. And there was a crowd of people, some of them she recognized, others presumably out for the weekend from England, all of them relaxed, sprawled together, talking and laughing, none of them paying the slightest bit of notice to her and Edouard. And now there was Nancy, lifting a hand to Carl in welcome, grinning up at him as if she hadn't a care in the world.

She stared at them all uncertainly. Was she wrong? Had she misunderstood the nasty intent that she'd seen in Paul's eyes, built it up out of all proportion? She turned back to Edouard, not sure whether to persist or to let it go, and saw on his face the wary half-smile half-frown that she hadn't seen for years.

Don't spoil tonight, he was pleading with her. Please don't let's fall out over Paul.

And looking up at him the outrage that had been bubbling up inside her calmed again and the words she'd been about to say dried on her lips and instead of explaining, telling him all about what Paul had said and done, her heart just softened and she reached up to his smooth brown cheek and kissed it, then took his arm and looped it over her shoulders.

'Everybody's here. Why didn't you say? When you said party I thought you meant a few people and some prawns on the barbecue.'

'And instead I've got a DJ and dancing

girls from Pacha. Seriously. Mark Ure is DJ-ing on the beach. City wide-boys expect nothing less.'

'Shut up.'

He laughed, bent and kissed her cheek. 'But you know what? I have to say *pinstripe arse* is perfect.'

She was serious again. 'Then why is he here?'

'Because he's important to me.' He shook his head. 'And I'll tell you why, but not tonight.' His arm tightened around her as he said it and she wondered just briefly why not and then let the thought drift away, forgotten.

4

Nancy, the girl from the pool in the Gold
Digger T-shirt had appeared from around the
side of the house and now she waved a bottle
of wine at Edouard and Honey and grinned.
'Hi! Coming to join us?' She spoke in a light
and happy voice and there was no sign of her
recent dip, her pale blonde hair now smooth
and dry and shining in the house lights.
'We're over there, please come!' And with a
little smile, she was gone again. Clearly the
girl knew who Honey was. Perhaps she'd
caught sight of her as she'd swum out of the
pool?

'We'll join everyone in a minute,' Edouard
told Honey. 'First I must show you the
house.'

She felt his arm tightening around her as
he spoke and looked up at him in surprise.

'What about it?'

But now they were nearing the doorway
and instead of answering he moved aside to
let her see and Honey strode on and then
stopped in shock because the first thing she
saw was that someone had cut out a large
rectangular hole in the sixteenth-century

front door and had inserted a piece of pink glass.

She turned back to him in wordless horror.

'Oh, good,' Edouard said drily. 'You love it already don't you?'

'How could you do this?'

'I think we used a hammer and chisel. Apparently we needed more light.'

She walked on in. El Figo was as familiar to her as Can Falco. With her eyes closed she could have navigated her way through the hall, turned left up the five steps, then right into Edouard's den, could have thrown herself confidently down on his sofa. But wide-eyed and silent now she walked on in and looked around at the complete transformation that had taken place since she'd been there last.

Under the care of Edouard's parents, this hall that she was standing in now had been an unconverted barn, complete with owls raising families in its high-arched ceiling. As a child she had often spent the nights here on a makeshift bed, fighting sleep, watching the moon through the gaps in the rafters, listening for the notes of a piano or guitar, gentle laughter, quiet conversations, all the soothing sounds of grown-ups outside having fun.

Then Edouard had taken on El Figo and

the hall had been incorporated into the main part of the house and had been given a simple going-over by Honey that had left it plain and white, a spectacular entrance to the house but unadorned. Now, since she'd been here last, just a few months before, it had been transformed again, finally into a room rather than an echoing unused space, its white walls painted in a burnt terracotta, the floors painted white and covered in bold modern silk rugs. On one side the enormous fireplace had been painted dark red, logs stacked ten foot high beside it, while stretching out on either side were two long sofas built out of the walls, their cushions deep and covered in a thick purple velvet. And between the sofas there was now a square stone table, fat white candles grouped artfully together in a round stone dish. There were new paintings, huge modern abstracts, on the walls, and in front of her there was a polished oak dining table laid elaborately for dinner with twinkling silver and heavy-looking glass, eight chairs around it, candles seemingly floating in mid-air above. Altogether it looked like an extremely expensive and rather hip private members' club, but certainly not the beloved El Figo she'd grown up with.

Who'd helped Edouard make such astonishing changes? When had it happened? Why hadn't she known anything about it? And was it just a misguided possessiveness that made her want to shout how much she hated it? How unbearable it was. Because actually it was spectacular, she couldn't deny that. But it was just . . . she walked forwards and leaned across the table to touch one of the candles and it swung away from her, revealing the fine wire that suspended it from the ceiling . . . It was just that every trace of Edouard's past life there, and hers, had been painted over. Had he realized that was what he was doing? She turned to him but couldn't find the words to ask, and then a telltale prickle down the back of her neck made her turn suddenly and she saw a woman standing quietly in the doorway, hands clasped, watching her.

'Anna!' Edouard immediately left Honey's side and moved towards her and Honey took in the expectant, hesitant look on the woman's face as she stared back at Honey, and understood a little more.

She managed to summon up a big enthusiastic grin. 'You've done all this, haven't you? It's amazing. It's completely transformed.'

The woman, Anna, nodded. 'I saw you coming in and I couldn't resist joining you.' She waited until Honey reached her then held out a thin hand.

Honey was aware of how Edouard moved, no more than a foot, just the tiniest of movements, and yet now he was standing quite definitely beside Anna not her, and in the context of the house it felt hugely significant.

While Honey shook Anna's hand, her brain clicked and whirled through a hundred possibilities. The immaculate black linen suit looked so out of place here, and yet Anna herself seemed disquietingly at home. Were she and Edouard together? She wasn't his type — attractive, yes, with long shiny chestnut hair tied back in a ponytail, but so humourless, so severe.

'And I'm Honey. I'm a friend of Edouard's.'

'I know who you are. So, tell me, do you like it?'

'It's beautiful.'

'But really not your style?' Anna smiled graciously, clearly not caring in the least. 'Don't worry, I can imagine.'

'Have you decorated all of the house?'

At that Anna laughed unexpectedly. 'Eddie wouldn't let me do any more until you'd passed this. I think he cares more about your opinion than anybody else's. Don't you, darling?' she teased, turning back to Edouard with a smile.

Honey looked at her as much in surprise at

the *Eddie* as at what Anna had said. 'That's definitely not true,' she retorted pleased all the same at the thought that it might be.

'Oh, trust me.' Anna gave another little laugh. She didn't sound jealous, if anything she sounded gently mocking as if she was teasing Edouard for being such a fool. 'So we've been out a few times this year, trying to get the place straight.'

'Anyway,' Edouard interrupted awkwardly. 'I should be getting Honey a drink. Bee, what'll you have? And Anna what about you?'

'You should have let me know you were here.' Honey told him off. 'I didn't even realize you were doing this. How could you not tell me?' At that Anna raised an amused eyebrow. 'I could have come around to see you, brought you some provisions.' Argued with this woman about putting purple velvet with terracotta.

Edouard didn't answer.

'We had everything we needed,' Anna said. 'I think we managed.'

Honey stared back at Edouard. 'Good for you.'

'Actually, we did come to see you at Can Falco,' said Anna.

'Did you? I'm sure I'd remember.'

'You weren't there. It was one evening, early, end of May. We only stayed for a drink.'

'I'm very sorry I missed you.'

'Edouard badly wanted me to see Can Falco.' And again it was as if she was teasing, making the point, *not you, Can Falco*. 'He wanted to show me what you'd done there.'

'Did you like what you saw?'

'Yes, what a pretty place.'

She sounded so patronizing that Honey couldn't resist a quick glance at Edouard. He was waiting for her, with a look, a mix of wide-eyed innocence and the sparkle of laughter.

'I left you alone because you were adding fifteen bedrooms to Can Falco and I knew you didn't have the time,' he told her.

'I should explain — I'm an interior designer,' Anna went on, completely unruffled. 'I have a consultancy in Great Portland Street called Green and Pleasant. We're very eco-ware. I think you'd approve of us.' She caressed the smooth polished oak of the table with the palm of her hand, and now she narrowed her eyes. 'So what has he told you about me?'

'Nothing,' Edouard answered smoothly. 'Not yet.'

Abruptly Honey'd had enough. She looked longingly to the door. She wanted to be away, running back up the steps to her car, giving up on the lot of them, Edouard most of all.

But Edouard followed her glance and knew

exactly what she was thinking. 'Don't go. There's lots of friends of yours outside, Honey, all waiting to see you. Please stay.'

'I'll go and find them.' She turned for the door.

'I'm so sorry, I should have asked before,' Anna exclaimed. 'Would you like a glass of champagne?'

A glass of champagne? She wanted to laugh because coming from Anna it sounded so pretentious.

'No, Honey's more of a cocktails girl,' Edouard told Anna. 'And tonight we have Danilo here, world-famous maker of strawberry daiquiris.' He turned to Honey. 'He's down on the beach waiting for you. He told me to tell you.' In his way, Edouard was apologizing for his awful woman, for letting her ruin his lovely house and be so rude. But still he couldn't bring himself to cast Anna adrift. 'Come and try one too,' he suggested, deliberately including Anna once more.

'Get one for me would you, Edouard?' Honey walked straight out through the door and didn't wait for an answer. 'I'll be outside. Do you mind?'

Skirting the side of the house, she told herself she was crazy still to be hanging around. What was she trying to prove by staying? Why didn't she simply walk away?

She stood at the top of the steps that led down to the first of many terraces. Below, the gardens looked like a lush and beautiful jungle, strings of lights swinging gently from the trees, the green grass of the pathways curving between spotlit palm trees and giant shrubs with leaves the size of elephant ears. And from far below, down on the beach, came the sound of seventies' soul, making her want to run down the steps towards it. And she knew there'd be friends to talk to, that if she made her way down she could pick up a drink and laugh and dance and talk and have a great time and probably carry on till the next morning without even seeing Edouard again. But she didn't want to do that. She wanted to know what he was up to because he was up to something. And what exactly had possessed him to turn to Anna for help?

'Honey!' a voice called and she spun around to see it was Paul's girlfriend, Nancy. She was sitting with her friend who'd helped her out from the pool, stretched out at opposite ends of a huge carved wooden sofa and beckoning her over to join them. Opposite them were two dark-haired men, and Honey wavered for a moment as she saw that one of them was Paul. They were laughing together quietly, their backs to the girls, and when Paul saw her he raised a hand at Honey's approach but didn't interrupt his conversation. And Honey saw that he'd changed into baggy shorts and a T-shirt, just like his friend, and the smoke that was curling into the air between them was now sweet familiar cannabis rather than nasty pungent cigar.

'Will you join us?' Nancy smiled. She touched her hand to her chest, 'I'm Nancy,' and then she pointed to her friend. 'And this is Belle.'

'Aren't you coming down to the party on the beach?' Honey asked.

Nancy yawned and stretched back against the cushions. 'We *were* on our way, weren't we Belle?'

'Stay for a moment,' Belle offered and jumped to her feet, stepping around the low table to reach Honey. She was tall, full of smiles, with thick reddish hair cut artfully in a choppy untidy bob and interested olive-green eyes. Then before Honey could move she'd crouched down to peer intently at Honey's feet.

'Wow. Totally beautiful. Just as I knew they would be.' She touched one sandal lightly with one finger, then smiled up at Honey. 'Do you mind? There was an article on you in *Red* last year and you were wearing some like this.'

'And she's wanted a pair ever since,' Nancy

explained, curling her feet up beneath her. 'I think she's engineered this whole weekend purely to be able to go and buy some.'

Belle turned back to her indignantly. 'As if I'd come just to look at shoes.'

'And dresses too, sorry.'

'She's being so unfair,' Belle told Honey. 'So, do you get them in Ibiza town?'

'And churches, and museums. You were saying you hoped to find some stained-glass windows, weren't you, Belle?'

'Ignore her,' Belle insisted, taking Honey's hand to guide her towards an empty chair opposite their places on the sofa. 'She's trying to make out I'm frivolous and silly and that she is cultured and classy, which, as you probably can see, could not be further from the truth. Here's to Ibicenco architecture — see, I can even say it right. And,' she went on solemnly, 'if there are any caves or churches I should spend some time in, on my *very short* break to Ibiza, I hope very much that you'll tell me where they are.'

'I will.' Honey laughed, overcome with the urge to stand up and hug her.

'But if I happened to pass the world-famous Las Dalias hippy market on the way, then I wouldn't object. And if there were any interesting little roadside shops, too, perhaps you could highlight them for me on my map?'

'Ideally little roadside shops with an authentic Ibicenco peasant woman inside, sewing tiny immaculate stitches and slowly going blind from the strain,' teased Nancy.

'In which case it would be thoughtless and selfish not to stop and buy something,' Belle finished for her. Then she looked down at Honey's feet. 'Just fabulous, take them off, let me try one.'

Honey dutifully stepped out of one of her sandals and Belle slipped it on her own bare foot, pulled up her floor-length green skirt to get a better look and sighed. Then she caught Nancy's eye and started to laugh.

'Oh, for God's sake, stop looking so disapproving, Nancy. Yes, I want to look like her. Honey's gorgeous and so is her hotel. And please don't you pretend that you don't think so too and that you haven't been dying to meet her and wouldn't kill for a night at Can Falco.' She swung back to Honey. 'To be honest, Honey, I didn't come here to pick up shoes, I came to meet *you*.'

'How nice of you . . . ' Honey looked at her uncertainly.

'We both wanted to meet you. We've been looking at Can Falco on-line,' Nancy joined in. 'We were imagining what fun it would be to come and take a yoga class in the Garden of Serenity.' She uncurled her legs and lifted her feet onto the low table in front of them, then reached for her glass and finished what looked like a strawberry daiquiri before she stretched back against the cushions. 'Hey! You haven't got a drink.'

'It's OK. I think Edouard's gone to get me one . . . '

Belle nodded. 'You know he was so pleased when he saw you were here tonight . . . '

Honey frowned. Of course it hadn't seemed quite that way to her.

'He was,' Belle insisted. 'I know how you don't get much chance to see each other now.'

'Not like it used to be. Now he has such a flat-out life.'

'I live with him in London, so I guess I know about that too.'

'You do!'

Belle grinned. 'I'm his lodger. I moved in with him about six months ago, into his flat in Islington.' She shook her head. 'You don't know the flat in Islington?'

'I guess I knew he had to live somewhere in London.'

'He bought it about two and a half years ago. It's gorgeous, especially now he's got me keeping it in order.' She leaned back, studying Honey. 'You should come and see us.'

'I know,' Honey agreed quietly, meeting Belle's stare.

67

Unexpectedly Belle held out her hand. 'I know, you can never get away,' she said. 'I've heard how hard you work to keep everything going. Edouard did tell me if I was ever going to meet you it was going to have to be here.'

'I must have sounded very boring.' Honey laughed.

'No . . . as if you need a holiday. It must be so hard having to work through the summertime, just when everybody else here is having fun,' Belle went on.

Her tone was still light and sympathetic but somehow she was making Honey feel as if she needed to defend herself. 'I love Can Falco,' she heard herself say, even though she wasn't sure if she did at all. 'And one day soon it'll start to run itself and I'll be able to travel again, take my holiday. Then I'll come to London and see you and Edouard . . . ' She shook her head. 'And you live with him, and I didn't even know . . . '

'We worked together on Trade Secrets . . . You must have heard.'

Honey nodded, but the truth was that again she was on shaky ground and she imagined Belle probably knew it too. All she remembered about last summer was that she'd hardly seen Edouard at all, and when she had done he'd been more distracted than ever. But she'd let it go. She'd never thought

68

to ask why, never tried to find out more.

'It was a big project he was involved in all last year. And now he's concocting evil plans with Paul.' Belle turned to include Nancy again. 'At least it means I get to spend time here with you! Nancy and I have been seeing quite a lot of each other, thanks to them.'

'The lovely Princess Anna introduced them,' Nancy explained. 'Have you met her yet?'

'Just now,' Honey said. 'Who is she?'

'She's a designer, with designs on Edouard's heart.'

'She'll have trouble finding that.'

'Poor Honey.' Belle laughed. 'Was she completely horrible?'

'Oh no, no, no. Yes.'

'You're a threat. Everything she can do you can do better.' Then she raised her leg to study her foot in Honey's shoe. 'And she's fallen for Ibiza. She says she loves the *whole vibe*. So you might find you're seeing more of her than you want to.'

'I'm sure I can keep out of her way.'

Belle smiled. 'Don't be. Not if you're in her sights. She's persistent. Look what she persuaded Edouard to do to this house.' She leaned forwards. 'You know he doesn't like it.'

'He doesn't?'

'He'll leave it a few months and then paint

over it all. He's sweet, he doesn't want to hurt her feelings, that's all.'

'For that have my shoes!' Honey reached down to pull off the other one and handed it to Belle, laughing at the surprise on her face. 'Six euros at Las Dalias market. If you like, I'll take you and Nancy there tomorrow.'

'We *would*.' Belle turned to Nancy. 'Wouldn't we? You'd be able to come too? Paul doesn't have other plans for you?'

'Of course not!' Nancy brushed her aside. 'And we could see Can Falco on the way ... Paul already said he'll be busy with Edouard all day.' She hesitated then and Honey saw the vulnerability in her face. 'You met Paul, didn't you?'

Honey nodded.

'Just as he pushed me in?'

'Yes.'

'Oh.' She nodded. 'You must have thought ... ' She looked up at the black night sky. 'It was no big deal. We were fooling around.'

Beside her Belle shifted in her chair.

'Don't worry, Honey,' Nancy insisted. 'I promise I'm in control and one day I will have my revenge on him. Now,' she went on brightly, 'how about we meet you at Can Falco tomorrow?'

'Perfect,' agreed Honey. 'We could join one

of my mother's yoga classes if you'd like to. Then I'll show you Las Dalias.'

'Brilliant,' said Belle.

'I know nothing about yoga,' Nancy warned.

'Doesn't matter at all. Tora loves her uncorrupted beginners best of all.' Honey hoped Claudio wouldn't mind losing his free Saturday morning if she joined Nancy and Belle for the class. 'And in any case it's a method all her own. My mother has a very special style. You won't have tried anything like a Tora class before.' She leaned into Nancy. 'When the fairies join us we must be very quiet.'

'She sounds brilliant.' Nancy giggled nervously.

'You'll fall in love with her. Everybody does.'

'*Tora?*' repeated Belle.

'She's Dutch.'

'But why do *you* call her Tora?'

'Because she never liked words beginning with *M*. Words like Mama or Mummy . . . or mature.' Honey laughed. 'She likes T words, like Tora and Tanit and Tai-Chi.'

'And Tickle,' said Edouard, from somewhere above Honey's head. 'She loves being the tickle-monster. I rather like her being one too.'

At the sight of him Nancy opened her arms and then Honey felt a pair of hands land gently upon her shoulders.

'I'm very sorry about Anna,' he whispered, tickling her ear with his breath, 'I don't know what got into her. Here . . . ' He passed her a tall pink cocktail then moved around so that she could see him. 'And Danilo says drink it slowly.'

'So where are ours?' Belle asked accusingly.

'Honey needed it more. Yours are waiting for you down on the beach. They're your reward for getting off the sofa and being sociable.'

'You need some time alone?'

'No, you can stay if you want to.' Now he was looking at Honey. 'I was wondering where you'd gone.'

'We're taking a Tora yoga class tomorrow morning,' Nancy told him. 'Do you think we'll survive? Do you want to come too?'

'Not sure I'm bendy enough for Tora.' He came and sat down between Nancy and Belle, tucked a strand of blond hair behind his ear and grinned across at Honey with warm brown eyes. Clearly absence had made his heart grow fonder.

'I never got the chance to ask. Do you like the house?' He stuck out his long legs on the table in front of him.

She sipped her drink. 'You know what I thought.'

'Subdued, classy, wonderfully tasteful?'

She prodded one of his feet with her bare toe. 'And I know you don't like it either. I'd have helped you if I'd known you wanted to change it. You should have asked me.'

'I didn't know I wanted to change it either. And, in any case, it turned out there was hardly anything to do, just an enormous lot of shopping.'

'And you know I'd never have managed that.' She leaned back, caught Belle and Nancy's eye and grinned at them.

At that Edouard threw his head back against the cushions. 'No. Stop those sneaky little glances. Nancy and Belle are *my* friends, *my* allies, Belle's *my* flatmate, Honey. What's going on?'

'Nothing.' Belle ruffled his hair sympathetically while sitting on his other side Nancy tried to uncork an obstinate bottle of wine.

'Poor Edouard,' Nancy said, handing Edouard the bottle before turning to Honey. 'He was very worried about what you'd think about his house. It's been bothering him all day.'

'No it hasn't,' Edouard insisted. 'Don't tell her that.'

He took the bottle of wine from Nancy's

hands, uncorked it and then poured her a glass and handed another to Belle before settling back easily between the two of them.

There he was, Honey thought, with his beautiful handmaidens on either side, pouring them wine while they stroked his sun-streaked hair and hung on to his every word. As he took a sip, she watched Belle push herself that little bit closer, laughing at something he'd said. She wasn't flirting, only being affectionate, but still an unexpected and unwelcome pang of jealousy shot through Honey.

Don't touch, she found herself wanting to snap at Belle. It was ridiculous, she knew it was. She liked Belle and of course she was just the right sort of housemate for Edouard. Happy, good company, able to hold her own, she should be pleased to think of him living with someone so much fun. And yet she wasn't at all. Watching him sitting there between Belle and Nancy, Honey couldn't help but feel childishly jealous and fearful that she'd lost her status as his number one girl. She'd known him all her life, had never been presented with competition before, but now she wondered if she could still make him laugh like Belle and Nancy did. She doubted he ever looked as happy with her as he did right now, with them. She'd seen him fall in love with other girls, but what she'd never seen or even thought of before were the ones who might have been his friends because there'd never been any who could remotely compete with her. Until this funny bright affectionate woman who lived in his present not his past and made Honey feel she hardly knew him at all.

She downed her drink quickly and made to stand up.

'Danilo said *slowly*,' he told her. 'Don't go away.'

'I want to. Come with me, we should all go down. I keep hearing the music on the beach. Why are we sitting up here?'

'Go with her,' Nancy encouraged him, 'take her down. She's an Ibiza girl. She can't sit on a sofa all evening talking when there's music on the beach! It's not her fault she's just met the two laziest and most antisocial people here tonight.'

'Come with us.' Honey held out her hands to them although the truth was she wanted a moment with Edouard on his own.

'In a while,' Nancy insisted. 'We'll finish our wine and be right behind you. Then you can introduce us to all your gorgeous, glamorous, boho friends.'

Edouard placed his glass on the table, pushed himself back to his feet and held out his hand. 'You can show them to me too. Come on.' He led Honey down the steps then stopped as soon as they were out of earshot. 'What's going on?' he asked. 'Are you angry with me?'

'No, with myself.' She was impressed by her own honesty. 'It's rubbish that I didn't know about Belle. She lives with you. How could I not even have heard her name before tonight? What's the matter with us, with me, that we've let it come to that? And Trade Winds. What are they? Why didn't I know about them?'

'Trade Secrets,' he corrected gently.

'Whatever. And Anna too. I know you don't like what she's done, but how has it got to that? Why did you let her loose on El Figo?' She paused, then added deliberately, 'How could you let her near *you*?'

'She's not got that close. I'd been working with her in London and one day we were talking about here, and then she came out and saw the house and she wanted to have a go at it, that's all. She had all these ideas and they sounded great.' He shrugged. 'And to tell you the truth I really didn't care what she did. You know I'm not precious about El Figo.'

'But you should be! Why aren't you? I hate that you can say that.'

76

'Bee.' He came to a halt and took her hands in his. 'All I mean is I don't care what colour my walls are.'

She threaded her fingers through his.

'What else?' he asked.

'I think it's you. You and me. Tonight I felt as if I'd lost you and worse, it's as if you've been gone a long time but I've only just noticed.'

'Come here.'

He pushed her down gently onto the edge of the next flight of stone steps that would take them down another tier, to a lower terrace. Below them was the sound of people, a beat of music, but here for the moment they were alone.

'Don't you know you'll never lose me? That however hard you try it's not going to happen?'

She let her head rest against his shoulder. 'But how many times have you been out here this year? How many days? How many years since we've sat here like this?'

'Too many. I know it's dreadful, such a waste of a house.'

She turned to look at him.

He laughed quietly. 'I can't quite believe you're saying you miss me.'

'But I do, I am. I've missed you for years. I want you to come back. I want you to spend some time here without a crowd of City bums to keep you company or even lovely friends like Belle and Nancy ... and Paul. I want you on your own. Because you need to spend some time here, you and me, together. You need to remind yourself of what you let go.' She could see it was the last thing he'd expected her to say and she felt suddenly self-conscious and yet at the same time relieved that she'd said it. 'I'm in a strange mood tonight.' She thought back to how she'd felt in the gardens of Can Falco, the restlessness and sadness that had forced her to her feet and sent her running to him and realized she'd been in a strange mood for weeks.

'Say some more. I like it.'

'I don't think so.' She stood up and held out her hand and he took it and stood up too, close beside her, and she thought he was about to say something else but then instead he silently led her on down the next flight of stone steps, along another path, past a square thatched gazebo, filled with people, more spilling outside. The music from the beach was louder here, she could feel the bass resonating beneath her feet and without thinking began to move in time to the sound.

As they rounded a corner they came across another group of people, her dear friends

Claire and Tony talking to a tall woman with a capuchin monkey around her neck, who called out to Honey in delight when she saw her but Edouard held tight onto her hand and didn't let her stop.

'But that was Claire and Tony, and Juno too,' Honey protested as they rounded another corner and disappeared out of sight. 'I haven't seen them for ages.'

'I don't care. We're going to dance.'

He was moving faster now, almost running down the shallow steps, down towards the sea.

'Did you see her monkey was wearing a little scarf around his neck? He looked so sweet.'

He turned back to her briefly. 'But if we'd talked to her we'd never have got away and I'd like to dance with you more than I'd like to talk to Juno.'

Her heart was beginning to race with the exertion but her feet picked up speed again until she was flying down the steps behind him. 'You saw Maggie and Troy were here too?'

'Maggie and Troy are always here,' he called back.

'They're not, they live at Can Falco. You must know that.'

'Not when I'm home.'

'Even when you're home.'

'No, Bee, they like me most. They told me.'

He led her down another flight of steps and past another clutch of people. She saw her new neighbours, a couple called Inca and Nash who'd just bought a house down in the valley below Can Falco. They were artists, working on all their *expressions* together.

'But I wanted to see Inca and Nash. And there was such a good-looking man talking to them. Who was he? I think I should go back.'

'Another time.'

'Did you hear they've finished the work on their house?'

At that he looked back at her once more. 'Do I care?'

'Yes,' she laughed, 'because it's all made of green glass. Don't you want to see it?'

'Find them later.'

'Tora's been modelling for them.'

'I heard.'

'Naked but for drawing pins. But don't worry because they stuck drawing pins *to* her but not *in* her. How do you think they did that?'

Edouard didn't answer and she stopped beside him because now they'd reached the last flight of steps before the beach and they were both out of breath. For the moment they were alone, standing side by side while their hearts thudded fast and in front of them the round white moon hung huge and low over the sea.

5

I'm with Edouard, she found herself saying in her head, over and over again. How strange it's Edouard standing here beside me, holding my hand, and I really don't want to let him go.

Still holding her hand, he turned away again to check his path and then led her down the last few steps and onto the beach.

Inaccessible but from Edouard's garden or by boat, the beach was almost the best part of El Figo. Only little, no more than three hundred metres long, it was covered in pure white sand and because of its location was completely private and for that almost priceless.

There were flares caught between the rocks that lit the path to a cluster of colourful Indian tepees with jewelled cushions and rugs scattered beneath them, while further out to sea the moonlight flickered on the rippling water. She'd seen the beach a million times before but it had never looked as beautiful as it did tonight. Beside the tepees their friend Mark Ure had set up his music and was mixing tracks for the fifty or so people spread out around them. Many people were dancing, some ankle-deep in the water, a few had even started to swim. Edouard took Honey's hand and led her towards the others. Mark raised a hand in greeting as he saw them approaching and Edouard slid his arms around her waist and together they began to dance on the sand, both of them already barefoot, Edouard in his long trousers, Honey in her very short dress that kept riding up high around her thighs.

Then following them down onto the beach came a rush of gorgeous-looking girls and glamorous men, none of whom Honey knew, the girls with sheets of long shining hair and beautiful floating clothes, fluttering excitedly down the rocky steps like nocturnal butterflies, out onto the sand, exclaiming with delight at what they saw, bending to slip out of shoes, then stretching up to slip out of their dresses, pulling each other by the wrists towards the sea. Others moved towards where Danilo and his two equally good-looking assistants stood waiting for them, dressed in identical purple silk shirts with red bandannas, long black hair tied back in ponytails. Several of the girls immediately swooped up their drinks and then went plunging on into the water to join their friends and Honey and Edouard, while at the same moment the music changed again, to a loud heavy bass.

'Who are they? How do I not know all these people?' Honey shouted, keeping her arms around his neck possessively as each wave seemed to bring with it another stunning girl determined to catch his attention. 'Where have you got them from? Have you trained them all to be like this?'

'Face it, Honey, they find me irresistible.'

She looked back up at him. 'No, you have to have paid them.'

He laughed. 'Most of them are here for the summer. They've rented a couple of big houses in Santa Agnes. I know most of them from London.'

She nodded. 'Your secret life in London.'

'Not secret,' he shouted above the noise of the music. 'You're just not interested in finding out about it.'

'I am. I want to find out now.'

'Then I'll tell you anything. Everything you want to know.'

She grinned back at him. 'So tell me if you've slept with Anna.'

'Quieter, Bee!' he exclaimed. 'And no I haven't.'

'Kissed her?'

'I meant that I'd tell you anything about my work.'

'But that's boring. Tell me if you've kissed Anna.'

'Nothing's going on.'

'Then I think that's even worse. Poor Anna, because I get the feeling she'd like it to be.'

'Not poor Anna. Perfectly fine, indestructible Anna. She's a business partner, that's all.'

She met his eye. 'I don't like her.'

'She has good ideas.'

'No, she talks rubbish. Eco this and green that without any sincerity at all. Surely you can see that?'

'She's very clever.'

'She's a fake.'

'She's been good to work with,' he said stubbornly.

'Oh, for God's sake, Edouard, please. Is that really all that counts?' She let him go. 'I don't know, why do I still care what you think, what you do? I thought I'd stopped, years ago, when you left me here and didn't even tell me why.'

'Bee, now you sound so sad. And I had to go. You know that.'

'But it hurt. I missed you.'

'Oh, darling Bee, you never said that before.'

'So I'm telling you now.' She looked

around her. 'Perhaps not the best time, perhaps not a conversation to have at the top of our voices, standing in the middle of the sea with a party all around us, but let's face it, there haven't been many other opportunities this year.'

He came closer and bent his head so that his forehead was almost touching hers. 'I'm sorry.'

She looked back up at him. 'You left and for six months I didn't hear from you at all.' Then she shook her head, and pushed him away. 'But don't worry about it too much because, of course, for years now it hasn't hurt at all. For years I've hardly thought about you.' She looked around them, at the sea, the people all about. 'But now that we're here doing this again it's all coming back to me, all the fun we used to have. We're dancing in the sea and you're getting your trousers wet, and it's as if nothing's changed at all.'

In answer he took her hands and pushed her slowly backwards deeper into the water. As she walked backwards she could feel it feel it touch the back of her knees, then her thighs, could feel it catch at the hem of her dress, and then rise up to her waist and slowly they walked further, out of the range of the flares, until only the light from the moon lit the water and the music suddenly seemed very far away and it was as if they had been left all alone.

She could feel his heart beating fast against hers.

'You've proved it now,' she heard herself say, her hands flat against his chest. 'You've shown how you can live without us all, so why don't you come back again? Loads of your old friends are coming back. Milo and Christian and Frankie and Tina, they can't stay away. Some of them are commuting, staying here for a few months at a time. Couldn't you do that?'

'Honey, have you got the first clue what I do in London?'

'No,' she admitted, laughing into his wet T-shirt. 'Something to do with Trade Secrets?'

'Hopeless. You know nothing. So just for the record, my job isn't one that would allow me to spend a few months of every year in Ibiza. My job involves me getting on the tube at six-fifteen every morning, in a suit, to be at my desk, in Golden Square, by seven. This,' he nodded out towards the water, 'Ibiza, is my most favourite place in the world but what I had here when I was sixteen without a care in the world, couldn't be found any more.'

'Yes it can.'

He shook his head. 'We're old now. I am an old man with serious financial responsibilities.'

'You're a pompous old man. It wasn't that we were only sixteen, it was a state of mind, and we could get it again if you'd only try. Of course we could,' she insisted, 'but better. Now we know what we like we'd do it even better now.'

'Are you so certain?'

'I am, because I know I'm right. I'll show you. Choose three places and I'll take you there again, but one of them must be Es Palmador. We have to go there.'

'Ride the horses into the sea at Cala Mastella?'

'Yes!' She took two steps back from him surprised he'd buy into the idea so easily and surprised by how much she wanted to do it too.

'Where else?'

'Santa Medea?'

She nodded again. But almost immediately thoughts started rushing in. Take up her precious time, it would mean nights away from Can Falco, how could she do it? The all-work-and-no-play Honey instinctively backed away, but only briefly because at the same time the old Honey was rising to the fore, knowing this was her chance to prove he'd been wrong, all those years ago, to leave her and Ibiza. More than anything she wanted to prove it to him, that the island he'd left was a jewel, heaven on earth, and he'd been a fool ever to have forgotten.

'Three dates,' she told him, serious now as she started to plan. 'Three weekends. We could start tomorrow evening with Es Palmador, but perhaps you shouldn't leave your friends at El Figo?'

'They wouldn't mind. Belle would certainly understand and Nancy and Paul will hardly notice I'm not there.'

'So shall we sleep the night on the beach?'

'Clay masks and hot springs.' He saw the happiness in her face. 'Bee, I hate that you think I don't remember.'

'Catch some fish for supper. We can take some mackerel lines.'

'Lie back and look at the stars.'

'Get bitten by the sandflies.'

'No, no, no!' Now it was Edouard defending the memory. 'That never ever happened on Es Palmador.'

She grinned back at him. 'Listen to you,' she teased. 'There's hope for you still.'

'So we'll do it, yes?'

She was enchanted by his enthusiasm. 'We'll do it.' She reached forwards and kissed him and he caught the back of her head with

89

his hand and held her there, trapping her lips against his cheek.

'Bee . . . '

She broke free again. 'And now, Mr Bonnier, you should join your party and all those other girls.'

Hand in hand they waded back to shore, to Danilo's daiquiris and Mark Ure's music and a cluster of their friends waiting for them on the beach, and minutes after having left the sea the hot night air had dried her dress, and soon she was joined by Belle and Nancy, Maggie and Troy, Inca and her friends Claire and Tony, until it seemed as if everyone from childhood and beyond was dancing on the beach, some people she hadn't seen for months, who reminded her, over and over again how little they saw of her now, how much they wished she could make more time for them all.

And when much later the sky began to lighten and the water turn to pink and gold, the drum and bass finally quietened and then the real drummers began, beating in the dawn of a new day. The fishing boats returning home to San Antonio heard their unique and wonderful sound and, as they drew nearer, picked up the smell of barbecued bacon and eggs and freshly baked bread on the air. And then, as the sun began to rise some more, some of them saw the moment when all the dancing abruptly stopped and almost as one the entire party on the beach dropped onto the sand to face the sun and sat in silence but for the beating drums, to watch its spectacular climb into the sky.

6

Honey lay under her sheet, feeling the weight of the sun like a bar of heat across her legs, watching through half-closed eyes as the brilliant pinpricks of light filtered through the cracks in her half-open shutters. She was thinking about boats, how a pretty sailing boat would be ideal, with a rug and a picnic already waiting for them, tucked into the locker on board. In the old days there'd been boats aplenty and no end of people to lend them to her too. Sometimes she and her friends would make their way across to the island of Es Palmador in a flotilla of dinghies and rowing boats, once even a yacht, but now that she really needed one there was only their own little fishing boat, *Baby Jane*, which had sat in the garages at Can Falco for at least ten years and was bound to be rusting and peeling, with rotten sails and a broken outboard motor. She'd go and have a look at her after breakfast, while she still had the rest of the day to come up with an alternative.

She checked her watch, stretched one last time, slid her legs off the bed and then streaked across the room to the shower. She'd ask Claudio to cover for her while she took Belle and Nancy to Las Dalias, she thought as she poured conditioner into her hair, trying to loosen the windblown tangles from last night. She'd catch him before the end of his shift.

After the shower she took a beautiful new kaftan made by an old school friend from her cupboard. It was pale pink and embroidered with translucent seed pearls and sequins and Honey was currently trying to persuade her friend to make enough to sell them in the boutique at Can Falco.

As she dressed she reminded herself that Claudio was reliable, that after a few months he knew the routines of a Can Falco day as well as she did. She told herself that she couldn't have picked a better Saturday to take off, with so few guests arriving and leaving, and that if she wanted to camp the night on Es Palmador, swim horses into the sea and sunbathe at Santa Medea, she'd only be doing what Claudio had been urging her to do for ages: take more than one day off at a time.

But first there was the class and Tora, she knew, would be utterly delighted to see her there. Tora loved getting her hands on Honey — she was, after all, her most recalcitrant, challenging pupil of all. And in return Honey enjoyed the classes, recognizing that they were the only times she'd ever felt the full focus of her mother's attention, the only times she felt Tora reaching out to her. The fact that Tora sensed Honey's *bad energy*, as she put it, but never seemed even to contemplate asking her about it had long since ceased to hurt. The fact that Can Falco had been so busy and Honey had had barely time for a cup of coffee let alone a class for the past three months had, of course, passed Tora by.

After breakfast she left Claudio manning the front desk and went to the garages to have a look at *Baby Jane*. The padlock on the garage doors was stiff and the key refused to turn until she'd split her nail to the quick, dripping blood onto her clothes, but eventually the lock clicked open and she pulled apart the heavy wooden doors and peered inside. Outside the heat was already intense and the sunshine dazzlingly bright. Inside it was cool and dark, the room smelling of wet cement and mildew, and it took some time for Honey's eyes to adjust.

Backed up against the far wall were boxes still waiting to be unpacked from almost twenty years before, enormous wooden planters from Bali, some terracotta pots, several cracked now, all of them bought while

Can Falco was still being planned, and which had ultimately found no place. And in front of the boxes, sitting on a trailer with two flat tyres, was the boat.

She approached her cautiously. The last time *Baby Jane* had seen water was at least five years ago and even then anyone sailing her had known to have a bucket to hand. Never the prettiest boat, there had at least been a cheeriness to her but now she looked tired and dispirited and Honey felt terribly guilty that she'd neglected her so. *We'll clean you up darling*, she whispered, looking down into sludge at the bottom of the hull and sniffing distastefully. The holes seemed to have been plugged with dead flies, long-dead flies. She went over to the locker beside the boat and unclipped it and pulled out a little of the sail, covered in mildew now, with a two-foot long tear, and the rest felt so fragile it would no doubt rip completely at the merest hint of a breeze. Was fate telling her that her trip was doomed, a lost cause after all? She kicked shut the locker, wondering if she dared look at the outboard motor.

'Honeybee?'

She turned to see her father standing in the doorway, shielding his eyes with his hand and peering in curiously.

She clapped her hands free of dust and

walked over to him. 'Hi, Dad. Just looking at *Baby Jane*.'

'Very good, very good.'

'No, not very good at all, she's a complete mess.'

He took her arm eagerly, starting to steer her away. 'Now, I was wondering what you'd think about a trip into town?'

'You mean you'd like someone to drive you in?'

Her father had given up driving a few years earlier, after he'd missed the edge of the road in a storm and had been trapped in his car for twelve hours.

'That would be marvellous.'

'I can't, Dad. Not this morning. Get Claudio to take you.' Then she remembered she needed Claudio at Can Falco.

'But I'm asking for your daughterly hand. I'd like you to come out with me. We could sit in the square and gawp at the grockles and their revolting pink legs.'

'I could do with a hand too, a fatherly hand, blowing up the tyres on that bloody trailer, emptying the gunge and the flies out of *Baby Jane*'s bottom.'

He burst into delighted guffaws of laughter. 'You're not serious?'

'Yes, I am. She'll sink if I take her to Es Palmador in the state she's in now.'

Es Palmador? he should have asked. *Darling girl, why are you sailing to Es Palmador?* And if he'd asked she'd have told him. She would have loved him to ask. Not that he'd have had the first clue how to respond. He'd have given her a sweet smile and would have wandered away, the thought of challenging anybody about anything utterly alien to him. The world beyond the white walls of Can Falco was not really his concern.

'But, Honey, I can't help you,' he cried instead. 'Look at my clothes.'

'So get out of the pouffy smock, help me clean up *Baby Jane*, blow up the tyres on the trailer and in return I'll drive you to Ibiza town. Do it while I'm at Tora's class and then we can leave as soon as I've finished.'

He frowned down at his feet. 'I'm not sure I'd know where to start.'

She shook her head. 'I don't believe you. You're just saying that because you don't want to get dirty.'

'No,' he said. 'It's not that. I really wouldn't know where to start.'

'But it's your bloody boat, Dad.'

'I know, I know. But I haven't sailed her for years. Honey, I'm an old man who wants to spend his morning with a beer in the square, not messing around with boats . . . ' He turned away. 'But not to worry if you're too busy, I'll see if Maggie and Troy fancy a trip.'

She came up close to him, belatedly took in the neatly parted grey hair, the freshly shaven jaw, the clean pink toe-nails in his open-toed sandals.

'So what's so tempting about Ibiza town, Dad? You hate the place in summertime. What's making you want to go in today?'

'Oh, no one, nothing at all,' he said, all of a sudden not meeting her eye. 'I need a change of beer, that's all. I felt like sitting outside Montesol, watching the world go by, just like the old days.' He turned to go.

'Dad?' He looked back at her. She waited.

'Goddammit!' He exploded into laughter. 'All right, I said I'd meet a woman.' Then he grinned at her mischievously. 'You should be proud of me, Honey. She's an absolute cracker, got the most marvellous eyes. She arrived the day before yesterday all on her own, came from Durham or Darlington or somewhere beginning with D, anyway and I feel sorry for her. I said I'd show her around.'

'You mean Marianne Darlington?'

'Perhaps.'

'Who's here checking out places for her honeymoon? Great idea to show her around, Dad. You'd be doing her such a favour.'

'Pah, of course she isn't here for her honeymoon!'

98

'Yes, she is.'

'If you're saying this just to upset me, it's not working. I'm telling you she watches me, Honey, all the time.'

'She'd eat you for breakfast.'

'To which I mightn't say no.'

She shook her head. 'You're impossible.'

'Come on, spoilsport,' he cajoled, 'it's just a bit of fun. It's all in my head, Honey, you know that.'

'So clean up the boat and in return I'll take you there.'

He looked back at her with the kind of wariness she saw more and more on his face these days, as if he couldn't quite believe she was his daughter, so alien was she.

'You're very tough on your old dad, you know.'

'You think so?'

'I do. And Marianne's a perfect lady.'

'I'm sure she is. I trust her completely.'

He stuck his hands on his hips and looked dispiritedly back into the darkness of the garage.

'Do I have to go in there? It really smells very damp.'

'Leave the doors open.'

'I'm sure Shimmy Roberts would lend you *Nervous Wreck*.'

'If I set off in *Nervous Wreck*, there's a

good chance I'll never come back.' Then she leaned closer in to him, grinning. 'But you'd chance that wouldn't you, if it meant you didn't have to clean out *Baby Jane?*'

'Honey, there's absolutely no chance of a mere boat getting the better of you. You're the most capable woman I know.'

It's lucky I am. It's lucky I am. She began to walk away, reached the gate in the wall that led her through to the Garden of Serenity. 'Bye-bye, Dad, I'll pick you up at three. Get those hands dirty.'

Their exchange left her feeling mean-spirited and horrible. She knew what he thought of her, how all work and no play had made Honey a very dull daughter. With her tight-lipped refusal to laugh at his jokes, cheer on his boozing, encourage his flirtations, innocent as they may be, she knew, in his eyes, she was slowly turning into a self-righteous kill-joy. And yet, honestly, she knew that she'd always treated him this way. She'd wagged her finger at him at ten years old. She'd never been the daddy's girl who'd thrown herself exuberantly into his arms. Perhaps she'd been afraid that he'd drop her, even then.

But now, as she walked towards the Garden of Serenity, she was filled with regret and a powerful longing for it to be different. This morning he'd asked her to sit with him in the square, something he hardly ever did, and she'd responded by making him pay for it first. Of course he wasn't going to relish the chance of helping her with *Baby Jane*, he was a fusspot in a new white smock, but as usual she'd been tough on him when, just for once, she could have been gentle. Yes, of course Marianne Darlington was at the heart of his request, but there was always a woman on the horizon. The prospect of a pretty new guest was what got him up in the morning. What was different about this morning was that after months when they'd hardly talked at all he'd come specially to seek her out and she realized how pleased she was that he had. She vowed there and then that she would surprise him, she'd join him outside Montesol and they'd drink a beer together and she'd let him chat, she'd let him relax.

She was the first to arrive in the Garden of Serenity, before even Tora. She went to the fountain, bent her head and splashed her face, then found a spot on the grass and laid out her mat, close to where her mother would be teaching, partly shaded by the hedge. It was almost nine thirty — late for a yoga class, with the sun already high and hot enough to make any movement hard work, but she was looking forward to it even so. She needed a channel for the restless energy that had been building since she'd woken that morning and wouldn't leave her until the night on Es Palmador was over.

She lay back on the grass, shielded her eyes from the sun with her hand and pictured the two of them, Edouard and her, sailing across the bright blue sky on a ship-shape *Baby Jane*.

Perhaps they should snorkel? She'd better bring kit for Edouard. She wondered what it was that he remembered best about Es Palmador, what it was that he'd liked best. She wished she'd thought to ask him. And then she pushed Edouard out of her mind, telling herself to relax, breathe and let her thoughts dissolve. *Better bring blankets too.* She forced her eyes shut, breathed slowly, in and out again, in and out, then let them flash open again. How far she'd come from her sixteen-year-old self! Because Es Palmador had never been about *doing* something, it had been about *being* something, being happy, being there, knowing that Paradise was a secret beach in the warm inky dark of the night, with a smoke and a beer in your hand and a snapping log fire at your side, while the sight of the stars and the sound of the waves wove their magic.

But it had also been about being sixteen.

Was Edouard really imagining she could re-create that? It was impossible. She sat up again in a flurry of panic. Being sixteen had been at the heart of the magic. How could she re-create having no care in the world, with Edouard lying beside her obsessing about the FTSE, while she, no doubt, fussed about Can Falco? She stretched out her legs in front of her so that the sunlight caught the rings on her toes and she imagined him pacing the shoreline in a pinstripe suit, begging to be sailed home. In agitation she stretched and pointed her toes until she gave herself cramp. Then she shook everything loose again, smiled at the nervous wreck she'd become. Tora and her Barely Yoga class clearly couldn't begin too soon.

She lowered her head slowly down to her knees and brought her arms high over her head in a careful stretching arc then rested them on her ankles and stayed there, breathing in through her nose, out through her mouth, and finally her mind began to clear.

And then, with a jolt her eyes flew open again as she heard someone calling her name and remembered at exactly the same moment that Belle and Nancy were supposed to be joining the class. She leaped to her feet, flicking a quick glance at her watch then ran back out of the Garden of Serenity, across the gardens and into the hotel, through the big open windows that led into the main hall. There they were, mats rolled up under their arms, talking to Claudio, who was sitting in Honey's chair behind the desk, staring with rapt adoration at Nancy.

Belle came forwards and kissed Honey's cheek. A navy polka-dot scarf held back her thick chestnut hair and she was wearing baggy white cotton trousers and a white T-shirt. 'Hello. Were you hoping we'd forgotten? Tell me I'm wearing the right clothes?'

'I'd forgotten,' Honey admitted, breathing hard from her mad dash to reach them. 'My brain's closed down today. And you look great.'

'Claudio was just telling us the way to the class.' Belle grinned conspiratorially at Honey and added quietly, 'Silly me, I mean Claudio was just telling *Nancy* the way to the class.' She took Honey's arm. 'Take your time,' she called over her shoulder to Nancy and she purposefully led Honey away. 'The sparks are flying between those two. When we walked in through the doors, into the hall, he saw her and she saw him and, Honey, his face . . . ' Belle shook her head wonderingly. 'There was this look of utter, complete . . . *besottedness.*

I've never seen anything like it.'

'She is very pretty.'

'Yes, but even so. Perhaps that's just him. Please tell me he's not like that with all the girls.'

'No, I've never seen him like that with anybody here before. And as far as I know he hasn't got a girlfriend. So — ' she shrugged, laughing at the bemused look on Belle's face, 'why not? Perhaps that's it. Love at first sight. You should be pleased you were there to witness it.' She saw Belle's concern and stopped, surprised. 'You surely can't mind if she falls for Claudio and finally dumps Paul?'

'No. Not at all, but Nancy is . . . ' she shrugged, trying to come up with the right words. 'Paul and Nancy are very complicated. I've seen other guys falling for Nancy, but it's never made any difference to her. He's bad for her, but she's been with him so long I sometimes doubt she'll ever get away.'

'How bad for her?'

Belle frowned. 'He's not violent, nothing worse than what you saw the other night, but he's a bully. You saw that too?'

They paused in the doorway of some French windows that led them out of the hall and into the gardens outside.

'I saw him push her in. Afterwards I wondered if I'd misunderstood. Edouard

105

clearly thinks he's great.'

'No, it happened just as you saw.' Belle looked serious for a moment. 'Don't underestimate him. He's been working with Edouard over the past few months, and he's been to the flat quite often, so I've seen more of him than I've wanted to. And he's always so charming and wonderful. He'll take the trouble to remember the name of my boss, make jokes, bring bottles of champagne. And he's careful and polite and easy to have around but I look into his eyes and I know he's trouble. I wish he'd stay away.'

The warning in Belle's voice touched Honey with unease.

'But what does Edouard see in him? He's not a fool. He knows this, surely. Doesn't he?'

But now Nancy was bearing down upon them again, pushing her way between Belle and Honey and the three of them stepped outside together through the windows and both Belle and Nancy stopped and shielded their eyes from the sun.

'My God,' Nancy breathed. 'It's so beautiful.'

'Could that be Claudio or Can Falco?' teased Belle, laughing and then running forwards. 'Where do we go? Aren't we late?'

'We are late,' Honey agreed. 'And Tora does not like people to be late.'

106

She led them on, round another corner but then Nancy stopped again as she saw the terrace ahead of her, people sitting at the various tables and chairs, sipping coffee, eating croissants, talking and laughing, while the stunning gardens stretched away towards the pool.

'Please can I live here?' she said in wonder. 'Does anyone do that? Book in for six months? Or perhaps I should come and work here. How about it, Honey? I'm extremely efficient.' She caught the questioning look on Honey's face. 'Oh, for God's sake, not you too. I only spoke to him for about three seconds.' But she'd blushed a deep pink. 'He's very sweet. I'll admit that,'

'Everybody's in love with Claudio.'

'No, Honey, please, not me!' And there was a plea in her voice. 'You know the score.'

Now they'd left the terrace and had reached the Garden of Serenity, where they stopped beside its arched entrance cut into the hedge. Belle and Nancy looked at it, curious and impressed, trying to see inside. On the other side Honey could hear her mother chanting with her class, 'One taste, one touch, one choice, one heart, one cry, one joy, one life, one world.'

Belle, hearing it too, suppressed a quick splutter of nervous laughter and then glanced at Honey. 'I will be serious,' she told her solemnly. 'It's an honour to be here.'

Less than two minutes ago Honey had been early, now the three of them were going to have to walk into a class that had already begun. Honey stepped aside to allow Nancy to go through first and then, when Nancy didn't move, gave her an encouraging push. But instead of striding forwards, Nancy took two steps back and spun to face Honey, her eyes round with disbelief.

'When did you mention they'd be naked?' she gasped.

Belle clapped her hands over her mouth.

Naked? Honey looked through the hedge and saw her mother sitting on her mat, facing her class, and she was indeed naked as were they all.

Barely Yoga. She'd imagined it meant stripped-down yoga, yoga at its purest. But, given Tora, how ridiculous ever to have thought that.

'Good morning,' Tora said, smiling at her from her mat, but the glint in her big blue eyes said, *You're late.* 'Bring in your friends, we've just begun.'

She was sitting in the lotus position, her grey blonde hair piled up on top of her head, a few stray tendrils curling softly around her serene and beautiful face, upturned hands

108

resting on her round brown knees, her breasts rising and falling gently with each inward and outward breath, her long legs wrapped gracefully around each other, the position of her feet and ankles, for now, leaving the rest of her to the imagination. Honey quickly looked around the class, there were about ten of them, a mixed class, all in the lotus position, following their leader, all naked. She stepped back through the hedge to Nancy and Belle.

'Did you know about this?' Nancy demanded from where she stood, pressed flat against the hedge, her yoga mat clutched tightly against her.

Honey shook her head apologetically. 'But as Tora spends most of the day naked I should have guessed . . . So, do you want to stay?'

'Of course we do,' Belle declared, bending down to take off her sandals. But Nancy suddenly crumpled to the ground in hysterical giggles.

'I can't, I can't,' she cried. 'I won't know where to look.'

'Don't be ridiculous, close your eyes,' Belle told her as she pulled her T-shirt over her head. 'Or stare straight ahead.'

'You're weird,' said Nancy. 'You shouldn't be so keen. Imagine doing the Downward Dog.'

Belle grinned up at her. 'It doesn't bother me.'

Far more confident than Nancy with her clothes on, for Belle it was just the same with them off, even if it was Nancy who had the perfect body. Belle strode through the group with her shoulders back and her head held high, apologized to Tora for being late, then unrolled her mat and took her place. Following her in, Honey sat down beside her, then came Nancy, shoulders hunched, biting her lip, looking straight ahead.

Tora sat quietly, for the moment saying nothing, a beatific smile upon her face.

The whole class must be in love with her, Honey thought. Three people down from Belle, a thick-set hairy man was sitting out of line and staring at Tora with love pouring out of his eyes. Barely Yoga, unlike some of Tora's other conceptions — such as Touch Me Yoga and Upside Down Yoga — was clearly going to run and run.

'Now, at first you might find Barely Yoga strange,' Tora said in her slightly sing-song voice that yoga classes always seemed to accentuate. 'You might find it feels funny. If you do, you are allowed to laugh.' She looked around at her class. 'Or perhaps Barely Yoga will make you want to cry?'

Nervous face stared back at her.

'I warn you, kneeling on your pubic hair can hurt.'

Tora was not a naturally humorous person and said this rather awkwardly but the group let out a little chuckle even so, and Nancy an uncontrolled, spluttering snort. Honey, risking a glance at her, saw her cheeks were very pink and her bright eyes wide open, fixed on the fountain ahead of her. But for the rest of the group it was clearly the right thing to say. All around her Honey could feel people start to relax and shift position, this poor buttoned-up class finally feeling fresh air all over their bodies and finding it felt rather good.

'These are the bodies we've been given,' Tora reasoned earnestly. 'We should be comfortable with them. We should celebrate their unique geometries, not hide them away ... because each fold of flesh, each line and wrinkle is as much a part of us as our thoughts and fears. Barely Yoga brings us one step closer to realizing that.'

From the corner of her eye, Honey saw Nancy give Belle a tiny, straight-faced nod.

'You will recognize many of the poses and breathing exercises from other classes,' Tora went on, 'but today you will experience them in a different way, in a naked way.'

All around Honey her class seemed to

shuffle in agreement. Honey risked a second glance at Nancy and this time Nancy caught her eye, glittering with fun and barely controlled hysteria.

And yet, Honey thought, Barely Yoga could still work. Yes, the class was naked. Yes the hairy man clearly wanted Tora for his wife. But so far her mother's words were making sense, and as long as she carried on this way, practical and devoid of sexuality, as long as Tora didn't go off on one of her specials and start talking about Indian temples and tantric sex, perhaps good things could come from such a class.

'And then,' said Tora, 'when we are comfortable in our skins, we will take a journey together.'

Ah, thought Honey, remembering the last journey, the one that had led them out into the gardens to sing to the olive trees and thank them for the joy they'd brought to the world. She couldn't quite imagine Belle and Nancy dancing naked through the gardens.

'But first let us stretch.' Tora paused, looking around her pupils for one, two, three seconds, and then she began, stretching her legs out in front of her. 'We shall bring our right knees in to our chests.' She looked approvingly around as the class, to a person, immediately followed her lead. 'Good, good.

We shall hold it, one, two, three, we will stretch out through our heels, point and raise, point and raise, then lower as we exhale again . . . '

And so they stretched and with each outward breath the class collectively seemed to relax some more, everybody committing wholeheartedly to each pose, clearly willing to follow inspirational Tora wherever she led them, from sitting to lying to standing to kneeling on all-fours, swinging arms, touching toes, legs wide apart, bare bottoms lifting willingly to the sun, so that it was only Honey — and perhaps Nancy — who remained certain that Barely Yoga was heading towards more than just a naked exercise routine.

Fifteen minutes later Tora abruptly brought the stretching to an end. Honey, who had been waiting for the moment, glanced up to see a definite look of anticipation on her mother's face as she sat cross-legged once more, waiting for the complete attention of her class. When she had it, she nodded.

'Now we are going on our journey,' she told them, eyes opening wider, 'a journey down to the ocean of our beginning, to where all our stories start.'

The class stared back with rapt attention at Tora. Honey risked another quick glance at Nancy, who nodded very solemnly back, but her eyes were on fire again and suddenly it was Honey fighting not to laugh.

'Dive deep,' Tora told them, 'clear your birthing spiral and allow your inner curiosity and delight the freedom to fly. Now that we are naked as babies, let us be reborn.' With that, she dropped her head to her knees and gracefully wrapped her arms around her body. 'We will dive deep and we will stretch to the sky.' She tipped back her face and flung her arms high above her head. 'Stretch to the sky, stretch to the sky, reach for the light. All of us, naked, let us be reborn. Let all the doubts and fears that have settled on our skin be cast away.'

'Not really yoga at all, is it?' Belle whispered to Honey out of the corner of her mouth as she reached, reached for the light.

'It's *Barely* Yoga,' Honey reminded her.

Tora threw her arms over her head again and all around Honey and Belle the rest of the class enthusiastically did the same, alternately ducking down, then lifting their heads, throwing their arms in the air and chanting with Tora. 'Let's fly, let's fly. Stretch to the sky.'

Then Tora rose to her feet and the class eagerly scrambled up after her, and now there was passion in her husky voice and her cheeks were flushed as she began a kind of breast stroke in the air. 'Come on, class,' she urged, 'chant with me the precious words and feel your rebirth begin. Stretch . . . pulse . . . undulate . . . reach for the light.'

'Stretch . . . pulse . . . undulate . . . reach for the light,' the class recited. Honey risked a quick glance down the line and saw that the hairy man had stayed sitting cross-legged on the floor and was now rocking gently with eyes wide open and a fixed blissed-out smile on his face.

'Stretch . . . pulse . . . undulate . . . reach for the light.'

And at this point the loudspeakers set into the fountain suddenly gurgled into life, filling the garden with a cacophony of flutes, drums, splashing water and calling birds. Honey, unable to risk a look at Belle, focused on the hedge in front of her and put her hands together, copying Tora. She'd never found the music funny before, but then she'd never had Belle beside her yet.

'She's hypnotized everyone,' Nancy managed to squeak out at Honey as around them the class chanted on. 'Does this happen often?'

'No, not so much. Not like this.'

'I love her. I love this class, but admit it, Honey. She's completely bonkers.'

Beside Nancy a woman was loudly

chanting with Tora, 'Stretch, pulse, undulate, reach for the light.' The woman was saying it over and over again, eyes closed, building herself into a frenzy, her arms diving forwards, reaching for the light, her hair dishevelled, breasts bouncing, her cheeks flushed. 'Reach for the light,' she cried, wobbling on her feet. 'Oh, Jesus, reach for the light.'

Nancy caught Honey's eye again, struggling desperately to smother her laughter and failing completely.

'Reach for the — ' And then, 'Oh — ' the woman gasped. 'Oh, God.'

'Is she?' Nancy said disbelievingly. 'Oh Honey, she is, isn't she?'

'Yes,' cried the woman, 'yes, yes. Oh Jesus, yes.'

It was too much. Doubled up with laughter they dived back through the hedge, and threw themselves gratefully, giggling uncontrollably, onto the grass on the other side.

7

Late the same morning Honey, Belle and Nancy wandered into the crowded Las Dalias market, and seeing it through Belle and Nancy's eyes, even the stalls full of tat had a magic that day. They wasted no time, swiftly plunging in, brushing their way through rails of hand-embroidered blouses and skirts, breathing in the bergamot and patchouli oil, moving from stall to stall, filling their bags not only with clothes, but also with dream-catchers, wooden toys, wind chimes and incense sticks.

'Where next?' Belle asked breathlessly when, an hour later, they'd finally completed the circuit.

'Nearly done,' Honey replied. 'And on the way out we'll pass my very favourite stall of all, but first . . . you have to meet Paris and Lucinda.'

'Is that a brand?'

'Almost,' Honey laughed. 'You'll love them. They've been here longer than anyone and they live in a white castle on a private island halfway between Ibiza and Formentera. They have elephants in their garden and they throw

117

the most badly behaved parties ever.'

'Darling, darling,' Lucinda growled, taking a quick last drag on a Cuban cigar before tossing it away as Honey steered Belle and Nancy towards her stall. 'How absolutely marvellous to see you here.'

She prodded at the shaggy, white-haired man asleep on a deckchair beside her. 'Paris, wake up. Darling Honey's here.'

Lucinda made jewellery, *because we girls like wearing something pretty, darling*. She had dyed jet-black hair, painted eyebrows and very red lips, and mesmerizing blue eyes that now turned with interest to Nancy and Belle.

'Friends,' Honey insisted, warning her off.

'No, customers, darling, customers, how exciting.'

Tentatively Belle picked up a fine jade necklace that had a little round ceramic disc in the middle, held it up closer to see that in the middle was a tiny ceramic hairdryer, brush and a pair of scissors.

'Hairdresser's necklace, darling,' Lucinda explained. 'But that one's not selling so well. Surfers and fortune tellers sell brilliantly,' she flashed her blue eyes at Belle. 'Two-four-five-O, darling, twofourfiveoh. Say it fast and it doesn't sound so bad.'

'That's two thousand, four hundred and fifty euros,' Honey said, slowly in case Belle hadn't taken it in.

'Yes, darling,' Lucinda said, completely unabashed, 'worth every penny.'

Belle put down the necklace and picked up a silver charm bracelet strung with taps.

'Does this have a profession too?'

'No, darling, I just thought it would be fun.'

'And this?' Belle had picked up a brown leather belt with a heavy silver buckle and a fringe of little silver books.

'You must have heard of the Bible Belt?'

Nancy laughed delightedly and reached out for it.

'I want it,' said Belle, grabbing it off her.

'So do I,' protested Nancy.

'I have more, many more. I have the corn belt,' — Lucinda pulled a belt made of plaited straw out from beneath her desk — 'and Orion's Belt — that has a sword of course. And the green belt.' She held out a belt made half of what looked like real grass, and half a succession of grimy-looking tower blocks and chimney stacks. They're two-six-oh, darling, all the same price.' She flashed them both a sudden kind smile. 'But as you're friends of Honey's you can have them for fifty.'

From his chair Paris opened one eye, took in the fact that three pretty girls had wandered in, and opened the other.

He stood up and looked at Nancy. 'Do I know you? Who are you? What time is it?'

'It's twelve,' said Belle.

'Oh, I don't recognize anyone until I've had my beer. What's your name again? Have we met before?'

A green belt, a bible belt and an invitation to one of Lucinda and Paris's infamous parties later, and the girls moved on, ambled their way back towards the exit and the main road, and then made one last stop at another of Honey's favourite stalls. This one was owned by a Spanish woman called Camila and it sold quilts and blankets, cot size to king size, cashmere and silk, fine and soft and incredibly warm, striped or checked in bright sea greens and turquoise blues then oversewn with wonderful collage-like pictures made from downy feathers or shells, scraps of velvet and taffeta, pearls and silver thread, all of them one-offs, each of them completely stunning.

Honey stood to one side, knowing Nancy and Belle were bound to love everything, and sat down in an empty deckchair just inside the stall, prepared for a long wait. And then, as she cast an idle eye around, immediately she saw what could only be *her* blanket right there in front of her, pinned to the sheet that divided the stall from the one next to it. It was big enough to cover her double bed in winter and so appropriate and so beautiful it had to have been made for her, with its aqua blues and greens like her bedroom and its picture was of her and Edouard, a boat sailing through a sunset streaked sky, two indistinct figures sitting at the prow, gold and silver fish dancing in its wake.

She forced herself to look down at her hands instead and told herself *absolutely not*. Not only because it was far too intricate and carefully sewn to survive a trip on *Baby Jane* and then a night on Es Palmador unscathed, but probably much too expensive as well.

And she truly thought she'd convinced herself, even as she stood up and found herself interrupting a surprised Belle, mid-haggle, to ask Camila to bring the blanket down so that she might look at it more closely. And then, with just a quick glance to confirm it really was as beautiful as she thought it was and without even an attempt at a haggle herself, she heard herself interrupting Belle again to say that she would like it. Much to her own surprise, she was then quickly opening her bag with sweaty fingers and bringing out a roll of euros, counting them off, ignoring the astonished look on Belle's face and, less than two minutes later, and almost as if it hadn't happened at all, she was sitting again in the corner of the stall with the beautiful blanket now clasped safely on her lap.

Ten minutes later Belle had bought one too and only Nancy was still undecided.

'Come on, ditherer,' urged Belle, looking as if the heat and the crush had finally caught up with her. She shifted from foot to foot, rolled her eyes at Honey and mouthed bitterly, 'Paul,' and belatedly Honey understood. She stood up and went over to join Nancy, who was standing over Camila's desk, looking anxiously at the blanket spread out in front of her.

'You're not sure Paul will like it?'

Nancy's choice was of a blanket that looked like an old English garden, sewn with clusters of roses, made of silk taffeta, beautifully finished in shades from palest baby pink to dark rugosa red. There was a fat bumblebee climbing the sky, and a cup and saucer wittily sewn into the velvet green grass, but Honey resisted the desire to urge Nancy on, understanding that, however lovely it was, that was not the point.

'A bit too girly for him,' Nancy decided regretfully. She thanked Camila and turned away.

'But you don't even live with him,' Belle

snapped from her place on Honey's chair. 'And it's your bedroom, your bed.' Nancy spun around and gave Belle a steely look. 'You should be able to put what you like on your own bed,' Belle insisted quietly.

'I know, but I'm not going to. Let's go.'

Belle stayed where she was, rubbed a hand across her hot forehead. 'The least you should do is buy it and stick it in a cupboard until you've got rid of him.'

'You think?'

Belle nodded and somehow managed to hold Nancy's angry stare. 'Yes, it's my bed,' Nancy said. 'But I want Paul in it too. So shut up.'

'All wrong, all wrong,' muttered Belle but she said nothing more, just pushed herself to her feet and Honey followed the two of them out of the market and back into the sunlight.

Heading towards the car, she hung back so that the other two could walk together. She watched Nancy, giggly, laughing, clearly ensuring the tension was immediately put behind the two of them. Was it lust for Paul that kept her at his side? Defiance in the face of too many people telling her to let him go? Either way Honey could no longer believe she was the defenceless little doll she'd witnessed the night before. However scary and threatening Paul had seemed, however much it had seemed she was in his thrall, Honey doubted it now.

Back at Can Falco Honey left them sitting on the terrace with glasses of iced tea while she caught up with Claudio. They'd only been away for a couple of hours but she'd had the briefest of handover chats with him before she'd joined the Barely Yoga class and, towards the end of their tour around Las Dalias, niggles of concern had kept leaping into her mind. Ridiculous niggles: there was a couple desperate to buy the bed from their room. Could Honey sell it to them? They were checking out that afternoon and Honey had forgotten to talk to them about the bed. And a young woman who'd fallen in love with a dog she'd met on the beach. Could Honey organize its return to England? And practical niggles, too. They were running very low on charcoal for the barbecues — had she remembered to ask Claudio to order more?

Claudio had ordered the charcoal and had tried to persuade the couple to let him order them a new bed, exactly the same as the one they'd been sleeping in, but they were having none of it. He'd begun the laborious process of bringing the dog to England and two new waitresses had turned up for work the night before so coked up he'd had to fire them before they'd even started. It was a familiar enough catalogue of events, Honey hardly needed to react at all.

'And can you work the next three Saturday nights?' she asked instead.

They were standing side by side, looking at the diary open on her desk and at that he turned to her in surprise.

'Of course,' he nodded then. After all the times he'd teased her for working too hard, he was careful not to say anything else.

'And tonight too? Would you mind?'

'Absolutely not. I would be delighted.'

'Claudio?'

He turned and looked at her solemnly. 'Yes, Honey?'

'It's nothing to get excited about. I'm going out — stop acting like I've never done it before.'

At that a grin broke across his flawless honey-gold skin, his eyes with their thick fringe of black lashes laughing into hers. *Gorgeous*, she thought, startled by his beauty. *You are absolutely gorgeous. Nancy would be a fool to let you go.*

'I understand.'

She put the diary away in a drawer. 'I'm sailing to Es Palmador.'

He nodded again.

'Dad's helping me launch *Baby Jane* this afternoon.'

'Now you make me nervous.'

She laughed. 'I wondered. Do you want to come and have lunch with me and Nancy and Belle?'

'You mean now?' He looked back at her startled but, instantly, transparently keen. 'This lunch? Lunch today?'

She grinned back at him. 'Angela can watch reception. We can eat on the terrace and then she can grab us when something goes wrong.'

★　★　★

Honey had to bide her time, but after lunch her opportunity came. Stretching in her chair, first Belle sighed at the heat, then fanned herself with the wine list and, taking her chance, Honey bounced to her feet.

'Come for a swim?'

'No, I'd drown.'

'Belle,' she said impatiently, 'I've got half an hour, then I'm back on duty. Claudio's taking the afternoon off, so come and swim with me now.'

At Honey's words Nancy stretched back in her chair and closed her eyes, clearly in no mood to move herself, and Belle belatedly got it. 'Swimming! Of course I want to go swimming.'

Honey turned to Claudio. 'Don't go back to reception, please. Angela knows where we are. If you're covering for me tonight you must take a proper break now. I'm going to tell her to give you another hour.'

She saw that he was aware of what she was doing and that he couldn't quite believe it. The look on his face made her laugh inside. She'd crossed a line with Claudio that day but all she could wonder was why it had taken so long. It had felt so right. They'd eaten together many times before, shared lunches, sometimes alone, other times with guests, but she'd never strayed into his personal life, certainly wouldn't have plonked the object of his affections down in front of him, actively gone out of her way to make it happen. And perhaps it had been triggered by the desire to prise Nancy away from Paul, but it was her affection for Claudio that she was aware of now. And having watched the two of them flirting over lunch, there was no doubt at all that she'd helped set something in motion between them. How far Nancy would allow it to go she'd have to wait to see.

When she arrived at the pool she found Belle already in the water doing lengths, her bag on a nearby sunbed. Honey pulled off her kaftan and sat down in a spotted blue bikini, then flipped up her legs and lay back, closing her eyes, trying to ignore the guilty voice telling her that she shouldn't be there, she should be inside, that whatever she'd said about Angela, Angela was next to useless and manning reception alone would terrify her. She closed her eyes against the sun and forced herself to lie still.

A few seconds later Belle lay down beside her, spraying her with welcome droplets of water. 'Do you ever go topless here?'

Honey shook her head, shielding her eyes from the sun.

'Not unless you're doing a Barely Yoga class, you mean?'

Honey grinned. 'Wasn't it fun?'

'Absolutely brilliant. I'll be there again tomorrow — if you don't mind. Your mother said I was a natural. I told her I'd booked my place. You know, I wonder if I could persuade them to take it up at Esporta.' Then moments later she sighed heavily. 'My God this is bliss. How do you ever do any work?' There was the briefest of silences while Belle waited for Honey to respond and then she went straight on.

'Ok, Honeybee Ballantyne, what are you up to?'

'What are you talking about?'

'I'm not talking about Nancy and Claudio. We both know the score there . . . have to cross our fingers and hope.'

Honey could think of nothing to say and so she just lay there, letting the sun beat down on her face, waiting for whatever Belle was going to say next.

'I'm talking about Edouard.'

The truth was she didn't want to talk or think about him. Edouard was about this evening. This was now.

'You'd have seduced him years ago if you'd wanted to,' Belle went on, forcing Honey to open her eyes. 'But I can't help thinking that's what you've got in mind for tonight.'

'Wrong, wrong, wrong.' She shut her eyes against Belle's inquisitive stare.

'I don't think so. You're taking him to a deserted island for the night. How romantic is that?'

'We have a history there.'

'Honey, please! Don't you think he's attractive?'

'Of course I do.' Honey sighed, took her time. 'But we've always been too close. We're like bro — '

'Oh no, don't say it.'

Now Honey turned her head back towards her. 'It sounds like a cliché but I mean it. For years he was much too important for me to think of him in any other way. Edouard and I have known each other all our lives and you have to understand how it was here. Both of us are only children. Both sets of parents lived in permanent la-la land. We only had each other. We'd spend all our time together.' Unconsciously she'd pushed herself upright in her chair as she spoke because from nowhere it was now very important that Belle understood how it had been. 'We'd go off camping, take a rucksack and come back after a couple of days and they wouldn't have realized we'd gone. Can you imagine that? How could they? We were only about ten. That's what I mean when I say we were important to each other.'

Belle didn't answer, but looked at her solemnly.

'Actually in a way it was fantastic. We used to have adventures, do amazing things.' She hesitated, wondering how bizarre her life might be sounding to Belle and how much more she wanted to tell her, after all. 'And then Edouard's parents grew up a bit, started to act more like parents, while if anything mine went even more loopy and unreliable.' She frowned. 'So what I'm saying is that if I hadn't had Edouard around I'd have become a very strange child and a completely deranged teenager.'

'And you never fancied him?'

'Probably I did. I've kissed him. I even went out with him for about a week, when we were about fourteen, until we both decided it was time we found somebody else.'

'He told me about that. Oh, I'm sorry.' Belle laughed at the surprise on Honey's face. 'Not in any detail. Just told me about the tosser you went out with next, Jerome? Was that his name?'

She giggled. 'I can't believe Edouard told you about Jerome!'

'Tell me about Edouard,' Belle insisted. 'So tonight you'll camp together, lie on some beach together, but, just to be clear, it's only for old times' sake?'

'Exactly.' Honey carefully lay back down on her sunbed and closed her eyes once more. 'Now talk about something else.'

'Haven't you ever wondered what Edouard makes of you now?'

'No.'

Belle dropped her sunglasses back over her eyes and lay back to the sun.

'I don't believe you. And I'm sure it'll muddle you up no end but I'm going to tell you what I think even so.'

'Please don't.'

'You *have* to hear it, Honey. Because if

131

you're not interested in him, what are you planning to do on that island? You'll sit him down on the beach, you'll talk, watch the stars, drink some wine . . . and then? What do you want to happen?'

'I suppose we'll fall asleep.'

'That's ridiculous.'

'No!'

'Be honest with yourself. Last time you were on Es Palmador you kissed him. I know because he told me.'

Honey put her hand over her mouth. 'Oh God, was it there?'

'You know it was.'

'So?' she asked defiantly. 'We were sitting by the fire. I'd split up with my boyfriend and I wanted him to see me kiss someone else. That's why it happened. Edouard kissed me as a favour. It may seem strange to you, Belle, but that's all it was.'

Belle wasn't convinced. 'So you're telling me, of all the places on the island, you two have just *happened* to choose to go back there? But it doesn't have any special significance for either of you?'

'Es Palmador is not our special place. We kissed each other, no big deal. That's what we did, that's what everybody did. I've probably kissed him on lots of other beaches too, only I can't remember doing it. So don't try and prove anything, Belle, because there's nothing to prove. Edouard thinks the same way as me. We chose Es Palmador because we had happy times there. The kissing does not come into it.'

8

There were two very different sides to Ibiza. In the south was the clubbers' paradise, around the bay of San Antonio, twenty-four-seven music and dancing. It was easy to spend a holiday there and never venture out of town. But high in the hills, the wind in the pine forests was still the only sound you heard and the wildlife was of the natural variety. Little had changed here since Tanit, goddess of fecundity, was first worshipped and the Phoenician and Carthaginian settlers sailed past Benirras Beach and stayed for the sunset.

Little had changed for two thousand years and yet in the last few decades Ibiza's peaceful and tolerant spirit had been stirred like never before and this time the marauding pirates were the money men, Mammon colliding with Tanit, greed colliding with generosity, bulldozers churning through the almond blossom to make way for new roads, threatening the Full-Moon and Petal parties with the all-night roar of a motorway.

And for Honey, sitting on the harbour wall

in her sarong, swinging her legs as she waited for Edouard and thinking about such things, the thought of Paul and Anna now also looking to make their mark on the island made her sick. Hypocritically clothed in eco-speak, it was as if Anna thought a cursory nod to the green lobby was all that was necessary to make her ideas attractive. The truth was it was the Annas and Pauls with too much money and too little sensitivity who could ruin Ibiza in the end. And where exactly did Edouard stand? Shoulder to shoulder with the two of them? Clearly there was some sort of relationship developing and she knew she wouldn't like the details if she was ever told what they were. She didn't want to doubt him, and yet wasn't that why she was here, waiting on the harbour wall for him now, knowing it was time to reimpress upon him the values that they'd grown up with? Because she did doubt him. He'd clearly been impressed with Paul and for all the brushing-Anna-aside when Honey had challenged him, Honey thought he rated her still. So taking him to Es Palmador was as much about proving how wrong he was to give Anna the time of day — let alone a free rein with his house, let alone any influence at all on Ibiza — as it was about their own past together.

With much affected grunting and groaning Hughie had finally launched *Baby Jane* into the sea, but because he had been so slow leaving Can Falco there were now just a few minutes left before Edouard was due to join her at the harbour. As Hughie had struggled to launch the boat she'd been tight-lipped with irritation, and all her good intentions of walking with him to Montesol afterwards, to put him at his ease and spend some quality time together, had vanished in her irritation. She hadn't even told him that she might join him and, understandably, Hughie had not hung around, almost running back up the hill towards a rendezvous with Troy and Maggie and, no doubt, Marianne Darlington too, as relieved to see the back of her as he was of *Baby Jane*.

She saw Edouard before he saw her, watched him slipping purposefully between the wandering holiday-makers, making his way down the street towards her. Today he was wearing shorts and a pink T-shirt and carried with him two fishing rods, and his air of purpose made him stand out. She could see people noticing him. Slipping off the harbour wall, she stood up to meet him.

'I thought *Baby Jane* had gone to heaven,' he said, peering over the harbour wall to look down at their boat.

'She's been brought back from the dead by Dad.'

'And was I hallucinating or did you invite Shimmy Roberts to join us too? I'm sure I just saw him making his way down here.'

The throaty growl of a Harley Davidson drowned out her denial and she turned away from Edouard to see Shimmy manoeuvring carefully through the crowds of people towards them. He was wearing just a pair of scuffed black leather trousers and his bare torso was as wrinkled and brown as a dried nut. A red spotted bandanna held back his rocker-length grey hair. With a final revving of the engine he arrived beside Honey then dropped his feet to the ground to balance the bike.

'Glad I caught you,' he said, scratching an armpit, directing all his attention to Honey, ignoring Edouard completely. 'Heard you'd got no flares. Heard you'd got no boat either, but you didn't fancy *Nervous Wreck*.'

'No, I didn't fancy her at all, Shimmy,' Honey agreed.

A reluctant twinkle came into his eye. 'I suppose I don't blame you, though I can't believe *Baby Jane*'s any better.' With a lopsided grin he unflipped a saddlebag, then dropped a firework into her arms. It was a rocket — *Triple Whistling*, she read on the

137

label — red and gold and looking big enough to reach the moon. 'Fire it if you need me. I'll come and find you if I see this in the sky.'

He spoke in a quiet drawl you had to strain to hear. As long as she'd known him, Honey had never heard him raise his voice.

'Thank you,' she laughed. 'And of course I'll have Edouard here to help me out.'

Now that he was forced to acknowledge Edouard he gave him a dismissive nod. 'Who'd a thought it?'

'I know,' agreed Edouard cheerfully. 'Look at us two, sailing into the sunset together.'

'You take good care of her,' Shimmy glowered at Edouard, as suspicious and resentful of him now as he had always been, with no more cause now than he had had before. He turned the key to his bike and the engine roared back into life. Raising a hand in farewell to Honey and lifting his feet, they watched and waited as he wove back through the crowd and disappeared.

'You know, I'd say he likes me now,' Edouard declared as he carried the cool boxes and blankets over to the boat. 'He really seemed to care.'

Then he took a running jump and landed heavily on the bottom of *Baby Jane*, causing the boat to tip violently from side to side.

'Pinstripe arse,' said Honey.

Edouard had brought the booze and she'd brought the picnic — apricots, figs, almonds and grapes from the gardens at Can Falco, bread, sweet round potatoes to cook on the fire, packets of butter and herbs, tomatoes and freshly caught fish that tasted like heaven when barbecued on the beach. And for breakfast the next morning she'd brought orange juice and rolls, a frying pan, bacon and eggs — for all that she'd never lived in England, she was an English girl at heart.

They sailed out of the harbour, the wind strong enough to fill *Baby Jane*'s sails and lift Honey's spirits just the same. They sat on opposite sides of the boat, Edouard's face turned to the open sea, and Honey watched him close his eyes to the wind as his streaky hair blew back from his face, and she saw that he loved it already and wondered if maybe Es Palmador was about to work its magic after all.

They crossed the water without a mishap and by the time they reached Es Palmador it was six and the sky was turning pink. In the shallows they jumped off *Baby Jane* and pulled her up onto the beach. There was a place in the dunes that they had always made for, sheltered and yet open to the sky, close enough to the water to hear the shush-shush of the sea, and now, years after they'd been here last and without even needing to discuss it, this was of course where they headed for.

After several trips back to *Baby Jane* to get everything up to their camp, Honey spread the old tartan blankets on the sand and finally brought out her new blanket, parcelled up in tissue paper.

'What is that?' Edouard asked.

In answer, she ripped off the paper and shook out the blanket, then laid it carefully down upon the other blankets.

Edouard spent a few moments taking it in, then came over to Honey and slipped his arm around her shoulders. 'It's us. It's you and me!' He bent down to see her face and she nodded her agreement. 'How sweet that you brought it. It's beautiful.' She grinned back at him. 'And so is here.' He raised his eyebrows at her, making her laugh. 'And so are we, *beautiful*, and so are you,' he dropped his voice again, '*beautiful*,' he said softly.

'Shut up silly man,' she replied, laughing still.

'You know we're going to have fun?'

'More than fun. We're going to make you sixteen again.'

He nodded. 'And you too.'

He turned away from her and dropped to

his knees beside the cool box. 'Beer, wine, champagne?' he asked. 'A little Vino Tinto? What did you used to like?'

'Bailey's Irish Cream,' she admitted, laughing again.

He rummaged, found a corkscrew and a bottle of wine, then sat back on his heels to open it for her, as completely at home as she'd known he would be, sand on his long brown feet and brushed up against his legs, his pink T-shirt wrapped around his strong muscular body by the breeze.

She turned back to the sea and undid her sarong. The cotton was so fine that the wind caught it and made it stream out from her like a long pink sail. Underneath she was wearing a white bikini, fifties style with a halter neck top and a big square tortoiseshell buckle between her breasts. Holding the sarong high above her head as the wind whipped against her hair, she fought it for a moment and she knew that Edouard had stopped what he was doing and was watching her. And then she let it go and the sarong dipped like a kite before the wind blew it upwards into the sky and away across the sand dunes.

'After it!' Edouard declared with a shout, dropping everything and running, racing up a sand dune, then leaping out of sight with a

141

rush of laughter, half cry, half shout. Honey tore after him, leaping and falling, running again. They found the sarong almost immediately but in an instant they'd become children again, climbing to the tops of the sand dunes to take it in turns to wave it and let it go again, then running, leaping into the air, rolling into the sand at the bottom, so that sand went everywhere, up their noses and in their mouths, their hair, their ears, down her bikini and Edouard's shorts.

Then, exhausted, they staggered towards the sea, Edouard stripping off his T-shirt and tossing it back onto the beach before diving into the silky warm water, disappearing underneath. They ducked under and swam side by side, Honey's long hair streaming out behind her like a mermaid's, opening their eyes in the salt water to grin at each other before bursting back to the surface. She felt for the bottom with her toes, then pushed her hair back from her face, eyes shining, and Edouard took two clumsy steps towards her and pulled her under again.

As darkness fell they lit a fire and lay on the rugs, opposite each other, propped up against the old cushions they'd brought from *Baby Jane*, watching the stars and the flickering fire, smoking a little grass and drinking wine from two crystal glasses Honey had purloined from Can Falco — after all, what was the point of having such beautiful things for all the guests if they couldn't occasionally be used by her?

'Last time I was here you kissed me,' Edouard said, lifting the frying pan onto the fire. 'Right there.' He pointed to a patch of sand a few feet away from him. 'You do remember that, don't you?'

'Belle reminded me about it yesterday.'

'But you hadn't forgotten.'

'No.'

On hands and knees she crossed over to him and kissed him again but this time on the cheek, not the lips.

He touched the place with his hand. 'First time felt better, you know.'

'Too bad.'

She turned and lay down beside him and stretched out, resting her head against his bare shoulder, knowing that she was being unfair coming so close, but unable to stop herself all the same. 'Roman Castilia,' she said, remembering the name of the boyfriend she'd just split up from, who'd prompted her kiss with Edouard. 'He deserved it too. I can't even think what he was like now.'

She felt his arm pull her closer.

'Hot and sweaty,' he said.

'What?'

'That's what he was like. That's what we used to call him, me and all your friends, when we used to laugh about him behind your back.'

She looked up at him. 'No, you did not laugh. He was a God.'

'You know he couldn't swim?'

'Of course he could. He was a fine swimmer.'

Edouard shook his head. 'I remember distinctly.'

She relaxed against his shoulder, sipping at her wine. He was making her laugh, and laughing made her want to kiss him so badly it almost overwhelmed her. She wanted to stretch out on top of him and kiss him and kiss him. And she wanted to tell him too. *I can't believe how badly I want to kiss you Edouard*, she wanted to say, but of course she didn't.

Years ago, when they'd lain here before a flickering fire, their friends had been close by. She'd leaned over him, catching him completely unawares. And as she'd softly touched her lips to his, she'd seen the surprise in his face turn swiftly to pleasure and passion and abruptly she'd stopped again.

'Why?' he'd asked, lying flat on his back staring up into her face.

144

'Because I know Roman is watching me.'

It had been a thoughtless thing to do, even if she hadn't seen until too late how much Edouard had cared. At seventeen he hadn't been able to disguise his feelings quite so well.

Now the older Edouard, mature, grown-up Edouard, who had got so good at hiding his feelings and thoughts she hardly knew him at all, shifted comfortably beside her.

'Remember James Bream's sunburnt buttocks?'

She laughed out loud in thankful relief. 'They had a baby, didn't they?'

He nodded. 'Him and Miranda Henson.'

'And do you remember the plague of wasps?'

'That wasn't here, that was Formentera.'

He nodded. 'The jellyfish were here.'

'Stung that American guy who was allergic to sand.'

'You'd think he'd have found that out before he came here.'

'Didn't he have such a bad weekend?'

'He did.'

Edouard gently disentangled his arm and sat up, stretching forwards to flick a knob of butter into the frying pan.

Honey sniffed appreciatively. 'Even butter smells delicious here. Have we died and gone to heaven?' Then she lay back again against the cushions, watching him as he rolled the butter around the pan. 'You have to admit, Edouard . . . We've proved it already. It's as lovely as it always was.'

'I do admit.' He opened the cool box and found the fish, dropping them one by one into the sizzling butter then squirting them with lemon.

'And we've only just begun. Remember, we haven't even touched on Cala Mastella and Santa Medea . . . So you have also to admit that you should spend some more time here, that you need to say, 'Sod the job'.'

'Oh, Honey,' he turned to her, shaking his head with disappointment, 'don't you realize you're going to have to try much harder than that?'

'I'm not so sure. I think Es Palmador's working its magic on you. Salt in your hair, sand between your toes, your sweet happy face . . . I'm beginning to recognize you again now.'

He sat back on his heels and looked at her with affection and amusement. 'Look who's talking, Bee Ballantyne.'

She knew what he meant. She felt different too, better, younger, sillier, ready to start again.

She looked around her, gave the sand an appreciative pat. 'It's true. I needed to come here as much as you did.'

He moved the fish off the fire and wrapped the end of a towel around the skewers and pulled their potatoes free from the fire too, then dropped them into a bowl. Honey pushed herself up and brought out the tomatoes from the cool box, chopped them roughly, then added olive oil and salt and ripped-up basil, and poured them both another glass of wine.

With their plates in their hands, they sat back against the cushions once more and Edouard gave her back his arm, eating his food one-handed.

'But what I've always wondered is why you had to go so suddenly.'

She'd started conversationally, not acknowledging that perhaps this was an area to be avoided, only realizing when the words were said and it was too late. This conversation had begun in the sea at Edouard's party, but this time there were no distractions and suddenly she wanted to know the answer, wanted to know why he'd gone, wanted him to tell her the truth.

'So why didn't you come back for nearly six years?'

'It was time to grow up.'

She frowned at him in surprise. 'You sound sad. Were you unhappy? Did something keep

147

you away?' And as she asked she was trying to remember the last days before he'd left but those days were hazy and indistinct. All she could know for sure was that by then she'd been thrown into the struggle at home. For her the halcyon days had already gone. 'At times I wondered if you were angry with my life at Can Falco, with Tora and Hughie for keeping me there all the time, but I can't believe it was that. You knew I couldn't be anywhere else — '

'Of course I didn't mind. I was sorry for you.'

'Then explain!'

'At times I was happier in Ibiza than anywhere else.'

'So why go?'

Her words hung in the air and all the laughter had gone from his face . . .

'Why do you keep asking that question when we've both always known the answer?'

She went very still because of course he was right. Probably she'd always understood but still she didn't know what to do about it. She couldn't meet him but she couldn't turn away, and after a few long seconds it was Edouard who got to his feet and walked away, climbing up the dune with his plate in his hand. He stopped at the top and looked towards the sea and the darkening sky and something in the way he was standing — so still, so close and yet so remote — made her rise to her feet and she would have joined him but he raised a hand, warning her to stay still, and she faltered and then she heard it too, the faint buzz of a motorboat.

At first it was intermittent. The sound occasionally carried on the wind, so that for a while neither of them spoke, both desperately hoping that they were picking up sounds from the mainland or perhaps the engine of a small plane, but as the moments passed it grew louder and more insistent. It was a motorboat heading their way.

'Shimmy?' Edouard suggested, clutching at straws.

Honey shook her head. 'No chance.'

The plummeting disappointment meant that for a moment she couldn't speak. Thunder, lightning, swarms of wasps or biting sandflies, nothing could ruin the intimacy of their deserted island the way other people would. And the sound got louder and louder as the boat came in to shore and then the engine was cut and for a few last moments there was silence before the sound of the engine was replaced by wild whoops and laughter, accompanied by loud, throbbing trance music.

'They won't have seen *Baby Jane*,' he said

moving on through the sand dunes to get a better look. 'They've landed around the corner. Our boat's out of sight.'

'Why does that matter?' She scrabbled after him. 'If they know we're here perhaps they'll leave.'

'No, Honey, they'll invite us to join the party.'

'And if we were sixteen again we'd probably say yes.'

'Will they notice our fire?'

'Probably not.'

As she spoke the sound crescendoed still more.

'If we were sixteen again they wouldn't be here,' he shouted back to her. 'People fucking knew not to do things like this back then. This wouldn't have happened when we were sixteen.'

'They sound as if they're coming right over. They're going to dance straight through our camp. Can you hear them talking? Are they Brits?'

'No, they are fucking not.'

'Spanish?'

'No!' he shouted furiously. 'They're not staying here. They're not doing this. They're going to leave.'

In sudden panic she ran to catch him. 'You can't, Edouard. Don't. They're not going to go, whatever you say, and, you don't know, they might beat you up for asking. You can't confront them when there's only the two of us.'

He hesitated, knowing it was true, and looked bleakly down to the beach.

'Hey.' She caught his arm. 'I'm sorry, I'm so sorry.'

But some of her wasn't. Some of her was grateful to them for the breathing space they'd just given her because their arrival had halted Honey and Edouard's conversation just as it had begun to make her heart thump with nerves, panic, excitement, just as it had begun to get serious, and of course Edouard had known that too. He had been right: she had known why he'd left Ibiza so abruptly, six years before. He'd left because of her, because six years ago, when she'd kissed him there in the sand dunes, so close to where they were standing now, she'd had a moment of choice: to kiss him some more or to pull away.

And now six years later, here they were again, and she'd been about to be kissed again, by a different Edouard, an Edouard who'd been gone a long time and had come home a different man.

He allowed her a small smile. 'Honey, if you start dancing to this music I will never

ever speak to you again.'

'It's Infected Mushroom. Don't you like them?'

She left him alone for a moment, turned and went back to their camp, picked up her beautiful new blanket and wrapped it around her shoulders, then climbed back up to join him.

Below them the group had stopped on the sand. There were about ten of them, a few already spread-eagled on the beach, two women dancing together, while back at their boat three men and another girl were bringing the last of their provisions ashore.

'Hardly anybody knows about this place . . . ' She looked down at them all. 'And those that do would never vandalize it like this. Everyone agrees you don't bring music here. You're right, this would never have happened before.'

He nodded. 'It's what I was saying, isn't it? Times are changing. Nothing's the same as it was.'

For a few moments they stood side by side, watching the beach. 'So shall we fire the rocket at them? Shimmy did say it should be used in emergencies.' He looked down at her blankly. 'Perhaps it'll scare them away.'

At least she'd made him smile. 'You're not serious?'

'Yes.'

He slid back down to their camp, found the rocket, lifted it up and waved it at her. 'You realize they'll probably love it?'

'Perhaps it'll bring Shimmy. That would surely scare them off.' She looked more closely at the box, reading the instructions. 'I say fire the bloody rocket, Edouard. Teach them a lesson.'

'Oh, Bee,' he sighed, coming forwards impulsively. 'You know that I adore you, don't you?'

'I adore you too. And not up into the air either. Aim it straight at them.'

'So is our conversation over?' He was standing so close, less than an arm's length away. 'The one about you and me, is it over before it even began?'

'No,' she looked back at him. 'It's not. But we're not having that conversation here, not now tonight. We've lost our chance. This lot have made sure of that.'

She could still have moved towards him but she didn't and in the end he took the firework and ripped off the red paper it was sealed in, then jammed the launching stick into the sand, steadied it, pointed it carefully straight up to the sky and well away from the crowd on the beach, fished in his jeans for his lighter and lit it. Together they took two steps back and held their breath, waited, waited and then with an exhilarating whoosh the rocket ignited.

'Go,' Honey encouraged it, willing it on. 'Go, baby, go!'

But it didn't go anywhere, just toppled onto its side and lay in the sand, hissing half-heartedly, spouting a miserable scattering of orange stars all of six inches into the air.

'Can you believe it?' Edouard said with disgust.

'The story of our night,' Honey watched it sadly. 'Not with a bang but with a whimper.'

And as if in response the music from the beach rose in volume drowning out his answer, loud enough to reach San Antonio.

'I hate them,' he said venomously.

'Let it go. They're only having fun.' She went over to him and opened the big blanket and pulled him inside, lifting her arms around his shoulders so that the two of them were wrapped together, on the top of their sand dune, silhouetted against the sky. 'Perhaps they'll get so stoned they'll fall asleep and we'll be able to creep down and turn it all off.'

In answer he carefully settled the blanket back around her shoulders, tucking it in around her throat, then gently turned her back towards their camp.

'You sending me off to sleep?' she asked.

'You want to try to go home?'

She shook her head. Slowly she made her way back down to their fire and sat down and waited for him to join her, but for a long time he stayed at the top of the sand dune, with his back to her, watching the party below. They'd come to the brink of the big conversation and she'd stalled and now, understandably, she could feel he was slipping away, all the intimacy that had built up between them sucked into the repetitious morphing beat that never stopped, music that made her feel as if she was spinning out of control, going mad with the sound.

Which was why when he finally came sliding back down the sand dune to join her, lay down on the blanket to face her, she felt she had to pick another subject, what felt like a safer, far less emotive subject. And so she asked him about Anna and Paul, and what were the evil plans being concocted by the three of them?

He took a long time answering, just propped his head on his hand and stared back at her for ages, so that eventually she gave up on waiting for an answer and started to study his face instead, his lashes thick as sable, his eyes so wide and serious, the skin across his cheekbones slightly flushed from too much sun . . . and then abruptly her thoughts came back to him, and she concentrated again, as she realized that he still had not answered her.

'Paul is planning a new club for the island.' He said it very quietly but he was so close of course she heard every word. 'He'd been waiting for a site for years and finally one came up about five months ago and I'm going to help him develop it. He and Anna have worked together before, there've been a couple of places in America and Monaco, super clubs that can take five thousand people a night. Pure will be much smaller than that.' He spoke quietly but she could hear the tension in his voice, and at that moment he bore no resemblance to the Edouard who'd been sitting with her just half an hour before. Now it was as if he thought he was speaking with a stopwatch, as if he imagined he had just a certain time to make his pitch. 'Paul needed someone like me, who knew the island but also understood the financial implications of what he was planning. You wouldn't believe his plans.' And it was then that she realized the truth of what she was hearing. It wasn't tension she was picking up in his voice. It was pure undiluted excitement. 'The returns are going to be over 800 per cent. It's a complete no-brainer.'

'A super club in Ibiza? Didn't a few others get there first?'

'Not a Privilege or even a Pacha, much smaller than both of them, but still with the best sound in the world. It'll be a club for the twenty-first century.'

'You mean it'll be green? Composting toilets and biodegradable foam parties?'

'Don't mock it, Honey.'

'I'm sorry but it sounds ridiculous.'

'You mean you've decided that already? I knew you would.'

'Why do you say that?'

Gone was the intimacy that had brought them so far. Wariness on Edouard's part and instinctive hostility on Honey's swept in to take its place.

'Because you don't like Paul,' he said. 'So you're going to hate anything he comes up with.'

'No, I don't.' She pushed herself upright so that she was sitting facing him cross-legged.

'Yes. You took one look at him, sitting there in his city-slicker pinstripes, and you decided you didn't like him before he even opened his mouth.'

'No, actually. It was when I realized he was a complete shit.'

She looked away from him finding it hard to believe he could be so ready for a fight, as if he'd been thinking and feeling all this for ages before, and was relishing the chance to say it now. She tried again. 'What are you accusing me of?'

'Being a snob.'

'No.'

'You're right about Paul,' he went on. 'But that doesn't change a thing because I'm talking about you. It started about five years ago. And since then you've got worse. It's what Ibiza's done to you, made you laugh at people who work in an office, carry a briefcase, commute, wear a suit.' She shook her head and opened her mouth to deny it, but Edouard had hit his stride and carried straight on. 'Of course you are. You think we're missing out on what's real, that we're living these shallow, two-dimensional lives. That we're all about money and greed. Come back to Ibiza and get a life, as if Ibiza's the only place where it's possible to *find yourself*. But the truth is that guys like Paul and everybody else staying in my house this weekend, they're not really any different from you. But you don't want to believe that, do you? You and your chilled-out friends want to clap around the campfires and despise everyone else, all those suits who haven't got hold of their inner rainbow. The truth is, Honey, we'd all quite like to give up our ride

158

on the tube on a Monday morning for a life here, banging drums, but it doesn't work like that for everyone, even if it has for you.'

He stared back at her, with a defiant look in his eye that told her she was right. He was glad he'd said it.

'Banging drums, I wish.'

'I'm not saying you don't work hard.'

'Longer days than you've ever managed, I'm sure. And I never get a holiday and I never go away and, yes, sometimes this place feels like a prison. But just because I don't wear a suit, and I have flip-flops on my feet and I work in the sunshine and don't live in London, Paris or New York, you think my hard work doesn't count. And you're saying *I'm* the snob? Paul's suit had nothing to do with it. I disliked him because he was a violent smartarse and I think he'd like to kill someone and I think his weasel of a friend would probably have sat back and watched that too. And the thought of him getting his hands on an inch of Ibiza makes me feel quite sick . . . And the thought that you are helping him do it makes it even worse.'

'It's a good idea. I've seen the plans and it will be stunning.'

'You've sold your soul to the devil.'

'Probably.'

She shrugged. 'So get building. It's your

choice. You knew how I'd react. You had your speech all planned.'

He looked uncertain for the first time. 'Even so I was hoping you might be involved . . . I was dreading telling you, but I figured if in the end I persuaded you to join me it would be worth the mauling first.'

'Sorry, but you'd better count me out.'

'Wait. Listen to me first. Yes, Paul is a complete bastard, loud, aggressive, massive ego, but he's also the most effective, energetic, imaginative person I've ever worked with and perhaps you shouldn't turn your back on him and me quite so fast. He has vision, sensitivity and bucket loads of cash, and what he's planning on doing, with me or without me, with you or without you, will be knock-out spectacular. I think you'd be proud to be involved. And he wants you, Honey, when he and Anna saw Can Falco . . . '

'He came to Can Falco, with you and Anna when I wasn't there?'

He nodded. 'Don't look like I was betraying you. As you say, you weren't there. And of course he was completely stunned by what you've done. It's what he wants for Pure. And he's right. Nobody could make it as beautiful as you could. Anna doesn't know it, but Paul would hand over all the design to you. You could have a free hand to do whatever you wanted. And Honey, please . . . ' now he knew she was listening all the antagonism had gone from his voice. 'Please don't reject it without giving it a chance. Come with me and meet them both, talk about it. Anna's design company Green and Pleasant is the best. Everybody wants to work with her. You shouldn't walk away without giving her a chance.'

She'd been too hasty. Edouard was right. She'd jumped at the obvious, behaved like the Ibiza snob he'd said she was, when what was wrong with another club on Ibiza, the island of clubs, especially one that at least attempted to be environmentally sympathetic? And if Paul wanted to involve her, what could she lose? Imaginative, effective, energetic businessman that Paul was, perhaps together they could make something special.

'So where's the site?' she asked.

'OK, Paul will build the club in Santa Medea.'

And instantly she was there. The pine forest rising steeply up behind her. She was standing on a rocky cliff path high above the sea, staring down at the tiny idyllic bay below her, the sliver of sand, curved like a baby's fingernail, cradling the turquoise water of the sea.

She said the first thing that came into her head. 'But it's so small and so pretty.' Her voice sounded small too, constricted by the shock. Then she came swiftly to her senses and grinned to show she hadn't been fooled. 'Where's the site, somewhere in San Antonio?'

He gave her a thin smile back. 'No, it really is Santa Medea.'

Somehow she managed to stumble out the words, 'But he can't build a club there.'

'Bee, don't get precious about it, please.'

Green and Pleasant, green and pleasant. Green pine forests, thousands of acres, stretching towards the sea, perfect in their uniformity. Didn't Edouard remember that Ibicencos shouted their news to the pine forests and would wait for the reply that would come shivering, whispering back in the breeze? Now she imagined the sound of bulldozers, the scream of chainsaws, clouds of smoke, open wounds across the hillside, huge cranes appearing on the skyline.

'There's nothing there, Honey, nothing to spoil,' Edouard insisted. 'It's not like Salinas. There's nothing to Santa Medea but a strip of beach below and the forest above.'

Who are you? She wanted to shake him. *What have you done with the real Edouard Bonnier?*

'Look at the campaign against the motor-way,' she said woodenly. 'People will fight.'

He nodded. 'Yes, look at the campaign against the motorway.'

She turned away because despite the protests and the marches, the placards and the banners, the motorway had gone ahead.

'Paul's on to it,' Edouard went on. 'He knows the right people. And Bee, what's there to ruin, I don't understand? There's nothing to spoil. What's so special about Santa Medea?'

It was as if he'd been waiting for exactly this response, for she was after all the small-minded child of the island, the hippy chick, so predictable, saying everything she was programmed to say. Of course he'd known he'd shock her, that she'd wave her arms around and protest a bit — it was, after all, exactly what she'd been programmed to do. But she'd come around, he must have thought there was hope that he'd persuade her to change her mind, for him to bother to tell her at all. She wondered if, after all, this was the only reason he'd brought her here. Not to seduce her but to make money with her, out of her.

'Have you been to Santa Medea recently?' she asked. He shook his head. 'So this strip of sand and a forest, that's just a memory, and a distant one at that?'

He stiffened. 'I do know the place, Honey. I may not have been there for years but I lived here, too.'

'Don't you think you should go there and see it again before you build all over it?'

'I'm going to.'

'Oh I see! That's why you chose it for another of our dates. What did you think? That we'd pace out the plans together while we were there? Decide where to put the dance floor? And what about that annoying little problem called planning *permission*? You do realize people will feel strongly about this, there'll be marches, petitions — '

'The plans were approved six weeks ago.'

'I don't believe you!' she shouted furiously. 'We'd have known. We'd have heard something.'

He shrugged. 'I can't help it if you didn't.'

Could it really be true? Could Paul really have managed that? She thought back to the man she'd observed at the pool, remembered his bulldozing force and relentless self-interest, and thought he probably could.

'So what did he do? Backhanders wouldn't work. Not at this level.'

'Not everybody thinks like you do. Lots of people support us.'

'How did he do it?'

164

'By being innovative, ambitious and exciting. Pure will be like nowhere else you've ever seen. Other people recognize that.'

'And that's the name?'

He nodded. 'Because the sound will be pure — we've retained the best acoustics designer in the world. And the structure will be pure too. That's what makes it unique. Anna will make it the most ecologically advanced, environmentally friendly building ever.'

'If you want to be environmentally friendly don't build it.'

'Biodegradable foam parties.'

She laughed bitterly. 'And you're serious, aren't you?'

He nodded. 'Pure will be solar-powered, of course, and there'll be minimal light pollution and everything will be built from natural materials.'

'Composting toilets?'

'Oh, for fuck's sake. I knew you'd be like this.'

He went to stand, but she caught his arm.

'No, don't go. It's too important.'

'What's the point in talking any more? I hoped you'd understand. I suppose I knew you wouldn't.'

'Edouard, please. You must have some doubts, any doubts at all.'

'Even if I did, it's going to happen anyway.'

'So you do have doubts, a doubt, even one?'

'Isn't it better that we're involved and can help control it?'

'People used that argument to go to war.'

'Oh, Honey!' he exploded. 'You're bright, you're brilliant but you're so predictable. I thought you might just want to work with me on this. I had this silly tiny hope you'd get it. But no, it's your little island because you got here first and you can't bear anything, anything at all, to change it! But you didn't get here first, Ibicencos were here before Honeybee Ballantyne and lots of them aren't quite as sentimental as you. They see that Ibiza needs places like Pure. Tourists bring work, money, infrastructure, new hospitals and schools.'

'But you have a doubt,' she said stubbornly.

'No, I don't.'

'Then save me the spiel,' she snapped. 'I bet you love the motorway too, carving the island in half, speeding everything up for all the clubbers.'

'Yes, I do. So beat me up about that too. And we'll probably need a bigger airport, with lots more cheap flights. And lots of islanders would like that, too.'

'And I'm not against change. I wasn't even

against your club until I found out where it's going to be. But Santa Medea needs protecting. Edouard, please! Don't tell me you can't see that. It's fragile and beautiful and you would never bulldoze it over if you'd spent more than three weeks a year here. You pretend it's not so but you have forgotten everything. You camped on beaches like Santa Medea, and swam with your horses in the sea. The old Edouard would have lain down in front of the bulldozers. Don't you remember how you felt?'

He stared stonily back at her. 'And then I left and got a different life.'

'And I lost you. I knew I had. I just didn't realize how completely. Or perhaps you were always like this, only seeing the worth in something you can buy and sell.'

'You're wrong.'

'So prove it.'

'But it's a good idea.'

'Not there it isn't. Listen to me. I am not against a new club in Ibiza. I am not automatically programmed to reject any change to the island. But listen to me, Santa Medea is special. Go and see for yourself. Go, go and look. You won't need me at your side to convince you, you just need to open your eyes.'

'Oh Christ, I knew you'd be like this.'

Dramatically he spread out his arms then toppled backwards onto the sand and lay silently looking up at the stars and she stared down at him waiting, waiting for more.

'Do you know you drive me mad?' he said at last, talking to the sky.

'Not as mad as you make me.'

'All the time I've been working, at my desk until midnight, night after night, taking calls from Anna, listening to Paul, meeting architects, trying to do my job, all the time you've been there, sitting on my shoulder, driving me mad.'

'Saying just what you expect me to say?'

He looked up at her. 'Yes, so why do I listen?'

'You don't listen. You've ignored every word I've said.'

He let a handful of sand run through his fingers. 'No, I've heard you say it in my head ever since Paul first approached me. You've been shouting at me all the time.'

'I'm sorry. Go and look at Santa Medea, then you won't need to listen to me any more.'

He kept his eyes on the stars far above. 'Will you come there with me?'

'We were going anyway. We were meant to be going to Santa Medea and Cala Mastella too. Remember our plan?'

168

'But you don't want to go any more?'

'No,' she took a deep breath. 'Not if you carry on with Paul. Not if you don't stop him building that club. If you stay involved then there's no hope for you and me.'

'But it's not so simple. I am involved now. I can't just walk away from Paul. I'm committed financially and I still think you're wrong. But I will go to Santa Medea and I hope you'll come too.'

'No, you should see it for yourself, you know what I think.'

'Then I hope I will still meet you at Cala Mastella next weekend.'

'We'll have to talk about that another time.'

He'd surprised her again. Later she lay on the sand, rolled tight in her blanket thinking about him as he dozed beside her, staring at his sleeping form caught in the dying embers of the fire. She'd so nearly kissed him and if she had would he still have told her about Santa Medea or would he have kept quiet, preserved the magic, betrayed her with his silence?

Then just before dawn he sat up suddenly and grabbed her hand.

'I want to make it happen. You and me, we've got to make it work.'

'What are you talking about?' she asked sleepily. 'Are you dreaming?'

'I want to make you happy. That's all that matters, you do know that, Bee?' He said nothing more, slipped down until he was lying flat again, still holding on to her hand, and she lay there beside him aware of his body slipping swiftly back to sleep, but in those few dreamy half-formed words, and in the way he still had hold of her hand, he had made everything OK again.

As the sun began to climb the music finally stopped and now it was light enough to see. They gathered together everything that they'd brought, stepped tentatively past the sleeping bodies scattered across the beach, slipped back down to *Baby Jane* and sailed away.

9

Two evenings later, Honey was at her desk when Edouard rang from London. Ever since she'd left him at the harbour wall in San Antonio, she'd been waiting for his call, telling herself it was all for the sake of Santa Medea, but knowing, of course, it was nothing of the sort. And at times she'd found herself stopping her work just to sit and gaze out of the window in disbelief that it was Edouard, Edouard Bonnier, whom she couldn't get out of her head, who'd done no more than hold her hand as he'd fallen asleep but was now, illogically, making her feel this way, making her want to dance through the French windows, throw her arms around her father, shower her guests with free drinks, her mother with flowers. She'd rung Nancy, who had stayed on in El Figo while Belle had had to return to work, and invited her for supper; she'd put Claudio on duty and bunked off for one whole morning, spending the time shopping in Ibiza town — something she realized she hadn't done for months — all because of Edoaurd, and the giddy anticipation of seeing him again the following

171

weekend, the expectation of what was about to happen next.

But then, when he did call, he immediately asked her to hold, and he kept her waiting on the phone for a good half a minute.

'Bee!' He said finally coming back to her with a great sigh of relief. 'I thought you'd have hung up on me by now.'

'I nearly did.'

'I'm having the day from hell.' There was a pause, then, '*No!*' He said it calmly, then exploded. '*Call him back and tell him no!*' Then only slightly more gently, 'I'm sorry.'

'Sounds as if you could have picked a better time to call me.'

'Yup.' He said it through clenched teeth.

'So tell me quickly, what's going on?'

'Do you want to know about the corrupt German backers, or the psycho American ones? Or do you perhaps want to know about the ridiculous Ibicenco planning laws? Or the fact that you can't tear down a dangerous building without getting it approved by health and safety . . . ' He gave a short bitter laugh. 'Or do you want to know about a shit-stirring journalist who seems to know more about what's going on in my business life than I do?'

'Sounds as if I should get off the phone.'

'Wait, I needed to talk to you about Friday

172

night. I can't do our date at Cala Mastella. I can't come out next weekend at all. I'm really sorry.'

Disappointment dropped through her like a stone. What's more, he sounded so preoccupied she wasn't sure he even cared.

'You want to rearrange?'

'Yes, yes, of course I do.' Again he paused. 'Deutsche Bank? Is he mad?'

'Edouard? Call me some other time and we'll make another plan.'

'No, wait,' still he sounded distracted. 'I was wondering if you were free on Wednesday night instead.'

'You mean, the day after tomorrow?' Instantly she pushed herself upright in her chair. 'Do you mean you'd come out especially?'

'Don't make it sound so strange.'

'I'm just surprised you have the time — '

'I don't. But the truth is, it's dark outside and tonight I won't be home before midnight, and tomorrow two of my clients are competing to give me the biggest nervous breakdown and I'm thinking how on Wednesday night I'd much rather be galloping along a beach at Cala Mastella with you. Crazy, isn't it? But I called Doon earlier this afternoon, because I presume that's where you'd get the horses from, and she said it would be fine, she can just as easily give us them on Wednesday night as at the weekend. So if it's all the same to you . . . ' He paused. 'Excuse me, Honey . . . ' There was another pause. 'Yes, if we can. Of course we'll sue.'

Her spirits raised, she waited patiently.

'Honey?'

'I'm still here. Sue who?'

He heaved a great sigh. 'Anyone who prints lies. Anyone who makes things worse than they already are. Anyone who gives me a hard time.'

'You sound so scary when you say that.'

'Good. So, how about Wednesday?'

'Wednesday would be fine . . . Edouard, can you tell me what's going on, with your work? I'd like to know.'

'It would be a long and complicated explanation and you probably wouldn't find it very interesting anyway.'

'It's interesting if you're in trouble.'

He didn't laugh. 'Then I'll tell you about it on Wednesday.' She could hear the weariness in his voice. 'When perhaps it will all be over. But you know, right now, Bee darling, I have to go.'

'You sure you don't want to leave the riding for another week, perhaps when you have more time? You might find you're tied to your desk — that you don't want to make a special trip here.'

'Erm . . . ' Another pause. 'No. I won't be. I'll be in Ibiza already.'

She flushed with embarrassment. Why had she ever imagined he'd fly all the way from England just to go riding with her?

'I have to be honest with you, Honey, Paul's arranged a meeting about the club and I've committed to being there. I'm meeting him in San Antonio. I could be with you afterwards, about seven thirty.'

She jumped at the snap of tension still there in his voice.

'Good!' she said hastily. 'I mean, good you can kill two birds with one stone. You'll be here anyway with Paul, so good you can fit in the riding with me at the same time. Although, I have to wonder why you're bothering meeting me at all if you're going ahead with Paul.'

'Honey, I can hear in your voice you think I should apologize for something and I'm not going to. I told you I'd listened about Santa Medea and I meant it, but right now I've got a lot on.' She felt her heart miss a beat. Edouard just didn't speak to her like that. 'And you should know that Pure is not going to go away simply on the strength of a couple of conversations with you.'

175

'I've hardly had a chance to say a word.'

'I know what you're thinking.'

'What I'm thinking is that you should call me back when you're feeling less bloody bad-tempered.'

He sighed. 'I'm sorry. And I'd like to ride on the beach with you on Wednesday. Will you still come?'

'No, I've got better things to do.'

She cut him off and pushed the phone away from her in disgust.

She'd hated the disappointment. She hated how he'd just spoken to her, the awful condescending tone, the unwillingness to try to explain, the implication that terribly important multimillion-pound meetings were taking place, way, way over her head. *So we need to shift the pony ride to Wednesday, Honey, surely you understand?* OK, he hadn't actually said that, but it had been there in the tone of his voice. As if the ride to Cala Mastella had been her treat, as if he hadn't talked her into taking him out in the first place. As if she cared whether they went on the sodding ride, and as if she gave a flying fuck about him and his bloody club that was so clearly still on course.

Resisting the urge to hurl the phone across the room, she pushed herself away from her desk. Thank God she'd got Nancy arriving for supper, thank God she'd got something to do, someone else to see. Nancy, who perhaps might not yet know about the disastrous project her boyfriend was involved in, who might find she was taken on a quick introductory visit to Santa Medea herself. Not that Honey had any faith in Nancy's ability to change Paul's mind.

All day Tuesday Honey wondered if Edouard would call back. Then on Wednesday morning, when she still hadn't heard from him, she rang Doon at the stable yard and found that he had called that morning to confirm that two horses would still be available.

'Benjamin and Sabrina,' Doon told her. 'He said you're taking them swimming so do make sure you dry them off before you bring them back.'

'Did he mention my name?' Honey couldn't believe his nerve. 'Edouard definitely said we were riding?'

'Honey, I wouldn't let them out with anybody else.'

She rang him on his mobile as soon as she'd put down the phone to Doon.

'I hoped you'd still come,' he said before she could say a word.

But he didn't elaborate. Clearly he wasn't about to apologize and he still wasn't about to give her an explanation and yet she had to hope that the problems at work were to do with cancelling the project at Santa Medea. Was it naïve to hope she was right?

She let a moment's silence hang between them. 'Then I'll be there at seven.'

'Thank you.'

'And when I see you, you can give me that huge apology you owe me.'

And so there she was a few hours later, loitering against a stable door watching dust boiling and building along the dirt track below, as Edouard's old jeep made its way at breakneck pace towards her.

'Bee, I'm sorry. I'm very, very sorry.' It was the first thing he said before he'd even slammed shut the door. 'I'm sorry, I'm sorry, I'm sorry.' He walked towards her. 'I was bad-tempered, I was rude. Work got to me badly last week. There.' He grinned at her. 'Good enough?'

She kissed him politely. 'Thank you. And did today's meeting go well?'

'It's too early to know.'

'Was Anna there?'

'Yes.'

'And was she bursting with great green ideas?'

'Please don't do this to me, Bee.'

'Then tell me: it's not going ahead. You've

managed to stop it. Tell me.'

'Paul is absolutely sure of Santa Medea. Getting him to change his mind is harder than you could imagine.'

'You probably put the idea there in the first place.'

He didn't deny it.

'So what next?' she asked.

'The three of us, Anna, Paul and I, are flying back to London together tonight. Bee, I'm still trying to work it out.'

'Nice of him to wait for you to finish your ride,' she snapped back.

She didn't want to be sarcastic, petulant. She didn't want to burst into tears, but Edouard was so frustrating, standing in front of her so calm, refusing to rise to her barbed comments, deliberately being obtuse, skirting around the issue of Santa Medea and still holding back from telling her exactly what was going on.

They tacked up the horses and Honey called goodbye to Doon and then led the way out of the gateway and into the setting sun, turning immediately off the road and up a steep sandy path that cut towards the pine forests and took them straight into the hills.

She was on Sabrina, a pale grey mare who picked her way carefully along the rocky path, forcing Edouard — on Benjamin, a tall black horse — to walk slowly behind, and his horse plunged and fussed at the indignity. Then as they entered the first forest and the path levelled out and widened, Edouard let Benjamin go and for a while the two horses raced side by side, splitting the pine needles that carpeted the ground beneath their flying hooves and filling the air with a wonderful scent, before Benjamin, bigger and stronger, passed Sabrina and streaked away. Honey pulled her mare back to a canter and then to a trot, patted her sweaty neck and laughed when ahead of her Edouard came to an abrupt halt at a fork in the forest path as he realized he didn't know which way to turn.

As she walked slowly up to them, he turned in the saddle with a grin, and she managed a tight-lipped smile in response and then they were leaving the forest behind, Honey leading them once more. They clattered down the rocky paths to the beach, the horses moving eagerly down over the stones as they realized where they were going.

Down by the sea, dusk had begun to fall and lights from the restaurants made the night sky feel darker. There were already people sitting outside at the bars and restaurants and they stopped talking and looked on in interest as she and Edouard came riding past silently.

They kicked on, ignoring the people and each other, straight out into the sea, threading their way carefully in single file through the rocks, the water rising to the horses' shoulders as they made their way around the side of the bay, then on to another tiny empty cove on the other side. Just a rock fall separated them from the restaurants and people on the other side. They could hear the laughter of children playing on the low walls outside the restaurants, but here their cove was empty of people and they were unobserved.

On the beach they both jumped off their horses. They undid the girths and slipped off the saddles and then the bridles too, following a time-honoured tradition, still neither of them speaking. Under her T-shirt Honey was wearing no bra, and under her jeans just a pair of skimpy green bikini bottoms. She glanced over to Edouard and saw that he'd stripped off down to a pair of boxer shorts. She kept on her bikini bottoms but took off everything else, then guided Sabrina towards a rock, slipped a leg over the horse's soft warm back then turned to see Edouard vault back up onto Benjamin. She leaned forwards, whispering into Sabrina's ears, guiding her towards the sea, and immediately the horse bounced forwards in an uncomfortable trot, Honey gripping on tightly with her knees, her back to Edouard as she and her horse plunged and splashed into the black water. Sabrina snorted as the sea-spray caught her nostrils, then struck gamely out from shore. And then Edouard was alongside her, his horse prancing as the water swirled beneath him. As they came alongside Honey, Benjamin curled his top lip comically at the taste of the sea-spray.

'He's expressing how I feel about you.' And then despite herself she caught his eye and started to laugh.

'I said I'm sorry. Let it go,' he demanded. 'There's nothing I wanted to do more than be with you tonight. And Bee, as far as the club goes, you have to trust me when I say I did listen to you. And I went there and now I'm doing what I can.'

'Do you mind me asking what you're discussing with Paul?'

'Think in the region of five, six million quid.' He nodded at the surprise on her face. 'You see now? Why it's not so easy to just walk away. I have a responsibility to him and to all my staff too. I'm on dangerous ground, Bee. I must tread carefully. So tell me, what do you make of Pineapple Beach?'

'I think it's the biggest dive on the island, why?'

Pineapple Beach was a battered, faded club facing a car park in San Antonio. Hip in the seventies, with each decade since it had gone further and further downhill and it was now, in Honey's opinion at least, Ibiza at its vomit-splattered, drug-infested, drunken worst and that was just in the daytime. At night she would think twice of walking within a few blocks of its open doors and the rare times she had been forced to pass by at night, she'd felt threatened like nowhere else on the island.

'That's what I thought,' said Edouard in relief. 'I was walking by earlier today and I looked up at it and suddenly it struck me, here it is. I thought *this* is Honey's kind of place. The problem with it is that the surrounding area is just as bad.'

'But we're not talking about Pineapple Beach, we're talking about Pure,' argued Honey. 'And we're not thinking about the rough edges of San Antonio, we're talking about the unspoilt perfection that is Santa Medea.'

He stretched out towards her with his hand. 'I know. And you find it very hard to understand and harder still to forgive me, I know that too. And I'm so glad you still came tonight, and if there was a neat explanation about what I'm going to do now you could have it, but there isn't. When Paul Dix put his business plan on my desk I thought it was fantastic. I listened to Anna and I thought she was fantastic too. I even bought into the idea that Pure could benefit Santa Medea, that the club would ensure developers didn't cover it in tacky hotels and golf courses, one little club open just four months of the year, it really didn't sound so bad to me.'

'You're not still trying to persuade me?'

'Not since I went back.'

It was good to hear. 'And now how do you feel?'

'Even worse.' He threw back his head and looked up at the sky. 'Now for once I don't know what the fuck to do.'

She came up alongside him. 'Yes you do. Because you're smart and you're savvy and you can run rings around Paul when you put your mind to it. I know you can.'

He smiled at that and took her hand and gripped it hard while below them the sea bed dropped away and the two horses breasted the water and started to swim.

'Can we forget about Santa Medea for the rest of tonight?'

'Thank God,' he laughed. 'Thank you.'

Now they leaned forwards and half floated, half sat on their horses' backs, hands buried in their manes, feeling the wonderful power and strength of the horses kicking out beneath them, their coats soft and slick with water, their eyes bright, nostrils wide. Without reins to guide them, they let the horses go their own way and for a few wonderful moments they struck out further and further from shore. Then, just as Honey was beginning to wonder if they shouldn't head back the horses turned together, snorting and blowing with exertion, and stopped where it was shallow enough for them to stand once more.

As soon as she felt the sea bed beneath her, Sabrina started to paw at the water and Honey shrieked and quickly slipped off her back and swam away, knowing just what the horse was planning. Edouard swam away too and came to join her and they floated out to deeper water while nearer the beach the two horses both began to paw insistently at the water and then, almost simultaneously, eight legs buckled and they went down, rolling luxuriously.

Further out to sea, Honey and Edouard stood neckdeep, keeping balance with their hands. From where they were they could see both sides of the beach. To the right-hand side of the rocks the horses were making their riderless way out of the water to stand and wait quietly, but on the other side of the rocks, to the left, the restaurants were now even busier. They could see children balancing on the walls that divided one restaurant from another, could clearly hear guests talking and laughing.

'Is the chef the same as last year?' someone asked, and Honey snorted at the well-heeled English drawl. It was as if this man was staking his claim. I've been here before, he was announcing. I do know the island. Please don't take me for a tourist, whatever you do. 'And do you recommend the sea-urchin?'

'Oh, absolutely,' Edouard replied in a perfect imitation of his voice, 'and you must swallow the spines, every one.'

He held out his hands and instantly she swam forwards and took them, just managing to dance on the bottom with the tips of her toes. He drew her closer, bending his arms so that he brought her body right up against his, and then as she struggled, laughing at her inability to stand still, he slipped his hands beneath her bottom to help her and instantly, without any thought of the consequences, her legs wound themselves around his waist and gripped him hard.

'Sorry,' she said, half embarrassed, relaxing her grip a little. But she was laughing too, at finding herself cradled so close, laughing at the wave of excitement that was building up inside her just from staring at his face, his perfect mouth, his perfect lips.

'Don't mention it,' said the lips.

And his shoulders, how brawny they were. How could she not have noticed before? How satiny smooth and brown his skin.

'So where were we, Bee, when we were so rudely interrupted in Es Palmador? Do you remember? You were about to tell me something, I think.' He came even closer and she stared into his eyes, his gold-flecked, warm brown eyes.

He bent and kissed her shoulder and she flinched, startled that he could be so sure of her. 'What were you going to tell me?'

'Why you went away,' she said nervously, unable to look away from him. This moment was upon her so fast, and yet she'd known it was coming, from the night on Es Palmador, she'd known what would happen this night, she'd been waiting for it.

'Tell me why I left Ibiza.'

His voice sounded husky and raw and she swayed towards him. She felt his lips brush her cheeks as he spoke. It's happening, she found herself thinking. Can I believe this is happening?

'You went because I didn't kiss you. Because I stopped . . . '

'That's right.'

Still he hesitated as if he wanted to be absolutely sure she knew what was about to happen. And then, at last, he bent his head and she heard her own muffled little cry as his mouth met hers and this time she clung to him and kissed him back.

Kissing her, kissing her all the time, he waded to where the water was shallower and he could stand more steadily and when they stopped she stroked his face, reached for him again.

'Oh my God,' she whispered, 'Edouard. Oh my God!' She had to break free to tell him, couldn't breathe or think. She put her hands on his chest to push him away, but found she couldn't bear to let him go and instead let herself fall against him again and for a moment he held her tight and they were still but for the gentle sway of the sea. Then she raised her head once more and he was ready for her, caught her mouth with his own, slipped his hand around the back of her head and kissed her back so blissfully that she had to put her arms around his neck to stop herself from sinking down into the sea.

'I can't believe this is you,' she muttered as he moved from her lips to kiss her neck and then her collarbone.

'I know. That's been my problem for a very

long time.' Then he stroked the palm of one hand against her breast, against her cold, hard nipple, making her arch her back and bite back a cry. 'How am I going to convince you?'

'You've done it.' She covered his face with kisses. 'I'm sorry it's so easy but I think I'm convinced already.' She ran her hands down his big strong arms that held her against him so lightly then let her teeth graze against his shoulder. 'Or maybe I'm not, what else will you try?'

He slipped his fingers inside her bikini bottoms and at his touch she cried out in shock.

'Edouard!' It was all she could say. At his touch her voice had gone, her mouth could speak no more words, it could only kiss and be kissed now her body had become so heavy she could barely hold herself upright. She felt his hand tugging down her bikini and she wriggled herself free letting it float away, then wound her legs higher around his waist as he pulled his own shorts clear, giggling as he lurched awkwardly forwards almost pushing her under, even as the passion built inside her, making her reach for him again, desperate not to let him go. Then his hands were holding her bottom again and this time she let herself lean backwards, away from him, far back until she was floating on the water with her legs still wrapped around his waist, keeping afloat with her hands. He stroked the flat of her stomach in idle circles, kissed her stomach until she felt she would dissolve with lust, holding out a hand to steady her when she thought she might go under the water, and not even care. She gripped his hand hard and immediately his other hand moved back into position once more, then stretched lower down her belly, then between her legs, touching her so that the spiral of lust and desire instantly began to build again, out of control. She felt him hold her hips steady, then slide inside her, making her gasp at the wonderful heat of him after the coldness of the water and then she felt his hands reach for hers and he held her tight as he began to move more quickly, sending them both spinning away together, both of them racing towards their moment, yet willing it never to end.

Afterwards they lay on the beach, their legs tangled together, waves lapping gently at their feet, Edouard with his arms around her, their faces inches apart, neither of them able to look away. And they'd probably have stayed there all night if Benjamin, bolder than Sabrina and growing restless at the lack of attention, hadn't finally come stepping down

190

the beach to find them, hadn't dropped his huge head between them and blown a long impatient horsy breath straight into their faces, telling them in no uncertain terms that it was time to go home.

10

Honey missed Edouard terribly the next day. She stood in the shade of the olive trees, watching her guests at Can Falco out by the pool, her father swimming among them, and wished savagely that she didn't have to be there; that just for once Hughie could get out of the ancient red swimming trunks, put on some clothes and settle down behind the desk to help her. It was his desk, his house, and yet she could count on one hand the times he'd done it. And she wanted help now, more than ever before. She wanted to sprint to her car, drive to the airport, catch the first plane to London, just to be near Edouard, for now, having found him, to lose him again so soon felt as if it might rip her in half.

She watched her father as he made his way to the edge of the pool, the strut in his stride telling her he was about to do something stupid. He was performing for someone and she cast a glance around the guests, spread out on the sunbeds, and saw Marianne Darlington facing the water, wearing a pair of Jackie O glasses, with a paperback in one hand. And then Honey's eyes flashed back to her father, and with a terrible shudder of fear, she saw him teetering on the edge of the shallow end, saw the stupid, crazy thing he was about to do. And so she began to run forwards, just as he leaped, into the air, into his dive.

★   ★   ★

Everyone says they hate hospitals. Honey loved them, white and quiet, orderly and calm, clean antiseptic corners, confident-looking nurses moving through the corridors on silent rubber-soled feet, patients all behaving themselves, keeping out of sight. She sometimes wished Can Falco could be more like a hospital.

She asked at reception and was given directions towards her father's ward and now, as she turned the last corner, she could see him, sharing a room with a couple of other men, both sleeping quietly while he lay back against his pillows in a pair of pale blue hospital pyjamas, with swollen, blackening eyes.

She walked on into the room and over to his bed. He turned and looked up at her and she caught the guarded, almost fearful look on his poor battered face. Her heart burst inside her and she sat down wordlessly beside him and took his hand, stroked the fingers and the shiny pink nails.

'Damned idiot, wasn't I?' he said sheepishly.

'You were showing off for Marianne Darlington, weren't you?' He nodded. 'I'm sure you impressed her. There was an awful lot of blood.'

'Don't,' he touched his nose gently with his fingertips. 'Aaaggh.' He closed his eyes.

'What did the doctors say?'

He kept his eyes shut. 'That I'm a lucky old fool.'

'Your skull's still in one piece?'

'Just about.'

'Tora did say you had a very thick one.'

He gave a tiny grin. 'She should know.'

She sighed. 'Glad to see you've still got your sense of humour.'

'I don't know how, Honey. I don't know how.'

She took his hand. 'Who's Rachel?'

She waited but he didn't answer, didn't open his eyes, appeared not to breathe.

'Dad?'

'I don't know,' he muttered but his fingers twitched briefly in her hand. Then as if he knew they'd given him away, he pulled his hand free and rested it on the sheet beside him.

'I don't know either, but you talked about her at the pool. You thought I was her.'

'Never heard of her before in my life.'

'Dad? I don't think that's true.'

With his other hand he moved his fingers to the bridge of his nose and touched gingerly. 'Aaaggh.'

But she wasn't distracted. 'If you wanted to tell me, you know you could. I wouldn't tell Tora, I wouldn't judge you.' She was stroking his arm gently as she spoke, feeling more tender and protective towards him than she'd ever felt before. 'I know you think I disapprove of everything you do, but it's not true. If she's someone you care about, someone you'd like to talk about, I'd like to listen. Perhaps it might help if you told me about her . . . '

He lay there motionless but she noticed that two fat tears had collected under his eyes, and as she watched they began to race each other down his cheeks.

'I can't believe I said her name.'

'Who is she?' His eyes opened again and he wiped the tears impatiently away. 'Tell me.' Confide in me, please. Here's our chance.

'She's an old girlfriend,' he told the ceiling. 'Someone I knew before I met your mother.'

Honey couldn't understand why this was

such a big deal to him. He was talking thirty years ago, after all.

'So you still think about her, do you?' He nodded. 'You've kept in touch? Have you seen her?'

Hughie shook his head, then clutched at it, screwing up his face with pain. 'Aaaggh.'

'Do you think you're still in love with her?'

His face cleared instantly. 'I was never in love with her.'

Relief poured through Honey. 'Then why do you still care? Why did you say her name?'

Hughie finally looked at her. 'I was concussed. I thought you were her.'

'Thirty years on?'

Now his look turned mutinous but she waited patiently, not about to give up, and eventually he went on. 'I feel bad about her even now. I buggered off. Left her.'

'So, who was she?'

'She was . . . she is Rachel. And we lived together.' He paused, picked at his sheet, and she could see how uncomfortable he was, frown lines etched into his forehead and cheeks. 'In Ladbroke Grove. We lived there for four years until I came here for the weekend and met your mother.'

'And then?'

'And then I behaved like a complete shit. Rachel loved me and I didn't love her and I stayed here and never told her I wasn't coming home.'

'You bastard!'

'Yes.'

'You didn't even call?'

'I never spoke to her again.'

'Dad! How could you?'

'Easily. It's the kind of man I am.' Hughie closed his eyes again, switching off the accusation in her eyes.

'But Rachel,' Honey said, 'she knew where to find you? She could have come here?'

Now Hughie was biting on his knuckles, fighting off more tears and she knew this time it was genuine and she shouldn't be pressing him. But if she didn't persist she'd never have another chance like this one.

'Why would she do that when it was so obvious I didn't want to be with her?' he croaked. 'You wouldn't do that, not if you had any pride at all. And my behaviour made it pretty clear I didn't want to be with her any more.'

His voice had broken, he'd had to force out the last words and now he lay back against the pillows looking exhausted. Honey gently stroked his hair, guessing that the concussion was making him all the more emotional. She'd come to the hospital determined to ask him about Rachel, knowing her one chance to get the truth out of him was while he was in this vulnerable state. But now, seeing him so upset, she wondered why it had felt so important to her. What exactly had she thought would be gained from pushing him? What was it she'd wanted him to say?

I've been looking for something that would help me understand you and me, she thought sadly, watching the tears seep again beneath his eyelashes — something that would tell me why we've never been close.

*   *   *

His plane touches down at Ibiza airport. He makes his way to the arrivals hall, knowing how out of place he looks in a dark suit, a briefcase in his hand, among the baggy shorts and the espadrilles. He's itching to get through the airport and out the other side, picks up the pace, leaving his friends momentarily behind. And then he sees her. She's standing directly ahead of him, a vision in flip-flops and a long lime-green skirt, sunglasses in her blonde hair, and he stops dead because she's so beautiful — more beautiful than he ever imagined any woman could be. Completely entranced, he finds himself staring at her as all around them there are happy reunions, tears, hugs and kisses.

He's dimly aware of his two friends coming up to join him but then she starts to smile at him and all at once she's full of mischief, daring him on, and he finds himself doing the bravest and simplest thing he's ever done in his life. Dropping his briefcase, he walks forwards and without saying a word opens his arms and pulls her towards him. He remembers the narrowness of her, the neatness of her head resting below his chin, her shiny hair, the madness in his heart.

'Who are you?' she asks, looking up at him, blushing and laughing.

And he remembers how he bent his head and kissed her before she even knew his name.

*   *   *

Hughie slowly opened his eyes again and the vision receded as he caught all the love and concern on his daughter's face. He found he couldn't bear to see it, looked down at his old man's hands instead and forced himself to let go of the sheet clasped between his fingers, then touched again his poor broken nose, felt the ache behind his bruised eyes and closed them once more.

And Honey looked back at him, saw the ageing hippy, weak and sentimental and yet still her lovely dad. She sensed his grief and the pain of a guilty conscience and felt protectiveness rising up inside her.

'If you want to apologize to her, to Rachel, you could still do that.' His eyes flashed open again but he said nothing. 'Would that make you feel better? If you knew that she'd forgiven you?'

'I would like to know what happened after I'd gone,' he conceded. 'I'd like to know that she's happy now.'

'Then why not write to her?'

'I did. I have done, on and off for the last twenty-five years. And she's never replied.'

'So go and find her.'

But even as she said it, Honey knew it was a fanciful thought. Her father could barely navigate the length of Ibiza, let alone fly back to England and find this Rachel. As if he knew it too, and was embarrassed, Hughie turned his face to the wall.

'And there's your mother,' he said quietly. 'I never told her. I certainly wouldn't want to hurt her now.'

Honey pictured Tora sitting cross-legged with her class in the Garden of Serenity, isolated from it all.

'I think it was what I first loved about Tora,' Hughie went on. 'How she could live entirely in the present — she was completely disinterested in what I'd left behind. And I was scared. I thought that if I confessed my regret about Rachel it would sound so bourgeois. I was in awe of Tora, intimidated even. I thought it would spoil what was happening between us. And you know what? In thirty years, she's never asked me anything about my life before I met her. And so I've never told her.'

It was the most intimate thing he'd ever told Honey and yet it was to Tora that Honey turned in her mind — how much easier it is to live in the present when you're young and beautiful and having the time of your life. Why did she think her mother was looking back to the past now?

She thought back to herself as a little girl, to the cliché-ridden sun-soaked days and her mother smiling and laughing, catching her hands and dancing her through Can Falco, fun, exuberant, wonderful. And she wondered when exactly it had all changed. Was Hughie wrong to think Tora knew nothing and didn't care?

'I could find her for you.' There was no sign of any reaction from Hughie. 'Perhaps it would be good for all of us if you had a chance to apologize? Because you never had a chance to let her go, Dad, and perhaps even after all this time you still need to?'

'Edouard's parents, Delphine and Tom, I think they kept in touch with her for a while.'

'Then I can ask them for you.' He nodded. 'Would you like me to do that?'

'You could go,' he said quietly.

'Leave the hospital? You want me to go?'

'Go from here, Can Falco, Ibiza. I know you should.'

She let his words hang in the air for a few seconds, but she didn't register them at all.

'You should have gone years ago.'

'Don't say that, Dad.'

'But it's true.'

'I love it here. This is my home.'

'It's your cosy, familiar cage. I don't need Maggie and Troy to tell me that.'

'Why are you saying this to me now?'

His eyes suddenly beamed into hers. 'Because when else have we had the chance to talk? Every time I try, you slip away.'

'I didn't know you felt like this. I had no idea.'

Now it was Honey who was fighting not to cry, simply and pathetically grateful that he wasn't as oblivious to her as she'd always believed, that he had thought about her, once in a while.

Hughie took her hand and held it between his own and they sat there quietly for a moment.

'Talking about Rachel makes me weep for England too,' her father said eventually. 'I haven't been back for thirty years. I don't think I'll ever see it again and I wish so much that I had taken you back to meet my family, to see what a glorious place it is. Why haven't we done that, you and me?'

'I thought it wasn't important to you. You hardly ever mention England. I used to think how I'd like to have met your parents . . . got to know some cousins, that kind of thing.'

'Poor lonely little Honey.' His face screwed up in pain. 'I was so ashamed of what I'd done. I wanted to blank it out of my mind.'

'But it's never been something I've worried much about,' she said, trying to reassure him now. 'England doesn't feel part of me at all.'

He shook his head. 'That's terrible.'

'So you'd like me to go? Pay a visit to your parents?' Find Rachel for you? The question was there, clearer than anything she'd said out loud, and even though the idea had only just occurred to her she was already feeling the anticipation, a tiny little seed, dividing and growing, blossoming inside her. Edouard, England. She could fly to him, be with him. He could help her find Rachel. With him she could go to Wiltshire, stay with her grandparents. She pictured Hughie's mother and father, ruddy-cheeked and windblown, standing in front of some cold, old manor house. Then she pictured herself walking hand in hand with Edouard through the London streets, him showing her his house, his life that she knew so little about.

'Oh no, you couldn't go to London.' Hughie had read her mind. 'Far too dangerous, chock-a-block with lunatics. It's not like here, you know. You'd be a fish out of water. You'd be like Crocodile Dundee.' He loved Crocodile Dundee, and stopped for a moment to savour the thought, distracted like a child.

'Dad, I have been away from here, remember? I'm not such an Ibiza bumpkin. I'd love to go, the season here is winding down and I could be back before you'd even known I'd gone. I could go for the weekend.'

'Don't go on my account. You don't have to do that for me. Not travel all that way, a telephone call's all you'd need to do. Go to England, but go for yourself, not for me.'

And she knew instantly that she would do it, of course she would. The idea had already seeded, blossomed in her mind. She didn't know when, but soon, and Hughie knew it. And when she was there she'd contact Rachel, and Hughie knew that too.

11

Back at her desk she jumped at the sound of glass hitting the stone floor of the hall just out of sight.

'We are under control,' a loud and imperious voice insisted. 'Stay where you are.'

Heart sinking because, much as she loved them, she really hadn't got the energy for them now, she looked up to see Maggie and Troy standing in the doorway. Domineering, sentimental Maggie, her Pekinese cradled tight against her chest, and just behind her, dapper cherubic Troy, with an overstacked tray wobbling in his arms.

Having stepped aside for Claudio, who'd appeared at their side with a dustpan and brush almost before the glass had finished shattering, Troy then came forwards once more. On his tray were three glasses, a bottle of sparkling rosé, tapas and a plate of lemon meringue pies, and Honey watched as they all made their slow hazardous journey towards her. Arriving safely, Troy dropped the tea tray onto the table with a crash and immediately took Honey in his arms.

'Oh my girl, what a super-hero you were.'

He immediately jumped back from her, wiping at his spotless white linen shirt.

Honey kissed his soft cheek. 'You were watching, were you?'

'We were indeed.'

He pulled out a chair for her and pushed her gently down into it, and then Maggie arrived at Honey's side, dropping the little dog straight into her lap. Meanwhile Claudio replaced the broken third glass as Maggie took the bottle of wine and started to pour, giving Honey a close-up of her spectacular mahogany cleavage as she did so.

'Now I know you don't like it but just this once — I promise, Honey, just this once — I told the girls to prepare me a tray because I think, in the circumstances, we all need a little drink.'

'They wouldn't mind if you occasionally paid for it,' Troy suggested mildly, helping himself to a slice of salami.

Maggie stopped mid-pour and gave him a contemptuous stare. Today she was dressed in a white turban and long white dress with a gold coiled snake entwined around her outstretched arm.

'I've had a horrible, stressful morning. I think they were pleased to help out. I thought Hughie had died. Honey flinging herself into the water like that was very alarming.' She placed a glass in front of Honey, then settled back into her chair.

'No, I can't stay,' Honey said. She lifted the dog off her lap and deposited him straight back into Maggie's, 'I'm off . . . Got to find Tora.'

Maggie took a careful bite of lemon meringue pie, then dabbed at her lips with a napkin. 'Such a good idea these are, darling, mops up all the alcohol and everybody absolutely adores them. They're a little taste of England, aren't they?' She went on without a pause, 'Honey, your father's such an old fool. You know not to listen to a word he says.'

Honey stared back at her. 'Did you know who he was talking about?'

'I'm sure there's nothing to know.'

'Oh yes there is, there's a great deal!'

'So.' Maggie stopped stroking her dog and laid her hand upon Honey's. 'I did wonder if he'd tell you.'

Honey sat back in her chair and took a sip of wine. 'What do you know?'

'I'm sure nothing more than your father's already said.'

'I wouldn't be so sure. I want to find her, Maggie. Do you know how I can do that?'

'Leave it be, darling. It happened thirty years ago.'

'Did you know her?'

'A little, back in London. Remember we all came out here at about the same time.'

'He left Rachel behind.'

Maggie nodded. 'Of course, I remember that.' She glanced at Honey uncomfortably. 'Oh, sweetie . . . I don't know what to say!'

'Now you're making me nervous.' Honey turned to Troy. 'Do you know Rachel too?'

He shook his head.

'Your mother is the love of your father's life,' Maggie said in a rush. 'Always has been, always will be.'

'Your father stopped thinking straight the moment he met her, and, as we know, has never managed to think straight again,' said Troy.

Honey reached forwards for a lemon meringue pie and nibbled it carefully around the edges. 'I'm thinking of going to England.'

Now there was a gleam in Maggie's eye.

'I'm not surprised. So tell us, we want to know all about him. And first of all, darling Honey,' she leaned forwards, 'we want to know why the hell it took you so long!'

'What!'

'Then we want to know *everything* you've been getting up to.'

Honey started to laugh. She was just so incredulous that Maggie could know anything, when it had only happened the night before and neither of them had had a chance to tell a soul.

'How do you know?'

'We're so happy for you, darling,' Maggie went on in a rush, hardly pausing for breath. 'You know, Troy and I, we adore him, we always have. We've always hoped this would happen, everybody has, Edouard's parents, Tora and Hughie. Have you told them yet?'

'No, I bloody haven't. And I want to know what you know and how you know it too!'

'I was there!' Maggie cried. 'Last night. I was there on the beach! I saw you.'

'You didn't,' Honey gasped.

'You went riding past me, straight into the sea,' Maggie went on blithely. 'It looked absolutely marvellous. She turned to her husband and took his hand affectionately. 'And I thought why didn't we ever do anything like that?'

'You saw we went riding,' Honey repeated in relief, grinning at them. 'Yes, we did, it was fun.'

'And what about the plans for his new nightclub?' Maggie asked. 'I must say that sounds like a very good idea. Pure.' She rolled the sound on her tongue. 'There was somebody telling us about it at Edouard's party, a very charming young man . . . what was his name?'

'Paul Dix,' offered Troy.

'That's right. He was telling us how Edouard's helping him put it all together.'

'No.' Honey said with complete finality. 'Edouard's not involved with that any more.'

'Oh, what a shame! Are you sure?'

'Don't look so crestfallen, they were going to build the club at Santa Medea.'

Abruptly she slid her drink into the middle of the table and pushed back her chair. 'But, you know, I can't talk about it now. Do you mind — I've got to go.'

She wanted to hear Edouard's voice. She wanted to tell him about Rachel, right then. Too much had happened that day for Edouard not to know about it all. She needed to get away.

Maggie looked at her sympathetically. 'Darling, of course. Send him our love. And come back for dinner. We're staying tonight so you should join us. We wanted to have Paloma's baby pig. What's the difference, do you think, between piglet and baby pig?'

'For God's sake, Maggie, let the dear girl go,' Troy finally interrupted. 'Go, Honey, go.'

'Thank you, Troy.' Honey smiled back at the two of them. 'I don't think there is a difference between piglet and baby pig,' she said. 'It's just Paloma's English.'

'But baby pig makes me feel so guilty.

Perhaps you should change it?'

'Perhaps I should.'

'We've booked for nine thirty,' Maggie called after her as Honey turned for the open floor-length windows running along the side of the room. 'And, Honey, why don't you ask Edouard to join us?'

Outside, she could hear chanting coming from the Garden of Serenity, and rising above it, the sound of her mother's gravely rock-chick voice singing *Om shanthi, shanthi shanthi* could clearly now be heard.

'Because he flew back to England last night,' she told Maggie from the open doorway.

'No, darling, he's here!' Maggie replied in surprise. 'I saw him just ten minutes ago. I thought you knew.'

Dappled sunlight poured through the almond and orange trees, and as she turned the corner to her cottage she saw him, dark against the light, leaning against the rounded whitewashed wall, in a well-cut suit that made her ache with wanting him, and with a mug of tea in his hand.

'I missed you,' he said, dropping the mug on the ground as she hurtled into his arms.

'You aren't meant to be here!' she cried, her voice muffled against his chest. 'But I am so incredibly pleased that you are.'

She lifted her face to his kiss.

'But you *are* going again aren't you? Now? You look as if you're dressed for work and I know you shouldn't be here at all.'

He nodded. 'I haven't got long, but I had to say goodbye. After last night I couldn't bear to go without seeing you again. They flew back without me. I got as far as the car to the airport but not the plane.'

'And, darling Edouard, you know I am so pleased you did.' She kept her arms tight around his waist. 'Until this moment today's been a spectacularly bad day. Everyone's gone mad.'

He stroked her hair sympathetically. 'I thought that happened years ago.'

She looked back at him. 'Oh yes!' She smiled up into his face. 'So it did.'

A soft look passed across his face. 'Poor Bee. Sometimes I forget what a hard time you have.' He kissed her again. 'What happened?'

'Dad hit the bottom of the pool . . . with his head.' Edouard winced. 'But he's fine — hallucinating, spouting gibberish, same as ever.'

'He'll be OK, then?'

She was outraged to see he was starting to laugh.

'It was bad!' she insisted. 'Lots of blood . . . And then we had a conversation in the

212

hospital. And, oh God . . . ' Suddenly the need to talk about her father was stronger than anything else and she slumped down on the ground and leaned back against the wall of her cottage and immediately Edouard did the same.

'Dad told me about a girl called Rachel, someone he knew a long time ago. I wonder if your parents ever mentioned her? Because they knew Dad in those days, didn't they, before he came out here?' She rubbed at her eyes and then let her chin drop down to her chest. 'He left Rachel behind in England when he first came over here,' she said, looking down at the ground through her knees. 'And I'd like to know more about her. But I'm not sure I have the energy to deal with all that now.'

He slipped his arm around her shoulders. 'Rachel the old girlfriend?'

'So you do know about her!' She looked up at him in surprise.

'I presumed you did too. She lived in London with your father, didn't she? And then he came over here for a weekend and met Tora and *Ka-Boom*! Mum and Dad were with him in the airport when it happened. And they were the ones who went back to London and had to go and tell Rachel he wasn't coming home again.'

'Yes,' Honey whispered, 'that's her. How did I not know anything about her at all?'

'I always thought you did. Just one look at Tora and he was completely, desperately in love. I grew up on that story.'

'And I didn't. I never heard a word of it until today.' She looked at him helplessly. 'Of course I'm happy to know they were in love, but why am I so shocked?'

'You mustn't mind too much. Remember your mother's the one he wanted, she's the one he fell in love with.'

'I know, I know,' she laughed sadly. 'You'd think with all that love they might have made a better job of being together.'

'They're not so bad.' He stretched out his legs on the dusty ground. 'I remember how besotted they were when we were very young. I remember how your dad was always picking her up. She was always in his arms.'

Honey shrugged dismissively, such images of her parents' happy early life somehow didn't touch her at all. 'Do you think your mother maybe kept in touch with Rachel? Might she know where she lives and what happened to her? Because if I could tell Dad I think it would transform him. All his life he's been wanting to say sorry.'

'I could ask them. I haven't heard her name for years so I guess they're not great friends.'

'Would you, please?' She waited, looking at him expectantly and belatedly he got it.

'You mean you want me to ask her *now*?'

She nodded, allowed him the smallest smile. 'Right now. Get out your phone, please, Edouard. Do it now.'

He dutifully reached inside his jacket pocket and brought out his phone. She watched him press in numbers, bit at her nails while she waited as he waited, flinched when he nodded to her as the phone was answered, waited again as he talked and listened, her heart banging in her chest as he then finished the call, said goodbye and snapped shut the phone.

'OK, Rachel got married about a year after Hughie left,' he said rapidly, getting the facts out while they were still fresh in his mind. 'She became Rachel Paget. She and my mother kept in touch for a while and the last my mother heard she was living in Oxford-shire, in a village called Lingcott.'

'Anything else?'

He shook his head. 'They've lost touch.'

She clenched her fists in agitation.

'Honey, what are you planning? What are you going to do?'

'Call directory enquiries and get her number.'

He looked back at her amused. 'You can't

just barge into her house.'

'Of course I wouldn't! I don't know if I'll get in touch with her at all but I wouldn't mind the option. I'd like to have her number. I'm going to ring directory enquiries and when I've got the number I might call it. And I might speak to her and if that goes well, I might even see her when I'm next in London.'

'You're planning on being in London soon?'

She grinned, fell against him affectionately. 'Very soon. How does this weekend suit you?'

She saw the answer immediately and she pulled herself free in surprise and sat back. 'It doesn't suit?'

'Please don't look so sad.'

'But I'm right? You don't want me to come?'

'Of course I do. But what I *want* doesn't come into it.'

'You couldn't see me at all? Not even for half an hour?'

'I'll be in Paris. But if you came *next* weekend I could see you. Please . . . ' He kissed her cheek. 'Come next weekend. This weekend I have work that will eat me alive if I don't take care of it. Please, darling Bee, understand. You surely see it crucifies me to say that, knowing that I could be spending

216

the time with you.'

So cancel the work. However important it was, surely it couldn't be as important as her? She knew it was childish to think it. She knew of course she couldn't expect his life to stop just because she'd decided to come to London. That of course he had a world that currently didn't involve her at all . . . But they had only just found each other, and so she wanted him to prove, with one sentence, that she was the only thing that mattered. She wanted him to sod his plans and his office. She wanted to be irresistible. But she wasn't.

'Next weekend,' he insisted.

'Perhaps.'

'Bee?'

'I do understand. I do. I can't expect you to drop everything just for me.'

'But you can and I would. Any other time.'

She didn't ask him what was happening in Paris. At that moment it didn't even occur to her that his work there could be connected to Santa Medea, and Paul Dix, and Pure. *Edouard's work* was a phrase, an explanation for why he wasn't in Ibiza, or for how he could afford to run such an expensive house as El Figo. In Honey's head, *Edouard's work* was still a vague world of black-suited men and ringing telephones, plush office suites and huge sums of money. But if anybody had

217

asked her what he did there she wouldn't have a clue. She knew he was good at it, knew that he moved rather effortlessly through his days, rarely saw the stresses and tensions in him that she so often experienced herself, but the details had always escaped her. And even now that she'd been given a glimpse into the world through the possibility of Pure; even though she had, for the first time ever, been shown the levels of money he worked with, the kinds of people he had to endure, still it didn't occur to her to open the door wider and walk on in, to ask him questions, look around, even to wonder if perhaps there was any practical way she could help.

He kissed her again, and she opened her mouth and kissed him back but almost immediately he was stopping her, taking her hands in his. 'I have to go now.' He kissed her hands held in front of him, then reached forwards, and kissed her mouth, her nose, her cheeks, her hair. 'I'm sorry. I'll miss the plane. I held on because I couldn't bear to leave without seeing you again. I've been here all morning waiting for you. I was just about to give up and then you appeared, and now I have to go.'

'I had to go to the hospital with Hughie. Did nobody tell you what had happened?'

'I sat here with the laptop and my phone

218

and didn't see a soul.'

'And I'm sure the hours flew by.' She couldn't help herself saying it, even though she knew she shouldn't. 'Go. You'll miss your plane.'

She kissed him again quickly, then watched as he walked away, turning all the time to blow her kisses as he went. She watched him until he walked out of sight, disappeared around the side of Can Falco and out towards his car and then she ran after him.

She caught up with him at the front door. 'I can take you to the airport.' And she led the way out to her car and he got in beside her. 'How long before your plane leaves?' She put her key into the ignition but he reached across and turned it off again then lifted her hand to his mouth and kissed her fingers.

'Bee,' he managed to mutter before she found his mouth with hers, kissing him desperately, winding her arms around his neck.

'Please don't leave me,' she said. 'I don't want you to go. Not yet. You can come back to my house, now. You have to.'

He kissed her lips, her cheeks, her hair. 'I could . . . You know I think I must do that.'

'Quickly before someone sees us, before someone catches me.'

They both got out of the car, looked

around guiltily, but the car park was deserted. Then Edouard took her hand and led her stealthily along the drive then back towards the main house.

'No, not that way!' Honey hissed seeing Maggie and Troy emerging through another doorway and turning straight towards them.

'Why does it matter? Tell them you're busy.'

'It's not just them,' she whispered back. 'It's everyone else.' She grinned at him. 'So keep quiet.'

They slipped along a pathway that took them around the side of the hotel and met nobody. But then ahead of them was the terrace full of guests taking their late-morning coffees and early lunches, all just waiting to tell her about their day so far and she knew there was no alternative but to make her way straight through them.

'I'm not going to speak to anyone. Keep your head down,' she told Edouard, 'whatever they might say.'

'Honey, darling,' cried the first voice, a woman calling from the nearest table they passed. 'Come and join us, we'd like to take a boat to Formentera today, could you recommend a skipper?'

But she ran on.

'Honey!' called someone else, another

woman. 'Could we have a word? Our room smells of — '

She didn't wait to hear what.

Then, seconds later it was a man's voice, the sexy, well-bred voice of Oscar-winning actor Damian Grant. 'Honeybee Ballantyne, stop right there. I need you.'

But she ignored him too, and ran on.

'Now I see,' said Edouard catching her up as they left the terrace and the guests and could finally slow to a walk. 'I had no idea. They want every bit of you, don't they? Tell me it's not like that every day.'

'It's worse,' she agreed laughing and breathing hard because now they had reached the front door of her little house, her haven and she was free. 'And I am on duty, and they are used to me always stopping and talking and listening to them. I don't usually have such a distraction as you.' She leaned back against her door. 'So, do you want to come inside?'

Once behind the door they fell upon each other, unbuttoning each other's clothes, pulling themselves free, then Honey led him into her bedroom, jumped onto her bed, then pulled him roughly down on top of her.

'I'm so glad you're here,' she whispered, giggling at his kisses. 'Now when you've gone at least I'll be able to remember you here, in my bed.'

She spread open her arms as he bent his head to kiss her again, tracing the line of her jaw down her neck with kisses, burying his face in the curve of her shoulder.

Afterwards he lay still as she sat up beside him.

'Bee?'

She looked down at him.

'We should go away. Go somewhere new for both of us, don't you think?' She ran her hand slowly down his bare smooth chest, loving the fact that she could. 'It's not that it matters that I've only ever seen you here because of course I'd feel the same wherever we were.'

'But I know what you mean about going away . . . Before us.' She stopped again because *Before Us* and *After Us* felt like two separate worlds. 'Before us I wanted to go away all the time. I thought I'd go mad with how much I wanted to leave. I think that was why I was angry with you — for being able to go so easily and leave me here. I think that's why I didn't want to know what you did when you were away, why I've never asked you . . . It was never that I didn't care, and now,' she let herself fall against his chest, 'I want to know everything, about your house and your office, who works there, who's left, I want to know about Paul Dix and what's happening with Pure. I want to know if you're happy there or if you're going to run away with me and build a new hotel somewhere else . . . '

'We could do that.' He took her hand. 'I always hated leaving you and yet for years I hated being here too, being so near you and yet so far away.'

Sadness crossed her face and abruptly she pushed herself off him again. 'And still it's just the same, isn't it? Because now you must go and I must stay. Better get dressed or you'll miss your plane.'

'Stop that.' He kissed her. 'Don't try to punish me. Everything has changed now. Don't be sad.'

But it was impossible to smile, the thought of losing him harder than it had ever been before.

She began to pick up her clothes, dress herself again, then stood in the doorway to her bedroom as he redid the laces to his shoes, slung his jacket over his shoulder.

'You don't have to come to the airport.'

'I want every last second.' She pulled herself together, made herself smile at him. 'Now, remember to ignore the guests on the way back, OK?'

When she got back home again she went straight back to her cottage, shut her bedroom door, sat down on her bed, picked up her phone and with the names *Paget* and *Lingcott* on a piece of paper in her lap, she rang international directory enquiries. And she did it at least partly because it was easier than thinking about Edouard, easier than acknowledging the pain she felt at him going, at the thought that it would now be almost ten days before she saw him again.

She wanted time to talk to him without looking at a clock. She wanted to sit in a restaurant late into the night and talk and talk about what had happened, how it could be that they'd taken so long to find each other and how perfect it was now they had. She wanted to hear him say everything out loud that he'd still not said. She wanted to hear from his lips that this monumental, life-changing event had been just the same for him. She wanted to hear him say it aloud, again and again, how now that he'd found her, he would never let her go. But he hadn't. He'd talked about taking her away and then he'd run to catch his plane, and had disappeared again without her, out of her life, just as he had always done before.

There was a Paget listed in Lingcott, a village in Oxfordshire, a Banbury code, and after the briefest of waits they smoothly gave her the number and she wrote it down. Just like that.

She sat some more, looking at her whitewashed walls, trying to collect her thoughts. She had the number in her hand. Edouard was making his way to London. And somewhere else in England, there was Rachel and bizarrely it was as if Rachel was suddenly the means of connecting with him again. Her head was full of images of him but there too was this woman whom she'd never met, but whom she could picture so clearly it was as if she was looking at her — the woman whom Hughie had abandoned, and in so doing he had changed her life and his, and Tora's and hers too. And she lived in England, pulling Honey towards her, to where Edouard was too.

For a couple of minutes more Honey sat on her bed, holding the piece of paper, telling herself how ridiculous it would be to dial the number now. That she needed to go back to her desk, back to work, that right now she wasn't thinking rationally, that she needed to give herself time to plan what she would say if the phone was answered.

She carefully and slowly pressed in the

numbers, still telling herself she could hang up before anyone answered if she changed her mind but after just three rings the call was answered and a man's voice said, 'Nick Paget.'

It gave her such a shock the phone dropped out of her hand and onto her lap and she had to scramble to pick it up again and get it back against her ear. He'd said it like a question and of course he needed an answer.

'You don't know me. I expect I'm mad to be calling. But don't worry — ' she could hear the shake in her voice and she was babbling because she was nervous and hadn't planned what she was going to say — 'it's nothing awful, nothing scary.'

At that, the man on the other end of the phone laughed a pleasant reassuring laugh. 'Go on then.'

And she responded to the friendliness in his voice, slowing down. 'I have this number for Rachel Paget . . . And you're Nick Paget.' She hesitated. How old was the voice? Was he her son, her husband, her brother? She was trembling with the need to get this right. 'I was wondering if perhaps I might speak to her.'

'Do you mind telling me who you are?' He didn't sound confrontational, only interested.

'She wouldn't know me. I'm ringing on

behalf of my father.' Did she dare to say his name? 'Hughie Ballantyne,' she blurted out.

'He's your father?'

'Yes.' She waited but Nick Paget said nothing, and yet she was sure he knew the name. 'I know it is thirty years since they last saw each other, and it's probably a ridiculous thought. She probably doesn't remember him at all . . . ' Nick Paget was quiet on the other end of the phone. 'But my father has been speaking of her.' She hesitated. 'If you think it's better not to tell her I called, then I understand. It was just a thought — '

'Rachel died just over eight years ago,' Nick Paget told her carefully and Honey's heart turned over. 'She was my wife.'

12

'Edouard. I am coming to England this weekend!' She knew she was loud with excitement and had consciously to think herself quiet. She'd caught Edouard still in the airport, about to make his way to his plane. 'I'm meeting the Pagets,' she explained. 'One phone call was all it took.'

'Bee,' said Edouard. 'I think you're crazy.'

'Yes!' she laughed. 'Maybe I am. I spoke to Rachel's husband, Nick Paget. He suggested lunch.'

'Oh, then you must go,' he said sarcastically.

'He said there was something I should know.'

'Then you definitely mustn't go! Please, Honey, can't you see? He wants you there but he knows if he tells you why you won't come!'

'He didn't say it in an ominous way. I think it's exciting, scary. I can't believe it would be dangerous to meet him.' She rushed on before he could answer. 'And whatever it is he wants to tell me, I'm ready and I want to hear it now — I can't wait another whole week.'

'Bee, you know nothing about him apart

from the fact that he married the woman your father dumped thirty years ago. He could be a nutter, out for revenge. *She* could be out for revenge. Of course that's it, Bee! This is how to get back at Hughie, after all this time.'

'Rachel is dead,' Honey said flatly. 'She died eight years ago. And her husband sounded extremely sane, rather kind actually. And it may be impulsive, it may be crazy, but you're away and I'm going to do it. I'm going to meet him this weekend.' She walked out of her cottage as she spoke to Edouard, the phone pressed hard against her ear, then while she waited for him to reply she strode off down the paths towards the main house. 'And I know you'd like me to wait so that you could be there too, but they want to meet me not you . . . And I have to do this, whatever you say.'

She'd reached the path leading to the pool, where there were guests, a couple floating on lilos in the water, others sprawled on the sunbeds. She'd been about to stride straight through them all as she talked and she hadn't even realized it. She stopped abruptly, then spun on her heel and turned back, repeating her strides, length for length, back along the paths, back to her cottage.

'He wouldn't tell me over the phone, but I'm guessing it'll be about Dad. I'm prepared for it to be something I won't like, but I'll be fine and I'm used to it. What could he tell me that could be so awful?'

Edouard's silence told her that he had lots of ideas.

'Listen.' She walked away from the cottage once more, this time finding her own path through the trees, moving forwards swiftly, not wanting Edouard's caution and reluctance to put her off her stride. 'Don't feel bad about not being there. I'll be gone for most of Saturday now, meeting Nick Paget in Oxfordshire and then on Sunday evening, I'll be flying back here.'

She was wearing a pair of leather flip-flops and she'd lost the path now, but still she strode on, scratching her feet on the thorns and the thistles.

He gave a short hopeless laugh. 'What a fucking joke. I've been waiting years for you to say you want to come to England and now you're coming and I'll be in Paris.'

Then cancel your plans.

'But Belle will be home.' At the thought he sounded almost buoyant again. 'You could stay with her. If you insist on coming at least *she'll* be there to keep you company.'

'I'd catch the train back to London soon after lunch. Nick Paget has agreed to pick me up from the station. And then perhaps you'd be back in time for us to spend the evening together?' She could hear the roar of a jet engine coming through his phone. 'Could you do that? Show me your street?' She shouted the question above the noise. 'And your house, and your bedroom. And of course I wish we had more time, but this weekend isn't about us it's about the Pagets. It's so important that I can tell Dad I've met Rachel's family, especially when I have to break the news that she has died. And I can't keep them, or her, a secret from Dad for long . . . I feel I have to go this weekend and for once I don't even care if Claudio can't cope without me, if the bookings are cocked up, if the sheets don't get changed and nobody gets paid.' She looked back to her cottage, to her little terrace, the pots full of geraniums, the pretty pergola, the hammock swinging merrily in the breeze. 'I have to get away from here and it's one weekend. Surely this place can survive without me?'

She really couldn't express it properly, the sense of urgency making her want to drive to the airport in the clothes she was wearing and jump on the first plane with a spare seat. Did she hope that, by finding Rachel's family for her father, somehow she'd break through to him herself? Or was it nervousness at what Nick Paget might have to say? Or was it

231

simply pure excitement at the prospect of spending even the littlest bit of time in England, even without Edouard there, but seeing his kitchen and bedroom, his bed, the whole of the rest of his life that for much too long she'd had no sense of at all?

'Dad and I got close this evening in the hospital, better than we've been for years.' The sound of the plane was dying away now and she dropped her voice, speaking more softly. 'I have such hopes for England. The way Hughie described it, he loves it so much and, although he didn't say so, he's desperate for me to go and see his family too — and I never even knew he still thought about them. And when I suggested coming to England it made me feel I was connecting with him for the first time in years. If I go, I know everything will be better between us . . . And Claudio can look after Can Falco, he only needs me to brief him and he could do it standing on his head. I think he'll be relieved to see the back of me.'

'Bee,' Edouard said shortly, grabbing a chance to speak before she began again, 'that was the last call for my plane.'

Belatedly she caught the strain in his voice. 'I'm sorry, please. Surely you can't be too cross with me? I'll come next weekend too. You know I only want to be with you, if you were anywhere I could get to, I'd do it.'

'It's nothing to do with you. I got a call just before you from Paul, that's all.' And now she heard the tiredness and defeat in his voice as he spoke. 'It's not important. Concentrate on Hughie now.'

She would have asked more. It occurred to her that she had to quiz him when he returned from Paris, find out what he'd been doing, make sure he didn't palm her off with the usual vague responses that it was work, it wasn't important. But still it didn't occur to her that he could be in any serious trouble, that the stakes could be sky high. It didn't occur to her that any of the strain she heard in his voice could be justified. When he'd first raised the question of Pure the weekend before, she misunderstood how advanced the project was, thought it was just that, a question, and so she had no idea how complicated and well advanced the plans were, just how many different developers and backers were already involved, how many thousands of drawings, hundreds of plans had been sketched and how much money had already been spent. Edouard's rather cautious descriptions had given her the impression Pure was just a thought, a fantasy castle based on air, but if she'd thought about it some more, she'd have known that it wasn't.

13
England

Honey was on a train from Paddington, looking out of the window at England.

She'd arrived at lunchtime the day before, after just one day of planning and packing, bringing Hughie home from hospital, convincing them all — and herself — that Can Falco could carry on without her. Then she'd found her way to Edouard's Islington townhouse and even though she'd been told where to look for a key, that there'd be nobody there in the middle of the day, Belle herself had opened the door and surprised her, throwing out her arms in welcome.

'I know all about you and Edouard and it's brilliant,' was the first thing she'd said.

Then she had led Honey through the door and into a wide, white-painted hall with a creamy limestone floor that led them on through an archway and down a couple of steps into a light-flooded square-shaped drawing room with floor-to-ceiling windows looking out onto a leafy communal garden.

Two squashy sofas faced a flatscreen TV, the bookshelves were crammed with books. There were interesting paintings on the walls and rugs on the floor and a Ganesh — the elephant head of Lord Ganesha, master of intelligence and wisdom, a favourite of Ibiza — up on one wall. She smiled at that, touched to see him there.

Altogether the house was uncannily similar to El Figo in feel, the two drawing rooms, at least before Anna got to work on the one in El Figo, were almost identical. Honey had looked around, greedily drinking in the signs of Edouard and his life in England as Belle gave her the quick tour, pointing out the sweet little private terrace, pots overflowing with flowers, the kitchen, *too much chrome but we haven't had a chance to change it yet*, and the three en-suite bathrooms, *gold plate and marble, aren't we so lucky*. She showed Honey the spare bedrooms, white-painted and innocuous, immaculately tidy, then slipped past her to open the door to Edouard's bedroom and Honey looked in, saw a pair of his battered navy Converse trainers lying on the floor and wished Belle would leave her alone to think about him.

Because surely Belle didn't know how it felt to see this empty space that still seemed so full of Edouard. She wasn't to know that by showing her his room, Belle was making Honey long for him so badly she wanted to climb on the bed to hold his pillows against her cheek. She nearly did it anyway.

After that, as they made their way back down to the ground floor, Honey saw him everywhere. In her imagination she was resting her hands on his shoulders as he sat at the breakfast table, bending down to kiss his head as he stared out of the window.

That Friday afternoon she and Belle spent shopping around London, using the open-topped tourist buses to link up their wanderings, sitting on the top decks, in the dusty August heat, breathing in the city fumes and ticking off the sights: the London Eye, St Paul's, the Houses of Parliament, Trafalgar Square. Then in the late afternoon they'd wandered down the Portobello Road Market, London's response to Las Dalias, and Honey had bought six Coalport china cups and saucers, hand-painted with roses and butterflies, and a rose quartz massage wand for Tora. And then, at the end of the day they'd returned to the flat and Honey had had a bath, soaking in the water with a glass of wine in her hand, as Belle had cooked in the kitchen downstairs, sending wafts of delicious Bolognese sauce up to greet her.

'He's still worried Nick Paget is planning a terrible revenge,' Belle had called to her up the stairs at one point.

'Don't sound so happy about it,' Honey had shouted back. 'Seriously, do you think I'm mad to be going there?'

'If you have to make a run for it, keep your head down and don't look back.'

'Shut up. I'm having lunch with him, that's all.'

'Still, charge up your mobile and call me if you need help. I could be there in a couple of hours. I'm not joking now.'

'Thank you.'

'I hope it works out for you.'

'Thank you, again.'

'Although — don't bite my head off for saying this — if Rachel's died, I'm not sure why you're still going.'

'I'm going because I can. And because Nick Paget is as curious to meet me as I am to meet him.'

★　★　★

And all the time, through every doubt Belle had raised, every second thought Honey had had, there'd been the anticipation of this morning, this journey that was now sending her flying through the fields and through the cities and towns ever nearer to the village of Lingcott.

It was as simple as that. She was going on a whim but it didn't stop the weight of expectation growing heavier with every mile, making her twitch in her seat, enjoy the sight of the countryside flashing past her window while not really taking it in at all.

Back in London, Honey had still been enjoying her bath when the doorbell had rung. Irrationally thinking it was Edouard, she'd leaped from the water then stood at the top of the stairs and watched Paul Dix stride confidently into the hall and then disappear into the kitchen, Belle frosty-faced just behind him.

She'd dressed quickly and had walked downstairs, filled with misgivings and Paul had turned delightedly at the sound of her approach. Clearly it was she who he'd come to see. Belle, now silently standing behind him, just didn't figure at all.

He'd come forwards with a broad smile and a kiss she didn't have a chance to decline. He'd looked glossy and smooth and expensive, his soft dark hair shining in the hall lights. At the sight of Honey his eyes had gleamed with satisfaction.

'I have something to show you.'

Without asking, he'd cleared the table of

the newly laid knives and forks, mats and glasses that had been put ready for her and Belle's supper and placed first a bottle of champagne, dripping with cold, then a large brown leather folder onto the table instead.

'The champagne is for you if you get all the answers right.' He'd turned from Honey to Belle. 'Any chance of some glasses?'

And he had then sat down without an answer, smoothing his hair back from his head, unzipping the brown leather folder and taking out a sheaf of papers and some photographs, either disregarding or completely oblivious to Honey's continued silence.

'Now Edouard tells me you've been having second thoughts.' He scratched his head, studying the pictures as he spoke. 'So which one to show you first?' He looked up at her. 'I can understand why, don't get me wrong, I can see what a special place it is, of course you're concerned.' He rifled through some more pictures, thinking aloud as he did so, ' . . . so I thought, I'd come and see you. Find out a little more.' He looked back at her again. 'Santa Medea — it's not spectacular, not even particularly beautiful, but it's got that special something, hasn't it?'

'What is that?' asked Honey politely.

'Oh I don't know . . . Its loneliness? Its calm?'

He doesn't have a clue, she realized. He can't see what makes me want to protect it, so he's having a guess, calling up the adjectives in the hope that one of them hits home.

'The place gives me goosebumps,' Paul tried again. 'Isn't it completely unique? You stand there on the cliff, you look out at the sea, and you want to protect it, keep it safe for ever. Not just for our pleasure but for future generations too.'

Couldn't he have come up with even one original line?

'And you think Pure can do that, do you?'

'Of course.' His eyes gleamed. 'Because the consortium that will own Pure will hold on to the surrounding land too, I think we're going for about sixty, seventy acres, and they will therefore ensure that the rest of that coastline never gets developed. If Pure buys the land around Santa Medea, you will never get those ruined hillsides, crammed full of identikit villas. You may hate the idea of anything there at all, but think about it, Honey, if we don't do it, surely someone else will. And if it's not Pure, how do you know it's not going to be several high-rise blocks of flats?'

He'd got a point. What she didn't know and wished she did was who actually owned Santa Medea and what sort of protection was offered to such coastlines and forest and how it was that Paul had managed to circumvent them. She would find out. But for now she knew she'd get much more out of the conversation if she sat back and listened.

'Look,' Paul went on again. 'When Edouard told you about Pure he had nothing to show you but the ideas in his head. No wonder you couldn't make real sense of what he was saying, but I have plans, detailed drawings and photographs, wonderful examples of the kinds of things Anna's been involved with in the past. And I promise you, Honey, when you see them you'll change your mind.'

She picked a photograph off the table. It was of a swimming pool, built in some sort of neo-classical style, rectangular and very plain with a column at each corner and flat stone edges and dark blue water.

Gently he took it out of her hand, pushed it out of reach. 'Don't look at that one, look at these.'

'Where will the swimming pool be?'

'It doesn't matter, it's got nothing to do with Pure.'

'It looked stunning.'

'Oh, did it?' He laughed, surprised. 'Then I'll tell you we're putting up a little boutique hotel alongside the club. Pure will be so beautifully soundproofed you won't even hear the music unless you want to. Isn't that amazing that they could exist side by side?' He went swiftly on. 'But what I want you to see first is the dance space.'

She let him hand her another photograph. 'By night mind-blowing,' he said and she looked and saw a huge round dance floor crammed full of people, arms above their heads. She caught a glimpse of a palm tree, half lost in the corner of the picture, and what looked like a series of billowing white sails strung across the roof.

She shrugged and handed the picture back to him.

'Exactly,' Paul cried delightedly. 'That's exactly how I wanted you to react. That's why your touch would be so vital, why I have to have you on board! It's nothing now but when you've waved your magic wand it will be mind-blowing.' He poked at another picture with his finger. 'Look at this. This is it by daytime, this is the broad canvas you'd have to work on. Look at that, isn't it utterly magnificent? That's what our guests will see first when they arrive. Now try and tell us what we're doing wrong.'

She saw a gigantic staircase, steps carved into what looked like rock, leading down and down to where the rock opened out onto the sand, and built there at the bottom was the most enormous glass-enclosed space, and what looked like the sea, spread out beyond the windows. And then with a start she saw that it *was* rock, that she was looking at the rocky hillside of Santa Medea; that the photograph was an artist's impression to show how Pure would look. The rocky flight of steps was genuinely carved out of the rocks, the gigantic dance floor, covered in glass, really would be built on the sand, on the beach, just a few laps away from the sea.

She couldn't hide her stunned, awestruck reaction and Paul saw it immediately and pounced upon it.

'You love it! I can see you do and why not? It's the most spectacular idea. We've mocked these pictures up. This is what it will be like, exactly how it will look. And there's nothing wrong, there is not a single thing you can pick out and say *change it*. That's the fucking beauty of this place, nature has done it all for us. Imagine it Honey. You will walk down the steps, down through those cliffs, a lemon vodka in your hand, and you will be transported to heaven.' He spread out his arms. 'Heaven! You will see the sun rising in the morning, you will look through the glass walls and on the other side of the glass will be the sea, right there, close enough to touch it.

It will be the most beautiful club in the world.'

He was right. It would be absolutely incredible. She scraped back her chair and stood up.

'Paul, is everything in place? You have the permissions? And I presume you've overcome the tree-huggers, the protesters. It's just I'm surprised there's been none of the fuss and publicity that you might have expected, nothing like the kinds of protests we saw for the motorway.'

For the first time she thought she saw a flicker of annoyance in his face.

'The motorway was an abomination. This will be nothing like the motorway. I don't appreciate you suggesting any comparison at all.'

'I'm sorry. And you have the bay, Santa Medea is yours?'

He didn't say yes and he hesitated briefly, just long enough for her to see there was a hitch.

'We have ninety-five per cent of what we want. To have you on board can only help us with the last five.'

She took a deep breath. 'But of course I can't be on board Paul, you know that. I'll fight to stop you developing Santa Medea with everything I have.'

He slapped his hand on the wooden table with a crack of sound.

'Don't mock it, Honey.'

'I don't. Pure would have been a stunning club, but people like you can't be left to rampage through places like Santa Medea. There has to be a point of control. Build your club in San Antonio, leave Santa Medea alone.'

'Edouard will be ruined if Pure fails.'

'No he won't be, because he'll have nothing to do with it.'

It was a mistake to say so. She knew it as soon as the words had left her mouth. But the need to shut Paul up, puncture his huge smug ego, had been irresistible.

In response Paul gathered up his papers and slipped them back into his case and stood up. And then at the doorway he paused once more and turned back.

'You might like to think you own Edouard, that because of your shared history you can persuade him to do or not do whatever you like, but unfortunately for you, and rather conveniently for me, Edouard pays less attention to you than you think. We are opening in a couple of years and Edouard had just agreed to take full financial responsibility for the next stage of development. Full steam ahead!

Keep the champagne, you might find you need it.'

And then he'd walked out, shutting the door quietly behind him, and Honey had sat heavily down in a chair, thinking she should call Edouard.

Now, looking out at the fat hedges and steep wooded hillsides speeding past, the grass bright green even in a drought-ridden August, the ancient churches and old red-brick farmhouses, she felt as if she was fleeing the lot of them, fleeing Paul Dix and fleeing Edouard too, fleeing her anger with him. A superclub, Edouard had told her back in the sand dunes on Es Palmador, one that would take up to five thousand people in a night. Different zones for different music, different nights for different music, rock, house, hip hop and pop, funky Balearic house, electro and trance, but listening to him then she'd thought he was talking about a castle in the sky, a proposal, nothing more, that could be over just as fast. She hadn't understood how determined Paul would be. And when, as they'd ridden the horses into the sea in Cala Mastella, she'd asked Edouard what had happened to the plans he had let her think he was in control. He hadn't deliberately misled her but he'd let her think the crisis was over and clearly it wasn't.

And now, remembering again the moment when Paul left the house in London, she felt the same sense of frustration with Edouard that he could get involved in the first place with a thug like Paul, frustrated that he chose not to tell her everything when she might have had a chance to help. And frustration that he would let her think he was extricating himself, when now she knew he was still involved and becoming more so with every day that followed.

After Paul had left the flat Honey had called Edouard's mobile and caught him in the middle of a dinner in Paris. He'd left the table to take the call, and she'd explained calmly enough what Paul had said, at that stage still expecting he would have an explanation she could live with. But there'd been none. Instead all he could tell her was that everything Paul had said had been true. He was still involved. He was still trying to come up with a way to get out. And she'd hardly listened to any more, so that in the end he'd sharply told her that he'd been away from his table too long and had to go. She hadn't spoken to him since.

Now the train slowed again and she stood up and made her way towards the door, smoothing her skirt down with her hands, nervously shaking her hair back into place, tucking a strand behind her ear. She took her sunglasses off and put them in her shoulder bag so that Nick Paget would be able to see her properly.

In her head she heard Belle's warning once more. *He's looking for revenge*, and at the same time the train came to a slow, screeching stop.

The doors opened and a push of people began to flow through the doors.

She jumped off too, hiding behind the other passengers as she walked towards the exits, wanting a first glimpse of Nick Paget before he saw her.

She immediately knew it was him, standing near the steps that led to a bridge over the track, the only man waiting to meet someone. He was scanning the crowd with the intensity of a customs official with a tip-off and she checked her pace, not quite ready for him to see her. Up closer, she saw he was tall with short dark hair, grey at the temples, attractive in an open-shirted, burnt orange-corduroyed English kind of a way, and she found herself smiling with relief because she thought he looked nice, the right sort of stranger to have waiting to pick you up.

She strode towards him, waiting for his reaction to confirm she'd got the right man but, when he did catch sight of her, his look of complete surprise made her stop in her tracks. Then, he quickly recovered himself and came striding towards her with a big smile of welcome.

She took his hand. 'Hi, Nick Paget!' she said shyly.

'Hello, Honeybee Ballantyne,' he said solemnly back but there was a twinkle in his eye and immediately she thought *I like you*. 'You must call me Nick, and may I call you Honey? I must say I think you're very brave to come.'

'Everyone keeps telling me that,' she agreed. 'But I have left letters to be opened if I don't return by night-fall.'

A quick flash of a grin. 'Very wise.'

He steered her towards a flight of steps that took them across the tracks.

'Everybody's dying to meet you as I'm sure you can imagine. I only just managed to persuade them all not to come with me.'

'So who are they all?'

'I have a son, Nat, and two daughters, Beth and Julia.'

'And who else?' she said suspiciously.

He laughed, looking at her approvingly. 'You're going to do just fine.'

Charming and confident, he had the manner of someone who found people generally behaved as he wanted. She'd bet that he was practical, resourceful and successful and always made things happen the way he wanted them to. Right now, today, he'd wanted to tell her something, he'd wanted to do it on home turf, he'd wanted his family to meet her so he was bringing her to them, brushing her fears aside. Tomorrow, no doubt, the focus of his attention would be on someone or something completely different.

'There are two others at home. There's my aunt, who we call Lettuce, and who is blind and ninety-two and lives at Lingcott. And there's my younger daughter Julia's boy-friend, Pete, who is a therapeutic masseur and who thankfully does not.' His eyes twinkled into hers. 'You're probably used to therapeu-tic masseurs in Ibiza?'

They walked across the bridge and came down the steps on the other side, walked out through the station doors and into the car park where a very clean, very speedy-looking vintage sports car sat waiting for them. He opened the door for her and helped her inside.

'Julia, the daughter with the boyfriend, is so very much in love we'll probably hardly see her,' he said as he walked around to his side and got in. 'The other one, Beth, will probably not leave you alone but don't worry, she's lovely. Lettuce will hardly realize you're there and Nat is extremely charming and will be delighted to meet you. They all will be. They're all so grateful you took the time and the trouble to come. OK?' He looked across at her, checking she'd done up her belt. 'Let's go.'

He drove like a bat out of hell, whipping them along the narrow lanes, through avenues of tall trees that dappled the light suddenly, and then they burst back out again, back into the brilliant sunshine. The wind tore at her hair, slapping it across her mouth as she tried to answer Nick's continuous stream of questions about her life, her family, growing up in Ibiza, running Can Falco.

'I must stop,' he said finally. 'I promised the girls I wouldn't quiz you until they could hear it all too. You'll have to tell them everything all over again.' But then, moments later, he started again. 'What does your mother look like? I imagine like you? In my head, I'll admit, I think of her as a siren, calling your helpless father to her island with her beautiful song, breaking my poor wife's heart.'

She looked at him lost as to how to respond. 'I'm sorry.'

'Oh, Honey, *I'm* sorry. I don't want to embarrass you. I'm very grateful to your father for giving me a chance. But I am glad if your mother is beautiful because I don't know why but it makes everything fit together better.'

She turned away from his piercing stare.

'How far from Lingcott are we now?' she asked instead, a nice bland question that might just keep him on track until they got back to the house and his family.

'About five minutes.'

They managed a minute more in silence.

'What was it you wanted to tell me?' she asked then.

He gave her another quick appraising look. 'If you don't mind I'd like you to wait for that until we get home, after lunch even, when you've met everybody ... Then I have something to show you.' And he moved immediately on before she could argue. 'Does it ever get boring, living on Ibiza all of the time?'

'How do you know that I do?'

He laughed. 'Looked you up on the internet. Read some article in a magazine called *Red*. It was interesting. I got to see your wonderful hotel, all the bedrooms, the gardens, the Garden of Serenity — where your mother practises her yoga.'

She didn't know what to make of him. Did she like him? She wasn't so sure now. He was almost too confident, bowling her along in his vintage car. She felt uneasy knowing that he'd been reading about her and yet, wasn't it rather enterprising of him, and the article was there after all for all the world to see. She decided, for now, to give him the benefit of the doubt.

'I used to think I'd never leave but recently . . . I don't know.' She let her hand trail out of the window as the car sped smoothly on. 'I've discovered how lovely it is to do what I like, just for a little while, every now and then.'

'So you're having fun in England?'

'Oh yes, I'm loving England even though I've only been here a couple of days.'

'You realize you're seeing it at its very best. It doesn't get more perfect than a day like today. The sun is hot. At Lingcott everybody will be out, lying by the pool.' He gave her another grin. 'Home from home.'

She shook her head. 'Nothing like home. I can hardly believe it's the same sun, the same sky.' She turned away from him, looking out of her window. 'Here there's such a lovely wash over everything. In Ibiza the sun's so bright and fierce. It makes all the colours seem sharper: peppermint-white houses, bright red soil, sharp blue sky . . . '

'You make it sound captivating. Tell me more,' he insisted, 'more about Can Falco and who lives there. Do you have sisters and brothers?'

'No, it's just me. And Can Falco's a finca, a farmhouse, very old. It was derelict when my parents found it, about thirty years ago.' She stopped abruptly. 'Of course,' she said quietly, 'you know when.'

'You don't have to choose your words so carefully. It all happened a long, long time ago, and you and I weren't involved. We didn't make their choices, even though we are here because of them. That's why I asked you to come. That's why you're here.'

She coloured and looked down at her skirt. 'Thank you.'

'So how did you find us?'

Just saying Edouard's surname aloud made her stomach lurch with anxiety and dismay. So many times she'd been on the verge of calling him again but she hadn't done it.

Minutes later they drove into the village of Lingcott, full of sleepy medieval-looking cottages built from a crumbling golden stone. The village was tiny and picture-postcard beautiful, with a pub and a village green, and even ducks swimming on a pond. She'd never quite trusted such places truly existed.

Off the village green, they passed through wrought-iron gates, 'LINGCOTT FARM' discreetly etched into a stone pillar on one side, then through more open fields and across a rattling cattle grid, a kink in the road and

254

they were there in a beautiful hidden landscape where fat white sheep grazed upon gently rolling hills and, in the middle of it all, stood a square stone house.

They drove around to the back. It was less manicured here than she'd expected, a proper farmyard with a couple of barns in an 'L' shape ahead and to the right of them, built in the same warm stone, and cobblestones on the ground. There was straw blowing out of an open stable door and hens scratching in the dirt. In the field beyond the barns were two ponies with their heads stuck through the fence stretching for the grass on the other side, and everything looked lived-in and English and welcoming. Then the kitchen door opened and two women came out, arms wide to welcome her. There was no question of awkwardness, it was as if they'd known her all their lives — which, after all, in a way they had.

The first sister to appear had shoulder-length strawberry-blonde hair caught up in a flower clip and a sweet freckled face and Honey saw with a start that her hands were covered in what looked like blood.

'It's all right, it's summer pudding,' she called, seeing Honey's shock. 'What a start! Silly me! I'm so sorry. I was just trying to put it together before you arrived.' She gave her hands a half-hearted shake then wiped them down the back of her jeans and stepped forwards again. 'Hi, Honey,' she said, her eyes shining and now Honey thought she might be crying a little. 'I can't tell you how much we were looking forward to meeting you.'

'Me too,' Honey said, smiling back at her.

The other sister had dark shiny hair cut very close to her beautifully shaped head. She had fine features, delicately arched eyebrows and brown, almost black eyes. She was wearing rolled-up baggy jeans and a scoop-neck white T-shirt and she had bare brown feet. She stepped from behind her sister and hopped gingerly towards Honey across the cobbles, went to take her hand and then said, 'Sod it' and caught her in a bony, heartfelt hug. 'I'm Julia. We're so glad you came.'

And then last out of the doorway came Nat, tall and dark as his sister Julia, in a pair of khaki shorts with a lovely lean face and eyes the colour of the sky. He broke into a delighted smile at the sight of Honey, came forwards to shake her hand and then, like his sister, changed his mind and kissed her cheek instead.

With Nat leading the way, the four of them took her into the house, through a messy farmhouse kitchen, washing-up piling several feet out of the sink, a chopping board covered in strawberries dripping juice onto the terracotta-tiled floor, and then on into a long low drawing room, which in contrast was tidy and quiet, serene and beautiful, where the mellow morning sun flooded across the bare brown floorboards and two squashy-looking sofas called out to them to come and sit down.

The dark-haired girl, Julia, did just that, flinging herself down, then turning back to Honey with an expectant smile.

'Do make yourself comfortable, Julia,' said the other sister waspishly and she gave Honey a quick flash of a smile. 'Now,' she announced with a flourish, 'I'm just going to wash my hands and fetch some drinks.'

'Nat will do that,' Julia called after her. 'Won't you, Nat?' she asked, turning back to her brother.

Nat nodded, walked back to the open doorway. 'Where's Pete, by the way?' he asked over his shoulder.

'Still in bed.'

'Good,' said Nick.

'He knows we don't want him around,' Julia told Honey. 'I said we'd call him down for lunch.'

Nat reappeared with a bottle of champagne and five glasses.

'Lamb for lunch,' Nick told her with hearty

relish. 'Does your father still enjoy a Sunday roast? If it was me, it's the kind of tradition I'd insist upon.'

'Insist upon what?' asked Beth back in the doorway again.

'Insist on my Sunday roast,' said Nick. 'Right from the moment I arrived in Ibiza I think I'd insist upon that.'

Honey looked to the doorway and seeing the way Beth was waiting so avidly for her reply, she faltered. I'm sure they're broadminded, she thought. I know they're grown-up, but what can I say about a Sunday roast? Imagine Nick's face if I told him that in those days, when Dad first arrived, he was sometimes tripping for several days at a time, and in any case he never got up before three. Or that my mother usually spent her Sunday lunchtimes feeding milk and honey to the spirits she imagined lived in our well. They'll be horrified or they'll laugh and either way they'll switch off from me and I don't want them to. And yet she could see from their expectant faces that she wasn't going to get away without saying something.

'Well,' she began cautiously, 'for a start everything in Ibiza happens a lot later than it does here. And so at lunchtime usually it's a question of finding my parents first. When it was hot we would quite often have slept the night before in the garden . . . '

'In tents?' Beth asked innocently, still standing in the doorway.

'No. I don't think we ever bothered with a tent. It's so warm.'

'But don't you get bitten?'

'You soon become immune. And some-times we'd hitch mosquito nets up between the olive trees, kind of like a tent.'

'It sounds lovely,' Beth said wistfully.

'Yes, it was. Other times we'd have ended up by the sea the night before and the mosquitoes aren't so bad there. When I was a child we'd often go to parties together, all of us, all the parents and the kids, and we'd build fires and camp and dance on the beach . . . '

She could feel the conflict bubbling inside her, half of her wanting to play it down, remembering that English girls and boys went to bed saying their prayers and surely long before sunrise, while the other half of her wanted to tell them exactly how she remembered it, idyllic, vibrant, eccentric, the whole island pulsing with its own hypnotic beat.

'When Tora and Dad were first in Ibiza, before I was born, there'd be wild parties but they've tamed down a bit now. There used to be animals wandering around the dance floor at Ku — Ku was the most famous nightclub in the world — and everyone would dance and dress up in fabulous costumes and parade down the streets before . . . ' She tailed off, still not wanting to let it go, wanting to tell them *I'm not ashamed of him, I know he hurt your mother, your wife. But he's my father and I understand how intoxicating it was to be in Ibiza, experiencing it all. I don't blame him for being too weak to turn away.* 'But it's not like that now, everybody's far too responsible.'

Julia sighed, stretching back against the sofa.

'I'm so jealous. Meanwhile Beth and I were at Pony Club camp and Nat was in the Beavers. Or was it the Cubs, Nat? Do you think you'd become a Cub by then?'

'You know,' Nat laughed, 'I think I had.'

Finally Beth came on into the room and sat down on the floor, leaning back against the sofa. 'It does sound spectacular, Honey.'

While Julia sounded as if she genuinely wished she'd tasted that life too, Beth seemed rather relieved that she hadn't. 'And we know it still is, of course. I've not been there yet but even I know about Manumission and Cream and Oblivious.'

'Amnesia?' Nat asked.

'Exactly,' Beth agreed.

Honey looked at Beth, at her clothes so co-ordinated and freshly pressed and old-fashioned English, her flyaway hair clamped down tightly against her head with a checked blue hair clip that carefully matched her blue T-shirt. But the fun in Beth's face told Honey that she'd love Ibiza. She was just waiting for her chance.

Nat worked the cork out of the bottle with a practised hand.

'Champagne, Honey?' Beth asked, eagerly fetching her a glass.

'Thank you,' said Honey, 'how generous of you.'

Nat leaned forwards and kissed her cheek. 'You're a good reason to celebrate.' He held up his glass to her then sat down on the sofa next to Julia.

'Here's to Honey,' Julia and Beth added their toasts. Then Beth leaned back against Nat's legs.

'I've been thinking what I'd have done if I were you,' she said, 'and I'm sure I wouldn't have come.' She had the same direct way of speaking as Nat but without his confidence, and even she could hear her words had sounded awkward. 'But I'm so glad you did,' she added hastily, blushing pink. 'Dad promised not to ask you too much in the car because we all wanted to hear everything you

261

said.' She looked up at her father as she spoke and he gave her an affectionate smile. 'And you're just like we hoped you'd be, not that we hoped you'd be anything particular. We just wanted to meet you.'

Honey looked at the four of them, all watching her intently, and felt that although it was friendly, it was an inquisition all the same.

'You wanted to meet me out of curiosity and of course I was curious to meet you, but actually I think there is something you could help me with too.' Instantly she had their attention. 'Until last week, when my father had a fall and concussed himself, I didn't know about your mother.' She glanced up at Nick, ' . . . About your wife. I hardly knew anything about my father's life in England, but suddenly he started talking about her and it was clear that there was a whole world he'd left behind here. He hasn't forgotten her and he hasn't forgiven himself for leaving her the way he did. And I came here to ask you just that, to forgive him.'

In her mind's eye she saw her father, back by the pool at Can Falco, talking too loudly, laughing and joking as he always did, a sunhat perhaps the only concession to his accident, with this secret of his still clutched tightly to his chest after so long. And suddenly it was unbearably poignant to be thinking of him back there in Ibiza as she sat here in England, in this house, on this sofa, telling his story to Rachel's husband and children, her spirit all around them.

'I think the memory of what he did has stayed with him all his life.' Honey frowned as she felt tears gathering behind her eyes. 'And when I realized that, I said I thought I might come and find you and tell you, on his behalf, how sorry he was.'

From his place in the corner of the room Nick came forwards and gently touched Honey's hand, and Honey saw tears in his eyes too.

'He shouldn't be sorry. You should tell him that Rachel was very happy. You might even say that during her life here your father was the last thing on her mind.' He smiled gently as he said it. 'And you could say that she forgave him a long time ago, because after all, she married me instead. She died too young and we miss her unbearably, but her whole life here at Lingcott was busy and happy and fulfilled, and if it helps to go home and tell your father that, tell him — it's the truth.'

Honey nodded. 'Thank you. I know it will mean everything to him.'

She looked at all three of the children in turn and Beth and Julia immediately wiped at their eyes, laughing as they did so.

'More drinks before we all start crying,' said Nat, standing up and quickly turning his back on them.

Beth got up off the floor and came to sit beside Honey. 'Please be OK,' she told her, slipping her arm around her shoulders and hugging her close. 'Nothing but good can come of you being here now.'

Honey looked back up at Nick. 'It's a very personal question . . . But do you mind me asking how long it was before Rachel met you?'

'She'd known me for a long while,' said Nick, 'but we started going out together about six months after your father left and we were married shortly after. We lived in London for a while and then came here.'

'And when did Rachel die?'

'It was eight years ago this summer. She was fifty-four.'

Abruptly Nick turned on his heel and walked out of the room.

'Don't worry,' Nat reassured her. 'He wouldn't have minded you asking. He likes to talk about her but, even so, sometimes it can still upset him.'

Now she felt responsible for his sadness. Facing these three siblings, so united and strong, so blameless, she still felt responsible

264

for Hughie whatever they said about their mother's happy life. Suddenly her own life in Ibiza felt flimsy and insubstantial by comparison. At that moment, looking at them grouped together, so mutually supportive, she felt alone and envious of their love for each other, envious of their big happy family and their lovely shambolic house, envious even of the grief they all shared. She looked uncertainly towards the doorway, wishing she knew Nick Paget well enough to go after him, to try to explain, but explain what she didn't know.

'Now, I'd like to know more about Ibiza,' said Beth.

'Half of Britain's thrown up on the streets of San Antonio,' said Nat. 'I can't imagine Honey's very impressed with us Brits.'

'Remember, I'm half Brit, too,' Honey insisted. She pulled herself together, forced out a smile.

'Nah,' Julia joked, 'you look nothing like a Brit.'

'WHY?' protested Honey. 'What do you mean?'

Julia pretended to consider the question and Honey looked self-consciously down at her feet, unpolished toenails, flat silver sandals. She was wearing a long olive-green skirt that had been in her cupboard for years and could have been bought anywhere, and a long-sleeved white shirt made out of very fine cotton and lace, which had, admittedly, been hand-made in Ibiza.

'Don't think it's a criticism, please,' Julia said. 'It's a compliment, you look gorgeous. British girls spend their lives trying to look like you.'

Honey shook her head. 'You can't say that.'

'Oh, she can, because it's true,' Beth agreed. 'It's the way you're put together, look at you and look at me.' As she spoke she looked down at her own very white legs, freshly shaved, the pink nail polish on her toes peeping out of her flowery flip-flops, and sighed. 'I tried, I really did, but I grew up in Banbury and it shows. Even though I live in London now, and I've got bloody hundreds of boho-boutiques to choose from, I still wouldn't know where to start. If I put some little plaits in my hair like you've done, I'd look like a fool.' She brushed at her hair with her fingers and laughed again.

'Whereas Honey's clearly spent her life running barefoot through the trees picking ripe figs,' said Nat.

Both Julia and Beth stared at him. 'How the hell did you work that out?' asked Julia.

'And I'm not sure it sounded very nice, Nat,' said Beth.

'She's a hippy chick, that's all I meant,' Nat defended himself laughing, pushing himself back on the sofa and grinning at Honey, then he raised his glass to her once more. 'She's beautiful.'

At that moment the door to the drawing room opened slowly and an old Labrador with milky blind eyes came stiffly walking in.

Nat immediately jumped to his feet. 'Lettuce, Pete,' he called towards the open door, 'we're in here. Come and have some champagne. Come and meet Honey.'

14

After lunch, Honey, Beth, Julia and Nat spread out around the pool outside.

While Nat, Julia and Pete immediately stripped off and stretched out on the sunbeds, side by side, facing the pool and calling for Honey to join them, Beth went instead to the shade of a big white sun umbrella, open above a wooden table and chairs. She sat down, kicked off her flip-flops and fanned her pink face.

For a moment Honey hesitated, then went to join her and sat down and Beth grinned up at her with pleasure and surprise.

'Don't you want to swim?'

'Not yet.'

'It's too hot for me,' said Beth. 'The whole summer long and I'm still not used to it. I'd never survive Ibiza.'

'Oh, you would, you would, you'd love it, and you know lots of people don't go into the sun at all.' Honey squinted out towards the pool to where Julia was now sliding slowly into the water and into Pete's arms. Inevitably it reminded her of Edouard and at that moment all the new hostility she felt about

268

him dissolved away and she thought only how she missed him, so much. 'We have houses made of stone six feet thick, they're beautifully cool inside all through the summer. Some days I don't go out at all.'

'I'd like to come to Ibiza some time.'

'Then you should!' She turned back to Beth. 'Come and stay with me.' It was so easy to offer it to Beth. There was something so sweet and undemanding about her compared to the angularity of her sister and brother.

'That would be wonderful and I could even put it down to research.'

'Why? What do you do?' Honey asked.

'I work for a wine merchant in London. Spanish wine is a speciality.'

'Oh, my father would love you,' Honey laughed. 'Spanish wine's his speciality too.' And as she said it she thought how for the first time it felt OK to be talking about him, especially to Beth. 'He has certain old friends he brings to Can Falco and they sit in the gardens under great big parasols, and I bring them the wine, and they sit there, and they research. They take it very seriously.'

'The best bit of the job.'

'Or, in his case, the only bit of the job.'

But Beth didn't laugh. 'Is it hard, living and breathing Can Falco while your parents have all the fun?'

'Oh no! Did I say that?'

'It's not what you say. It's the disapproving look when you say it.'

'That's really bad,' Honey winced. 'I thought I was making a joke.'

'But is that how it is?'

'A little, if I'm honest . . . but it's my own fault. It's easy to blame Can Falco and my parents, but nobody *makes* me work the way I do.'

'You should find someone to give you a hand.'

'I do. I have gorgeous Claudio to help me. He's looking after everything now. And certainly, coming to England again has made me ashamed at how little I've been here. I suppose, through the guests we have, I've always felt in touch with England, even though I've hardly been here myself.' She stretched out on her chair. 'It's also made me see how it is possible to get away for a weekend. I'm surprised how little I'm thinking about them all, how little I worry what I'll find when I go back.'

'Honey, you've come here for one weekend, not even a proper holiday.'

'I know. I've been programmed to think I'm essential, and I'm probably not at all.'

'So do you ever think of going anywhere else? Doing something different?'

'One of the guests, a rather rich guest, has a plantation in a place called Hue, somewhere on the Perfume River in Vietnam. I know nothing about it at all, but it sounded so beautiful that I thought I would like to go there one day, set up another Can Falco.' She laughed. 'His idea not mine.'

I want to go with Edouard, she thought privately, not elaborating to Beth. *That's what I'd thought, that we'd go there together.*

Out of the corner of her eye Honey could see that Pete was now lying along the diving board, stretching down to Julia, who was in the water below him holding on to his arms. Their heads were close together, noses touching as they talked.

Beth followed her gaze. 'Well, that certainly puts me off swimming. Do you want to go in? I'll tell them to stop if you do.'

'No,' Honey laughed. 'You can't do that.'

She stretched out her legs to the sun, slipped her feet out of her sandals and pulled her skirt up to her thighs and sat back and thought how ironic it was that she'd flown to England only to end up beside a swimming pool in the hot, hot sun. And yet how right it felt to be here with them all, how welcoming they'd been, how glad she was that she'd made the decision to come. She wondered if she'd ever see them again after this day.

In front of her the gardens spread out from the pool. Patches of the lawn were burnt and brown but the deep borders and beds were still full of colour, and roses and clematis in full flower climbed the old stone walls of the house. And there were so many wonderful trees, hundreds of feet high, bigger than any she could remember seeing before, beautiful bluey-green, their branches widely spread, elegant and symmetrical, casting long shadows across the lawn, the grass beneath them still spongy and green. She thought how perfect it would be to sit there and practise her chakras and how funny that she'd thought such a thing, how fitting that here in England she felt so much more her mother's daughter, whereas in Ibiza she behaved, at least in her mother's eyes, like the archetypal uptight Brit.

'OK?' Julia called to her from the pool, arms around Pete's neck.

'Perfect,' Honey told her. 'I might borrow something to wear and come and join you.'

In answer Julia gave her a thumbs up then swam over to the side, resting her arms on the stone slabs that surrounded the pool and looked up at Honey.

'You know, it's so great to have you here.'

'That's very nice of you to say.'

'Exactly what I've been telling her,' said

Beth, reappearing beside her and dropping a swimming costume onto her lap.

'Exactly what I've been telling her too,' Nat said from his sunbed. 'Don't leave me out.'

'Thank you, Nat. Thank you, Julia, thank you, Beth. You are all being extremely nice.' She got off her sunbed and picked up Beth's offer of a costume. It was pink and white gingham with a little frilly skirt.

'Oh, I get it,' she grinned at them. 'Now you're going to have a laugh.'

'No, not at all. You don't have to wear it,' Beth said anxiously. 'I had it when I was about twelve, but I don't think anything else of mine now will fit you.'

'Beth, how could you?' Julia giggled.

'You're right,' Beth was now acutely embarrassed. 'What was I thinking? Of course Honey can't wear it.' She looked pleadingly at Julia. 'I'm such a fool. I should have got her one of yours.'

Honey wished she hadn't made the joke. Standing in her own tight, white, rather see-through costume, Beth looked as if she was about to run away and cry.

'Honey will look sweet and she's certainly thin enough to get it on,' Julia comforted Beth.

'I love it,' Honey confirmed forcefully.

With the costume on she sat down beside

Nat, then lay back and through half-closed eyes watched Beth swimming a length, moving powerfully up the pool. Upon reaching the far end, she turned immediately for another. Meanwhile Julia had slipped away.

'I should go soon,' Honey said to Nat, 'even though I don't want to.'

He looked over to her, shielding his eyes from the sun. 'Can't you stay this evening?'

She shook her head.

Beth climbed out of the pool and made her way over to the diving board.

'Got better plans?'

She grinned back at him. 'Maybe.'

'Where are you staying?'

'London, Islington.'

'With your boyfriend?'

'None of your business.'

Up on the diving board Beth walked to the edge and held her arms up high.

Nat stretched in his chair, brought his arms above his head and sighed. 'I didn't mean to be nosy.'

But Honey wasn't listening, wasn't really aware that he'd spoken at all, because up on the board, gripping the edge with her toes, Beth was getting ready to dive. She thrust out her chest, her hands pointed up to the sky then she bounced once and spread out her arms and was launched up, up into a perfect swallow dive.

And for a moment Beth seemed to freeze in midair, held by invisible lines in the perfect blue while Honey gripped the sides of the sunbed, feeling as if it was she who had been tossed high into the sky . . . There was no doubt at all that she'd seen that dive before, back by the pool at Can Falco. Beth was her father's daughter from her freckled face and strawberry-blonde hair to the way she'd flexed her fingers and tipped up her nose as she prepared for take-off.

Beside her she felt Nat touch her and she turned to him blindly, unable to breathe for the shock.

'Honey,' he said, gripping her wrist tightly as he spoke, 'it's all right. We know.'

15

Beth's Dive made hardly a splash and now she was swimming the length underwater, her disjointed, rippling body moving her swiftly towards the shallow end, every stroke bringing her closer to the moment when she would burst free of the water and Honey would have to react . . . but she didn't know how, she really didn't know how.

Nat still had his hand gripped tightly around her wrist as if he was physically holding her together. 'Honey, it's OK.' She couldn't speak. 'We didn't know how to tell you.'

'My father doesn't know,' she managed to stumble out.

'No, of course.'

'She's my sister.'

'Yes.'

She pushed free of Nat's hand and walked stiffly towards the shallow end of the pool, but Beth got there first and rose to the surface in a shower of glittering water. She pushed her wet hair back from her face and swung around and Honey thought again, *this is my sister*. She felt her knees give way and

276

she sat down heavily at the edge of the pool.

Beth sprang out of the water and was there at her side, slipping a wet arm around her neck and hugging her close.

'Oh what a shock,' she breathed as Honey stayed stiff and unresponsive. 'I've known about you most of my life. You're not the surprise I am to you. But how must it be for you, coming here, walking straight in among us all, with no idea?'

Still Honey couldn't make her brain move beyond the one thought, *she's my sister.* Before Nat had spoken there'd been a few panic-stricken moments when her mind had moved shot ahead in urgent leaps and bounds. *Tell them or not? How can I? How could I not? If I tell Beth, would she want to meet Dad? Of course she would. How would he cope? And what about Tora? What would she make of a stepdaughter she didn't know she had? Am I wrong to guess she wouldn't like it at all?* All these thoughts had tumbled over themselves in their struggle to be heard. But then as soon as she realized Nat already knew about Beth and that Julia knew too, all the questions in her head abruptly stopped and everything went quiet. It was as if her brain acknowledged she didn't have to take control and as a consequence could no longer move at all.

Beth kept her arm around Honey. 'Ever since you got in touch with Dad, I've known I was about to meet you. I've had time to prepare, whereas you've had none at all.'

No time to prepare, Honey thought, watching the drops of water from Beth's wet body find the cracks between the slabs of stone and race away. *I've had a whole lifetime of not preparing.*

'We, Nat, Julia and me, we couldn't say anything on the telephone. Once we knew you were coming here we were so delighted. It felt as if everything was falling so perfectly into place. But since you've been here there's been no time to tell you properly. I nearly did, that moment when we all started to cry, but then Lettuce walked in and then it was lunchtime and . . . I hope you don't mind.'

Honey was aware it was funny. Not, *I hope you don't mind you have a new sister* but *I hope you don't mind I waited until after lunch to tell you.*

'And then,' Beth went on, 'sitting out here with you just now, talking about Ibiza and your dad, I knew it was the right time to say something.' She bit her lip. 'But I was just so scared . . . '

Beth's admission made Honey lift her head in surprise. In the brief few moments she'd had to think, it hadn't occurred to her that

Beth could be scared.

'When you dived it was as if I was watching him,' she told her. 'You look very like him, you know.' It was the only thing she could think of to say.

'What will he think when he meets me?'

'I don't understand. When do you mean?'

'I'm sorry, I'm sorry, I shouldn't have said that.'

But she had and immediately a surge of protectiveness swept through Honey, making her want to stamp down on Beth straight away, leave her in no doubt that Beth might be her sister but she could not simply invade her life, Hughie's life, Tora's life too.

'Of course I'll do whatever you think is best.' Beth lifted her arm from around Honey's shoulders and sat back on the stone. 'I've been waiting for this day for so long, and it's turned out so brilliantly. I'm sorry if I'm getting bits wrong, rushing you, saying the wrong things. You have to understand it's only because I'm so happy to meet you, to know you. I'll do whatever you want, of course I will.'

Honey nodded.

'When you arrived, when you got out of the car, I couldn't help crying. I know you noticed but of course I couldn't tell you why.' She stared at Honey, eyes shining again. 'I was so proud of you. It was the first thing I thought, before you'd even said a word.'

'I thought you were crying because of your mother.'

'No, only you.'

She was being generous and sweet and the fact that Honey couldn't respond in the same way didn't seem to matter to her.

'It's always been Nat and Julia, Nat and Julia,' Beth continued. 'You can see what they're like, how close they are. They look the same, sound the same, whereas I don't at all. But I've always known that somewhere there's you: there's Nat and Julia, but there's Beth and Honeybee, too.'

'You even knew my name?'

She nodded. 'I've always known your name.'

'I suppose your mother would have heard from the Bonniers. You know them? They're a family on Ibiza your mother kept in touch with. Their son is a friend of mine . . . '

And I wish he could be here right now helping me hear all this.

Beth shook her head. 'My mother told me about you when she was ill. She thought I might have wanted to find you one day, you and your dad.' Beth stopped abruptly. 'I would like him to know about me.'

'Of course.'

'I mean soon. I've waited so long.' Beth bit her lip, eyes wide. 'I don't mean this very moment, but, yes, I'd like you to tell him where you are. Tell him about me.'

'No!' she said it sharply but then some instinct told her to play along, not belittle Beth or her idea. 'I understand why you want him to know now, but you see, the problem is he's just been in hospital and perhaps it would be better if — '

'He's been in hospital!' Beth cried in horror. 'Why? What happened to him?'

'He had a little fall, he hit his head.'

Beth leaped to her feet. 'Oh my God, but that's terrible.'

'No, no. It really wasn't so bad. He dived into the shallow end of the pool. It's the sort of mad thing he does quite often.'

She took Beth's hand trying to persuade her back to the ground.

'Please, Honey, no!' Beth insisted. 'He could have broken his neck, fractured his spine. When did he do this, did you say?'

'On Thursday.'

'And you're here!' Now she was incredulous. 'He's only just out of hospital, with concussion and you've come here?' Now she shivered uncontrollably. 'Perhaps you think I'm getting all hysterical, over-reacting, but what if he dies? Now I'm having this terrible thought that I'm never going to meet him. I've waited so long, all my life and you tell me he's in hospital.' She clutched at her head, gave Honey a wobbly helpless smile and then her eyes abruptly filled with tears. 'Now you're telling me he's had an accident and wouldn't it be such a perfect bloody tragedy. I can see it happening. He's going to die and I'll never meet him.'

'No!' Honey got to her feet and pushed Beth back down so that she was sitting beside her once more. 'Listen to me. I promise you it was not bad. Do you seriously think I'd have left him if I'd thought it was?'

Beth wiped at her eyes, and sniffed. 'I'm sorry, probably not, of course you wouldn't.' She sniffed again. 'It's just I'm furious with myself for not thinking this could have happened years before now. He might have died, mightn't he? After all you came to find my mother and she's not alive. It would only have taken one accident, one illness, in all the years I've been waiting to meet him, all those years while I've been listening to everybody telling me to wait. *It's too soon after my mother's death, don't go now. Finish university, don't go now.* I've been waiting all the time for Nat or Julia or my father to give me the go-ahead. Why did I do that? Why should they make the decisions? I've hated it.

And then, last week, Dad said you were coming . . . It was as if you were his gift to me, when I'd always wanted to find you for myself.' She paused for a shaking, wobbling breath, and Honey held tightly to her hand, waiting while Beth slowly brought herself back under control.

'I used to imagine coming to Can Falco to stay, walking around as a guest with none of you knowing who I was. It's all right, I wouldn't have really done that,' she added hastily, seeing the look of alarm on Honey's face. 'It was much too devious for me, not how I wanted to do it at all. And when Mum was alive you and your father were out of bounds. She'd done such a good job of forgetting. I always felt it would be a betrayal of her and Dad to come looking for you both and I suppose, even after her death, that's what stopped me. That and knowing what it would do to Dad. But then out of the blue you called us, and now, having met you, it changes everything, doesn't it?' She sniffed again. 'And all I have been able to think about, apart from the fact that I was about to meet you, was that also I'd meet him.'

Come to Ibiza, come to Can Falco, Beth. Come to the home of the wonderful, the incomparable, Mr Ballantyne, thought Honey sadly. *Watch him split his skull on swimming pool floors, watch him fight with his neighbours, fall off harbour walls into the sea, or through the roof of someone's gazebo, or out of a car window. Watch him trip over someone's chair in the restaurant and land face-first in their food.*

'When I go home I'll talk to him,' Honey promised. 'I think it's best if I tell him about you first. But you should meet him as soon as you can. And then, there's my mother, Tora, too . . . ' who could either scoop Beth up in her arms with cries of joy or ignore her completely.

'Oh, of course,' Beth exclaimed. Honey's concern was understandable, but not putting her off her stride in the slightest. 'I didn't think I could just walk into Can Falco, catch them at the bar. *Hi, Stepmom! Hi, Dad!*'

At that Honey let out a splutter of appalled laughter. 'He'd know straight away you were serious, too.'

'I could give him a heart attack to go with the concussion.' Now she was joking, trying to reassure. 'Look, it's too soon for you to trust me, I can see that, but all I want is to be your friend, as good a friend as you'll let me be. I know I might have freaked you out then, saying I had to meet him straight away; of course I don't. I'll meet him whenever you want to introduce me. He's your dad in a way he'll never be mine. I've never known him and, back there in the house, I already have a father who's looked after me and loved me all my life, and whatever I say about feeling different from Nat and Julia, I know they're still my family and I do adore them too. And so the last thing I want to do is take anything away from you. I want to add to it, that's all.'

She had moved in seconds from bordering on hysterical to being reassuring and calm.

'For a while Mum said she had to fight the urge to go out to Ibiza to find Hughie and try to persuade him to come home,' Beth went on. 'She was sure he would have done if he'd known about me, but the truth was that their relationship was falling apart months before and she knew it would never work.'

And Honey thought, already she's calling him Hughie. She has a 'Dad' and now she has a 'Hughie'.

'I don't know why they let me happen at all but they did.' Beth shrugged. 'Anyway, she never did tell him.'

And so Beth talked on, telling Honey how her mother and Nick Paget had married very quickly, that Beth had been born only a few weeks after their wedding, but every time Honey took a breath to respond, to say something caring and kind, instead the mean, vicious fears circled overhead making her hesitate. She worried that Beth would come to meet Hughie and he would break down or even reject Beth completely. How shattered Beth would be if he did. There she was, sitting on the stones, bravely facing Honey, telling her over and over again how she expected nothing and could cope with anything and Honey knew it wasn't true. Of course Beth was looking for something, just as Honey had always done herself.

And she saw too, that it was more complicated still, that alongside the genuine worry for Beth, there was also a desperate reluctance to give up her own roles as only child, only daughter. Even if it was a role she'd always complained about, it was *her* role all the same, it was what made her who she was.

Honey met Beth's eye, really focused on her for the first time, and prepared her words, thinking how to say the right things, whatever they might be, but all she saw was Hughie staring back at her with the same wide-eyed, pale blue eyes, a little bit hurt, a little bit wary. Seeing him and Beth all mixed up, so familiar and yet so new too, she didn't say a word but burst into tears instead.

'I'm happy,' she insisted as Beth immediately threw her arm back around her. 'I am.

You mustn't think I'm not.'

'It's OK,' Beth soothed again. 'Second by second, minute by minute, hour by hour, you'll get a little bit more used to me. That's all you have to do.'

With Beth's arm around her, she looked out at the great gardens of the house, shadows from the trees lengthening along the beautiful soft curves of the lawns. She breathed in the sense of calm serenity, along with the excitement and expectation that her visit had brought to this thriving family, and among all the tumble of emotions there was fear for all of them, fear that by becoming involved with the Ballantynes, not just Beth but all of them would lose so much more than they'd gain. Because it seemed to Honey that they already had it all, everything that they could possibly want, apart from Rachel, of course.

'I wonder if the Bonniers knew about you,' she said through her tears, 'they were her friends.'

Beth shook her head. 'Nobody knew. My mother left London very quickly and moved back in with her parents. She went to ground. Granny and Grandpa were very supportive, although they hardly approved, and then she found Dad. And very soon after I was born they moved here and had Nat and Julia. Nat's just eighteen months younger than me, Julia came along a couple of years after him. And so to most people I'm one hundred per cent Paget too. I've grown up knowing that Dad isn't my father but I've got his name and, to be honest, for years I hardly thought about it at all.' She grinned. 'But I did think about you.'

'And then, suddenly, here I am, walking into your house with absolutely no idea what I'm about to find.'

'Not too horrible a surprise, I hope.' Beth laughed.

She's so in control, Honey thought. She's planned for this and now, after that one understandable outburst of panic, she's dignified and warm and happy about it too.

Honey sat back uncomfortably and looked around to find that they were still alone, then turned back to Beth. She knew what she wanted to do. She wanted to leave here, have a chance to think and take it all in before she made the wrong move she knew was just waiting to happen. She wanted to be back home in Ibiza, working out how best to break the news to her father, and most of all she wanted Edouard beside her.

'It's time for me to go, you know. I should get Nat to take me to the station.'

'Honey, you're not serious!' Beth looked at

288

her with disbelief and hurt. 'I've only just found you. Please, please don't go.'

But I want to. I want to be with Edouard. I'm all over the place, can't you see? I'm in shock. I want to run away from you all, find somewhere to hide and go over everything that's happened this day, think how best to deal with it. She remembered a little phrase of Tora's: *Let me find my moment of stillness. That's what I need.*

But here beside her was Beth, expectant, saying nothing but clearly desperate for Honey to stay and Honey knew she couldn't refuse her, that if she rejected Beth's plea, her sister's plea, that she'd never be able to make things right again.

So she made herself smile warmly and say that she'd love to stay.

'But I should call my boyfriend, Edouard, and let him know I'm not coming back. He was expecting me tonight.'

She pushed herself to her feet.

'Are you going to tell him your news?' asked Beth, following as Honey walked back to the sunbed and found her handbag underneath her clothes, waiting expectantly as Honey took out her phone.

She swung away from her not answering, wishing that Beth might understand she wanted to make the call alone.

'Bee, I've been trying to reach you all day,' Edouard said straight away.

'Why, what's wrong?'

'Nothing! Everything's right. I'm home, I'm waiting for you.'

She felt her cheeks burn. Hearing that lovely familiar voice, it didn't matter now that they'd spent the last conversation shouting at each other, that they'd allowed Paul Dix to shove his way between them. It didn't even matter if Paul had won. All she knew was that she wanted Edouard there beside her so badly. And she knew that if she only asked him, he would come straight away . . . and she couldn't do it.

She half-turned away, knowing that Beth was listening still.

'I want to tell you about my day. And why I have to stay here tonight.'

At that Beth immediately held up her hand in apology but still didn't leave her alone.

Honey started to walk slowly across the lawn.

'No, Bee!' he laughed. 'Don't say that.' He wasn't being serious. She could hear from his voice that he didn't actually believe her.

And then, when she didn't deny it, he spoke again more quietly, his voice full of disbelief.

'You'd rather stay with *them*? I've worked

day and night to finish early and you're staying with them?'

'I have to.'

'Why?'

She told him why.

16

It was as if Beth had privately had a word with Julia and Nat, even though Honey knew that she hadn't had the chance. When the four of them met again just inside the house — Honey still in the ridiculous pink swimming costume — thankfully neither Nat nor Julia chose to fall upon her in floods of tears. Instead Julia immediately suggested she would take Honey upstairs and show her where she would sleep and seemed instinctively to understand that Honey could do with some time alone and was certainly not in the mood for another big heart to heart.

They passed a landing on the first floor and climbed the stairs again, Julia scampering ahead in her bikini bottoms and a little T-shirt, and eventually the staircase opened out onto a second floor just like the first, their bare feet soundless on the oak floor boards. First Julia led her to her own bedroom, which was a large square room painted white, with more bare floorboards, a big rumpled, unmade bed, and a green velvet chair piled high with what were presumably Pete's clothes. There was lots of oak furniture, and gauzy white curtains blowing at the window and a glass vase crammed with blowsy pink roses, their petals blown to the floor by the breeze.

Julia ran across the room and shut the window, picked up the vase and gave it to Honey.

'Here. Let's take them for your room.'

Honey, still standing in the doorway, took them carefully from her. She felt very close to tears now, knew that once she was alone, in her own bedroom with the door shut, she would succumb.

'Sit on the bed while I find you some things.' Julia moved to her chest of drawers, opened a drawer and tipped out a pile of clothes onto the floor and Honey did as she was told, moving to the bed and putting the flowers carefully on the bedside table before sitting down.

On the floor Julia shook out a round-necked grey T-shirt. 'You can sleep in this.' Then she opened a smaller drawer at the top and with a grin swung a tiny lace thong around her index finger. 'And you can wear this tomorrow. It was a Christmas present, I never wore it. It's all I've got.'

'Better than nothing.'

She threw it across the room and Honey caught it one-handed.

'Toothpaste and brush,' Julia said next, disappearing through a doorway and then reappearing with Colgate and a toothbrush in her hand. 'Now, what else do you need?' She paused, looking wonderingly at the pink swimming costume. 'What was Beth thinking?'

She jumped up beside Honey on the bed so that they were sitting side by side, four brown legs in a row. 'Your clothes are still by the pool but you can borrow something of mine if you like, but you don't have to,' she added hastily. 'You're not on show and tonight we'll all watch telly together and hardly talk at all, I promise.' She gave Honey a sympathetic smile. 'We must remember we don't have to cram in every important conversation into this very first afternoon.'

Honey nodded and allowed herself to fall back against the mattress. She felt exhausted. Sinking back into the soft squashy mattress, she'd have been happy not to move again.

Julia looked down at her. 'I could leave you here? I could cover you up with a blanket? You could have a sleep?'

Honey gave her a grateful smile back. 'Not such a bad idea.'

She didn't want to admit to Julia that actually it was someone else, completely unrelated to all of them, who was taking up most of her thoughts right then.

Julia tucked a stray strand of black hair behind her ear and put her head on one side like a bright-eyed blackbird. 'I keep wondering what you're making of us. I can't imagine how strange it must be for you.' She shifted on the bed so that she could see Honey properly. 'I hope when you've got used to the idea, you'll be pleased to have us around.'

'Of course, I am already.'

'But how can you know?' she looked at Honey seriously. 'It's time that will tell how close we're going to get. We're grown-ups, we're not kids who are going to be forced to live with each other. No one will judge how much time you spend with us, how much of your life changes because we're around.'

'Yours will change too.'

'Of course, but let's not pretend we're as affected by this as much as you are.' She smiled suddenly. 'That sounded nothing like I wanted it to.' Then she surprised Honey by falling down on the bed beside her. 'The truth is that Nat and I are just as pleased about you as Beth is. You do know that, don't you? We have all lost our mother, and I think we're all closer to you because of that. I suddenly listened to myself and sounded rather detached, but that's not how I feel at all.' She shrugged then gave Honey a wide easy smile. 'I want to welcome you but I don't want to swamp you.'

'You're not at all.'

'So what did your mum make of your coming here?'

'She said may the rainbow of truth and love bring me home again soon.'

'You're joking?'

'No!'

'I mean it's as if she knew,' Julia said delightedly. 'How absolutely brilliant of her.'

Honey shook her head. 'She didn't know. She wouldn't have kept quiet about it if she had done. Tora doesn't believe in secrets.'

'So what will she make of Beth?'

'I really don't know.'

'Here are your clothes,' said Beth from the doorway and Honey quickly pushed herself back upright to see her sister standing there with an armful of clothes and Honey's handbag clutched between two fingers. The look on Beth's face made Honey feel as if she'd been caught out. She immediately jumped off the bed and took them from her.

'Honey,' Beth said, now looking determinedly down at the floor. 'I was wondering if you'd like a cup of tea?'

'Sure,' Honey tried very hard not to let on how uncomfortable Beth was making her feel. 'Julia was just going to show me my room and then I'll come down.'

Beth nodded. 'That's fine then. I'll see you downstairs.'

'Thanks so much,' Honey called after her as Beth ran back down the stairs.

'Oh, dear Beth,' Julia sighed. She pushed herself upright and looked at Honey. 'You see how careful you're going to have to be?'

'So far she's been amazing, very sweet and only concerned about me.'

Julia nodded. 'That sounds like Beth.'

'What do you mean?'

'It's just she can be a bit intense. And she's been fixated about this day . . . and you. Not in an unnatural way,' she added hastily, 'in a perfectly understandable way.' Abruptly she bounced back off the bed. 'We'd better go back, they'll be wondering what's happened to you. The best thing you could do right now is go and drink her cup of tea, reassure her that she's your number one.' She looked at Honey and smiled. 'Sorry, but that time on your own we were talking about? Forget it. I think my father's waiting to talk to you too . . . But wait! I nearly forgot. Let me quickly show you your room.'

Honey's room, very similar to Julia's in the way it was laid out, was two doors down and was next to the bathroom. It had one window that looked out across the gardens, and another to the right of the bed that looked down to the farmyard below. They looked in for just long enough for Honey to place the vase of flowers on her bedside table then strip off the un-swum-in swimming costume and replace her T-shirt and skirt. As an after-thought she picked up her phone and dropped it into the deep pockets of her skirt.

Outside again Julia pointed out Nat's bedroom, which was opposite Honey's, and the one next door to that belonged to Beth. Down on the first floor, Julia explained, all the rooms were laid out in exactly the same way and housed Nick's bedroom and one for Aunt Lettuce.

When they got back down to the kitchen it was to find Beth making tea. Everybody but Nick had reemerged to join Nat and Beth in the kitchen. Honey was appalled to see blind Aunt Lettuce standing at the table carving large pieces of fruit cake for everybody with a bread knife while beside her Nat and Pete sat reading the papers, oblivious.

'Don't worry, Honey. I do it by touch,' she told Honey, passing her a slice, then she took her own plate and a cup of tea and went to sit down at the other end of the table.

'Honey!' Nat looked up at her.

'Hello, Nat.'

'Edouard Bonnier?' he demanded. 'Who is

that? Did you say you knew him?'

Honey froze. 'What about him?' She saw Nat was reading the business pages of the *Saturday Telegraph*.

'Does he run a management company called Masterplan?'

'Yes he does.'

He nodded, turned back to the paper. 'Spells his name with 'ou' not 'w.' '

Beth came across the kitchen, passed her a mug of tea. 'Have this.'

Honey took it from her. Now the kitchen was suddenly stifling and she felt sweaty and hot. She crossed the room to join Nat.

'His mother's French. Why, what does it say? If it is *my* Edouard Bonnier, you'd better tell me what you've read about him.'

'It's only some mucky gossip columnist stirring up trouble,' said Nat. 'Nothing important. You haven't heard of a guy called Paul Dix?'

'Yes I have.' She leaned over his shoulder to read the paragraph he was highlighting with his finger.

Edouard Bonnier says it is business as usual, but Paul Dix would have it otherwise. Word has it another major player will desert Masterplan on Monday. Business as usual perhaps, but

299

right now that's hardly reassuring news for the shareholders.

'Don't take this journalist seriously,' Nat said. 'I'm sure Edouard Bonnier doesn't.'

'Honeybee!' said Nick, walking into the kitchen and straight up to her. He patted her gently on the shoulder. 'Tell me you've survived.' He picked up a mug of tea for himself. 'Shall we take a walk around the garden while we drink these? Would you mind?'

'I need to make a call.' She touched a hand to her hot cheeks.

He looked surprised at her abruptness. 'Are you all right? Do you want to use my study?'

She pulled herself together. 'I'll go outside. Then I'd like to walk with you.'

She held out her phone in front of her without waiting for his answer and keyed in the numbers, then took it out into the yard outside, willing Edouard to pick up.

It went straight to answerphone.

'I wish you were here,' she said rapidly. 'I wish I was with you. What cheap stunt has Paul Dix pulled now? Are you OK? Are you surviving?' She hesitated, looked out across the sunlit peaceful hills. 'I don't even know where you are. In Paris? Did you come home? Perhaps you're in Ibiza. Let him build all over it if it means he will leave you alone. I just care about you.'

She went back to the kitchen and picked up Nick and they walked together across the front lawn, Honey grateful to be outside, then gingerly made their way one by one across the cattle grid that divided the garden from the fields, Honey following him as he led them along a little track close to a high hawthorn hedge and then immediately over an old wooden stile.

'I want to show it off to you,' he told her with a smile. 'I want you to see how perfect England can be.'

It was a golden early evening with just enough of a breeze to cool the air, the sun still warm, casting everything in a beautiful light. In the distance Honey could see the rooftops of the village, the spire of the church, heard the distant whinny of a horse, while alongside the path they were following, the hedges were unexpectedly full of move-ment and sound. A blackbird sitting on a bramble, belting out its full-throated song, staying put as she walked quietly by, while all around her she could hear the rustle and snap of twigs as other animals and birds, hiding in the undergrowth dived back to safety at the sound of her passing feet. She looked down at her feet covered in dust, at her white shirt now grey, a day's worth of dirt. She felt battle-worn, vulnerable in her grimy clothes, wary of Nick as he led her on, aware that he'd brought her outside to talk some more and too tired to want to hear it.

'First, an apology,' Nick said, 'for bringing you here under false pretences, for no doubt giving you the shock of your life.'

She gave him a shaky smile. 'Tell me Beth was the something you should know? Tell me there are no more secrets still to come out.'

'She was my secret and I'm very sorry I couldn't be clearer, but I thought it was the best way. I thought it was wise to allow you to have a chance to get to know Beth and see what a sweetie she was before we spilled the beans. I'm presuming, I mean I suppose I'm hoping, that she was a good surprise?' He broke off a dark gold ear of wheat, broke it open and passed Honey a single kernel. 'Try it.' Honey bit hard and it split open, the floury texture familiar and yet it was sweet as a nut. 'That's perfectly ripe. They should be harvesting here tomorrow. I always love watching them, don't you?' He gestured to the second tyre track running alongside her. 'Come and walk beside me.'

They reached a five-bar gate that led them out into a grassy meadow, this time full of buttercups blowing in the breeze, another archetypically English scene, and Nick stopped, leaning over the gate and sipping his tea.

'I'm still shocked,' admitted Honey. 'But Beth is so sweet and kind. I could see that straight away. I'm lucky to have found her. I know we'll be good friends.'

He smiled in relief. 'Good for you, Honey.' They walked on. 'You saw that Beth's got a great deal resting on meeting her father?'

At his words Honey looked at the baked and cracked ground under her feet, knowing that she wanted to be loyal and faithful and true, wanted to champion Hughie not tear him down but that she wanted to be honest too.

'I don't know if he'll live up to expectations.'

'Did you ever think you might have had a sister or a brother?'

She glanced at him in surprise. It seemed such a strange response.

'Of course not. I didn't know anything about any of you until last week,' Honey answered. 'My father never said anything to lead me to suspect . . . '

'And your mother? Did Tora say nothing either?'

'I don't think she knew any more than I did. Why do you ask?'

'I fear that perhaps Beth won't be such a surprise to your father.'

'He definitely didn't know,' Honey said vehemently. 'He would never have left her if he had.'

That had to be true, didn't it? Please? Hughie wouldn't have been so cowardly as to run away knowing Rachel was carrying his child. 'Why do you say that to me?' She didn't want to believe it, but already she was starting to. 'Don't tell me that he knew. Did Rachel tell you that? Did she say so?'

'She said she never did tell him. But seeing her pregnant with our other two children I can't believe he wouldn't have known. I'm sorry, Honeybee, but I'm telling you that because I want you to help me keep Beth safe. In good time she will meet your father, but before she does you must make sure that he understands it would be devastating for her ever to learn he abandoned her.'

Loyalty made her not want to admit to Nick Paget that it could be true and yet the knowledge fitted everything she knew of her father, not just in the way he had always run away when things got tough, but in his uselessness, as if he'd always hated himself as a consequence. And telling Beth was the kind of impulsive thing he would do. Catch him off guard and he might admit it to her in their very first conversation.

'I know you've misjudged him but even so I'll make sure I talk to him, find out what he means to say.'

'Thank you.'

He opened the gate and they walked on, along a tiny path that led them down to a stream where a couple of sleepers and a guard rail stretched across as a footbridge, and here Nick came to a halt again, leaning over the rail and catching his breath, looking down at the running stream below.

'Rachel and I would often come here.'

Honey leaned her arms over the wooden guard rail and watched the journey of the water flowing below. In places it sped past, splashing over the pebbles and rocks, nearer the bank it pooled, moving so slowly that long-legged insects were sitting on its surface, splayed on the water, their feelers gently testing the air.

'She needs you to keep Beth safe.'

'I will,' Honey insisted. 'Know that I wouldn't take a chance on something so important.'

At her words his ready tears plopped down into the stream below. 'I must sound so desperate, but I feel as if I'm handing her over. She's my daughter, Honeybee. She's never been anything else. But in this I have to let her go with you.'

She put out a hand and touched his. It felt a curiously intimate yet very natural thing to do. The confident almost abrasive man who'd met her at the station was unrecognizable now.

'I'm repeating myself, I know, but you have to watch her,' Nick went on. 'She's vulnerable. She's told me already how Julia has tried to lend you clothes, how she's found you in Julia's bedroom having a chat and hated it so. You can see she wants you all to herself.'

'We've only just begun,' said Honey. 'She can't outguess me. She has to learn to trust me . . . I'm sure it's been hard living with the pair of them, always that little bit happier, that little bit different to her, but she has to let me spend time with them, laugh and joke with them too. It would be unnatural if I didn't. I have to be free to sit on Julia's bed and I want to be able to have a drink with Nat without guiltily looking over my shoulder in case she's watching. She's got to learn to have faith in me.'

'I know, I'm just telling you how it is.'

He led the way back off the footbridge, back into the wheat field and this time Honey stayed behind him and they walked in single file back towards the house.

Once inside Honey desperately needed some time alone. She motioned to Beth that she was going upstairs, slipped through the kitchen door and up the stairs, opened her bedroom door and flung herself upon her bed, filled with pain at the thought that Hughie could have known about Beth all along.

Much later, long after suppertime, long after the house had gone to bed, she was still thinking about it, puzzling over everything she knew, all the time edging closer to the knowledge that of course Hughie had known about Beth. She sat in her bedroom, looking through the open window, and held out her arm to the night, feeling the air cool against her skin, there was none of the heat of an Ibiza night. She thought how back at Can Falco at eleven o'clock people would be beginning to stir and think about dinner. But here it was very much time to sleep, around her the whole house was falling asleep, and she too was so very tired. She drew the curtains and returned to her bed, sank wearily down onto the old bouncy mattress and pulled the sheets around her.

Her head started spinning as soon as she closed her eyes. Whether it was because of the wine or tiredness or confusion or a combination of all three, she was immediately awake again. And thinking of Can Falco had made her sad. She'd been gone two days, it felt like years. But somehow, now that it was night time, it was easier to accept that not so far away the same moon was shining down on her hotel and on Hughie and Tora, and for all the sadness suddenly she felt a huge pang of missing them too, a massive love for them, just as they were, and a longing for nothing to have changed after all. She feared the future. She felt cold at the responsibility now not just to them but to Beth too. It was no longer going to be enough to be a good daughter, now she had to be a good sister too.

Lying in her bed with eyes wide open, now she longed for Edouard, who expected nothing from her at all. She rolled against the pillows burying her face, then twisted again, lying on her back, staring up into the darkness.

Suddenly she sat up in the bed, finding the walls of the bedroom claustrophobic. She wanted to get outside, to walk in the moonlight, pace the gardens and think what to do, and once the idea had come to her she couldn't stay in bed any longer.

Quietly she opened her door and walked out into the shadowy hall. She slipped along the corridor and then down the main hall stairs. At the bottom she felt her way towards a doorway and to where she imagined there would be a light switch, patted blindly around the walls but found nothing. She stood in the silence, listening for clues but there was no sound at all. She moved on into the darkness, and slowly her eyes adjusted to the light. Then she was in a hall that she thought had the kitchen at its far end and once she decided that it did she walked boldly down the length of it and opened the door at the far end, to find herself not in the kitchen at all but in another hallway that seemed exactly like the first. Now she looked back the way she'd come, then forwards once more and it felt as if she was in a dream, that if she walked on she would find another door and another hallway, and then another and another and another. So she turned back the way she'd come, paced back the length of the first hall and then stopped because she'd passed a window sill, waist-high, the moon bright and hanging low in the sky, three-quarters full. She opened the window wide, breathed in the soft cool darkness of the beautiful gardens outside, grey in the moonlight, where nothing moved at all, then sank down cross-legged on the stone floor, tucked her T-shirt beneath her, held her hands together in her lap and tipped up her face to the light. She closed her eyes, rested her hands on her knees and imagined the moon's delicate silvery light bathing her face, its warmth gently slipping through her body. She breathed slowly, in and out, thinking only of its light and its gentleness and gradually she felt its peace settle upon her shoulders.

She stayed there for about five minutes and when she opened her eyes again it was because she could hear someone breathing. And then a side door squeaked open halfway down the hall, and suddenly there was Beth peering through it.

Honey stayed where she was, waiting for her and she came cautiously through the door. When Honey didn't rise to her feet at the sight of her, Beth hesitated and then sat carefully and silently down opposite her.

'For a moment I thought you were a ghost,' she whispered. 'You looked so pale, with your hair and your grey T-shirt. I'm sorry. I didn't mean to interrupt you.'

Honey shook her head, wondering if she was in the middle of a dream, It all seemed so strange.

Beth nodded towards the open window. 'You're watching the moon?'

'Yes.' She smiled, amused by Beth's chatty tone.

'I can see why, it's magical isn't it? Sometimes at night, when I can't sleep, I go out into the gardens and I lie under the cedars and I watch the light through the branches. Have you ever done that?'

'Never,' said Honey, thinking how in Tora, Beth might find a kindred spirit after all. 'One day you'll have to let my mother get her hands on you. She has excellent tricks for getting to sleep.' Honey scrambled back to her feet, hesitated a moment. 'I couldn't sleep either. I thought I might have gone for a wander outside but I couldn't find the door.'

'Easily lost and I've lived here all my life.' Beth rose back to her feet. 'I'll show you if you want. Can I come with you?'

'I'd like you to.'

Beth reached behind her and pressed a switch and immediately the hall was bathed in light, and Honey saw the grey stone floor she'd been sitting on, the heavy curtains on either side of the open window and further down an oak-studded door. Beth went over to the door and carefully turned its iron key, opened the door. And the two of them stepped outside into the wonderful night, the sky packed with stars.

'Come on,' Beth said, dropping her voice to a whisper.

Barefoot they padded across the garden. In the moonlight Honey could see the way towards the cattle grid and on to the path she'd taken with Nick that afternoon. Now it seemed a completely different place, the garden grass slightly damp and soft and springy between her toes. They walked on towards the tall dark trees. Cedars of Lebanon, Beth had said. They moved between them, pacing deliberately, hardly needing to speak and yet here in the darkness, with each unspoken word, she felt closer to Beth than she ever had in the daylight.

Beth walked to one of the tallest trees and laid her hands flat against its trunk, then pressed her cheek against its scratchy bark.

'I lie beneath it like this . . . ' She sank down to the ground, then lay on her back looking up into the dark branches. 'I love the balance of the earth beneath me and the weightlessness of the night above.'

Her clear musical voice was loud in the silence of the night. Tora will work on you, thought Honey, lying down beside her. She will mould you and guide you, lead you down the pathways to fulfilment and inner joy. Perhaps of the two of her parents, it would be Tora who'd influence her most. You will love her. And you'll love Ibiza too.

'Beth?' she whispered a couple of minutes later, when the grass had become a little colder and the sky had begun to lose its attraction. There was no reply. 'Beth?'

Honey shook her awake.

'Honey!' She opened her eyes. 'Did you feel it too? Wasn't it great?'

'You were asleep, Beth.'

She stood up first then helped Beth onto her feet and together they walked back across the lawns to the house.

Back inside at the top of the stairs Honey paused to say goodnight, leaned in to kiss her, when Beth caught hold of her arm.

'Forgive me if I make life difficult for you.'

Honey shook her head. 'Of course you don't.'

'No,' said Beth, 'I don't mean now, I mean later.'

★ ★ ★

Honey slept late the next morning, had a lazy bath. Then, wrapped in a towel, she found her way to Beth's bedroom to ask for some clothes to borrow. When there was no response to her knock, she quietly opened the door expecting to find her still asleep, but the bed was made, and even before she logged that the room was completely empty, no sign of Beth at all, she heard voices downstairs calling her name and Beth's too and she knew something was wrong.

She left the room, crossed the hall and stopped at the top of the stairs. She could hear Nat and Nick at the bottom and she leaned over the banisters to see what was going on. Below her she could see Nick looking vainly out through the open front door.

'Has her car gone?' As he spoke he moved towards the window to see.

'I don't know.' Nat came into view, moving closer, to look out of the window too.

'I think it has,' said Nick quietly. 'She's left without a word. So why would Beth do that, Nat? Where could she possibly have gone? And why wouldn't she want to tell us first?'

At his words Honey flew back to her bedroom, and dressed in the same dirty clothes that she had worn the day before, then came back to the top of the stairs, took a deep breath and began to walk down.

Below her Nick was now sitting in a hall chair with his head in his hands.

'She wouldn't want to tell us because she'd know we'd try to stop her.'

He looked up to where Honey was standing halfway down the stairs and stared at her in horrible surprise.

'What can you mean? Where is she Honey, do you know? Is she safe? Is she in trouble?'

'I think she's on her way to Ibiza.'

Honey stepped forwards down the last stairs and stopped to face the two of them. 'Yesterday, beside the pool, all she could think about was meeting my father . . . Hughie.'

'Her father,' said Nick.

'She wanted me to call him straight away to tell him that she was here, who she was, and I didn't want to brush her aside. I didn't want her thinking she didn't have a right to see him as soon as she wanted to, but I wanted time to prepare the way, so I told her how Hughie had been in hospital. I thought it would make her see she shouldn't rush him, but it did the opposite. She couldn't bear it. For a while nothing I said made the slightest bit of difference and then suddenly she calmed down again, apologized even, and so we stopped talking about him, about when she'd meet him and I forgot about it. Perhaps she sensed that if it was left to me, it would be a while because I wanted him to be well again, I wanted to prepare him. Perhaps it was wrong of me to think I had any right to do that. Perhaps she knew even then what she'd do this morning. And then later last night she asked me to forgive her if she made life difficult for me and again it makes me think she had to have been planning this. We were up at two or three in the morning, we'd been walking in the garden. Perhaps she even left last night, after she said goodbye to me. Two, three o'clock in the morning, she could be there already.'

Nick looked back at her uncomprehending.

'Dad,' Nat said awkwardly, clutching his arm, but Nicholas immediately shook him off.

'And will Hughie tell her?' he demanded, rising from his chair and striding up the stairs to face Honey, all hostility now. 'Will he tell her that he knew about her before she was born?'

Honey looked him in the eye. 'I don't know. Why would he want to hurt her? He's not that kind of man, but if she surprises him, perhaps. I don't know.'

'I think he is that kind of man.' Nick laid his hand against his chest. He was a strong, confident, vital man but now his hand trembled uncontrollably and he crumpled down onto the stair below Honey. 'My poor little Beth.' He looked down to where Nat waited silently. 'Please find her,' he begged him. 'Please don't let her be hurt.'

Nat nodded. 'I'll make some calls.' And immediately he left the room, leaving Honey alone with Nick.

'You promised me you'd keep her safe. Oh this might not seem so important to you, but

Beth is so uncertain, so unsure of herself. You have no idea how she's blossomed already in your company because you've never seen her any other way, but she's not strong, Honey, and I dread her meeting him, blurting out everything without you at her side to stop him rejecting her again.' He closed his eyes. 'Oh, Honey, what did I do bringing you into our lives? Did I make the most terrible mistake?'

'She's my sister. And it was the only thing you could do. Secrets have a way of getting told.'

'It's true. I know and I'm sorry. Lashing out at you doesn't help anyone.'

'I want to look after her too, I want to help her, make her happy.'

As she said that he dropped his head back in his hands.

'If she's gone to Ibiza I must go too.'

'Let me take you to London,' said Nat, returning to the room. 'I'll drive you. And Dad?' Nick turned agonized eyes towards him. 'Beth will be fine. You know she will be. You're acting as if she's in terrible danger, but you must know she's more likely to be sitting in her car in a traffic jam on the M40 or perhaps she has no intention of going to Ibiza. And, Dad, she's not so fragile either. Stop making out that she can't stand up to anything without one of us at her side.'

'I know,' he whispered. 'I know you're right but I have to look after her for your mother, that's why I worry so.'

'And you must stop blaming Honey for what happened to Mum. Don't turn this little family drama into something that's her fault. Blame Hughie Ballantyne if you have to, but don't even think of blaming Honey.'

'I don't!' he cried defensively. 'I was the one who brought her here.'

'But she's his daughter, and now you're terrified that he's about to take Beth away from you.'

Nick couldn't reply. For a moment Nat looked at him, as he slumped to sit down on the bottom stair, then awkwardly dropped his hand on his father's shoulder.

'We'll follow her, Dad, and you'll see everything will be fine.' He turned to Honey. 'Cup of coffee, then pick up your bag and we could leave straight away, yes? We can call from the car and find out where she is.'

Julia and Pete had joined Nat when she returned from her bedroom and Nick had disappeared. She stopped, looking at Julia from the third from bottom stair, wondering if she felt the same way, whether secretly all of them blamed her for what had happened. But in answer Julia took one look at Honey's face and ran up the last few stairs to meet her.

'Poor Honey. You know, she does this sometimes. She likes to watch us run around after her, prove how much we love her.'

'I'm ringing her,' Nat told Honey, phone against his ear. 'She might answer and tell us where she is.' He grinned. 'Then we could stay for breakfast.'

He waited, waited, but got no reply and eventually he put away the phone. 'It's gone straight to answer. She's not picking up.'

'She's such an awful drama queen,' said Julia, leaning back against the wall and addressing her comment to her father, who'd reappeared from the kitchen. 'She'll know exactly what she's doing to us all, running away like a kid. I'm cross with her Dad, not particularly worried, I'm pissed off.'

Nick looked back to her. 'I don't want to know.'

'She won't have gone to Ibiza. She's gone back to London. She's got the day off tomorrow so she can do what she likes. Tuesday morning she'll be back at work and we'll all be expected to forget all about it.'

'Beth wouldn't have left Honey here without a good reason.'

'And if she has gone?' Julia challenged him.

'So what if she does make it to Ibiza? Whatever she hears from her father, she'll get over it.'

'Stop it, Julia,' said Nat ending the conversation sharply. He nodded to them all. 'I'll take Honey with me now. I'll drop her off and then I'll go on to Beth's flat, find her, or at least see if she's been there.'

'And if she hasn't?' asked Julia.

'Then we talk and we decide what to do next.'

Nat put his arm around Honey's shoulder. 'OK?' he asked her. 'I'm very sorry your first visit here is ending this way, but you know this is a hitch, that's all, and when we've got her back then we can begin again.'

Nick bit his lip at his son's words, but as they passed him by on their way to the front door he turned and she moved stiffly towards him before he caught her by the shoulders and held her still.

'I'm ashamed to say I'm still furious with your father. I have been angry with him for thirty years, but that's no justification for lashing out at you. You couldn't have handled this weekend better than you did.'

Then he moved aside for the two of them and Nat took her hand and ushered her through the door.

When they moved out onto the drive and

to Nat's car, she turned to see Nick standing in the open doorway to watch them go, and as the car leaped into life and Nat pointed it towards the drive, saw him raise his arm in sad farewell.

17

Back at Edouard's flat Belle was waiting for Honey. Tight-lipped and hardly meeting her eye she was a different person from the woman Honey had said goodbye to only the day before. And still feeling buffeted from the fears about Beth, at first Honey thought it had to do with the Pagets and what had just happened, that somehow Belle had heard about it all and also blamed Honey for Beth's flight.

She let Honey into the house and then stalked back into the sitting room, leaving her alone in the hall. So seconds later Honey stalked in after her. After everything that had already happened that morning, she was in no mood for Belle's unexpected and completely inexplicable bad temper.

'You need to tell me what's going on,' said Belle.

'So do you,' retorted Honey.

Belle cleared the long brown leather sofa clear of newspapers and magazines to make a space, throwing them in a big pile onto the carpet, then she sat down, crossed her legs and waited.

'No,' Honey said flatly. 'First you tell me what's pissing you off.'

'Absolutely I will. Edouard's in trouble, but you know that, don't you, you just don't care that much. You worry about Santa Medea, what happens to darling Ibiza and all your new friends, the Pagets, but it doesn't cross your mind to worry about what could be happening to Edouard.'

'Belle, what's wrong?'

'When Paul threatened Edouard, here in this house, did it occur to you that he was powerful and dangerous and that if things didn't go his way he could make trouble?'

'Of course it did.'

'So what did you do about it?'

'Nothing.' Honey shrugged helplessly. 'What did you have in mind?'

'Anything at all. Because you've let Edouard run around after you, watching out for you, understanding, putting up with you. Six days he's gone without sleep. He's flown all over Europe, he's been sweating in his office, twenty-hour days, trying to pull this around, trying not to lose El Figo, trying to pacify Paul, trying to find him some other place to build on. And you haven't even thought about it, have you? You certainly didn't mention it to me yesterday. I don't think you even realized there was a problem until Paul came marching in here. Honey, as Edouard's friend, I'm saying it's not good enough.'

'I don't care what you think.'

'You have to because it's true! You just presumed that Edouard had sorted the whole Pure fiasco out for you, didn't you?'

'No. I knew it was worse than that. And I read something in the newspaper today . . . '

'Oh, well done.'

'No, don't. I've explained to him, we've talked about this.'

'You didn't know!' Belle exploded. 'And I'm so angry with you on his behalf because Edouard's never going to be angry with you himself. Before we came out to stay with Edouard last weekend, Nancy and I knew about every last detail of Can Falco. We knew the grass seed you use on the lawns because Edouard told us, we knew about the wild asparagus you gather in the hills and serve in the restaurant and what date your mother's birthday is. We knew you liked quince jelly with your Ibicenco lamb and that your friend Hayley Boston makes jewellery for Barneys in New York. He cares about you so much he can be *that* boring about you. He knows the date of your anniversary of when you opened Can Falco, and you have to admit he always remembers it too. But, Honey, you didn't even know his address. You tell him all your thoughts, your hurts, he cares about every one of them, but what do you know about him?'

She hadn't finished.

'You know Edouard considered opening a club with Paul Dix, but only because he told you, because he had to tell you, because he wanted you to become involved. But you didn't know about it because you were interested in finding out about *Edouard*. It wasn't as if you'd asked him one question ever about what he does here, what his world is about when it's not to do with you. For all your life, Honey, as far as I can tell, Edouard has been there for you and you haven't even noticed. What do you give him in return? Not your time, your concern, not a single thought when it's not directly related to you. What's his middle name, for example?' Belle demanded.

'Fabien.'

'Where did he go to school?'

'At home until the sixth form . . . ' Honey faltered. 'Then a boarding school in England. I don't know its name.'

'What was his first job?'

'I don't know.'

'Where did he live before we moved here?'

'I don't know.'

'You see?' Belle asked more gently. 'You can do his life up to when he left Ibiza and then it's as if he only existed when he was there on the island in front of your eyes.'

'But that's not true! And in any case this is nothing to do with you. I don't need you to tell me how to behave around him, I know it for myself. And we're happy Belle, really happy. Perhaps that's your problem with me?'

'Don't even think it's like that. You're only together because of me, because I suggested he could trigger some reaction from you if he took you back to Es Palmador, and Cala Mastella and Santa Medea and I was right.'

'But we chose those places. I can't believe you think you had anything to do with it.'

'I've worked with Edouard for the last five years, and all I've heard about is you. I've seen girlfriends come and go, other women try to get his attraction, but it was always you. And so finally I persuaded him to invite me to Ibiza to meet you. We talked, remember that day when we were lying out by the pool and I was asking you what you thought? The night before you went to Es Palmador? Even then you weren't having it, even then you weren't ready to see him for what he was.'

'So what's it to do with you?'

'Honey! I loved you, everything about you, you know I did. Everything but how you were

326

behaving around Edouard. And he's my friend.'

'And Nancy? Did Nancy know what was going on too? Did she feel the same way?'

'No, she knew nothing about you at all. She had no idea what she was getting into. And oh, by the way, you'll have to talk to Nancy.'

'Why? What's happened?'

'Let her tell you.' Belle nodded. 'Although you can probably guess.'

Angry as she was with Belle, still she cared enough about Nancy to keep talking. 'Claudio?'

'Something like that.' Then Belle smiled for the first time. 'Paul's lost her, anyway.'

Honey nodded. 'Good for her.' She stood up, started pacing the room. 'Where is Edouard now? Do you know?'

'He's flying back from Paris. You'll see him soon.'

Honey dropped her head in her hands. 'It's none of your business, but I'll tell you anyway. He's all I've been thinking about. Everything else that's happened and he's all I care about.' She looked up at Belle. 'Once I deserved what you said but I don't any more. I saw it myself without you saying a word. Everything's changed.' She wasn't angry with Belle now. In the scheme of everything else, what did it matter what Belle thought of her anyway?

Her mobile rang and she saw that it was Nat, picked up the phone and closed her eyes, waiting for his news.

'Beth has gone to Can Falco,' Nat told her and Honey felt the floor drop away beneath her. 'Julia's just spoken to Beth's flatmate. Apparently she came home to pick up some clothes and her passport. Her phone's switched off, she's had too much of a head start for me to be able to catch her now. I can only say that she's a good person and she won't be looking to hurt anybody. And I hope when she tells your father who she is that he'll be a good person too.'

'Let me go. Put down the phone and think what to do. Then I'll call you back.'

She dropped her phone and turned back to Belle, having to fill her in on the whole story but struggling to find the words to explain, whilst at the same time driving forwards, knowing that she wanted to be there, supporting them both, Beth and her father, but at the same time knowing too that her place wasn't at Can Falco. It was here in London, waiting for Edouard to join her.

'She'll walk into Can Falco. What will she say to them, how will they cope?'

'You can catch a plane home, right now.'

'I can do that, I know.' Honey looked back at Belle wide-eyed. 'But I'm not going to. They're not my priority any more. I've always presumed Edouard would be able to sort anything out in the world, given a chance, because that's how he's always been and I'm sure he'd understand if I left for Ibiza now. But I'm not going to presume that. I want to be with him now.'

'You know he'd understand.'

Honey shook her head. 'Yes, he would, but I'll wait even so.' She rang him straight away, caught his answerphone again and this time she took the plunge.

'Edouard. It's Honey. I want to tell you again.' She swallowed, suddenly overcome with what she wanted to say. 'Actually, I want to tell you for the *first* time that I love you. I really do.' She laughed, suddenly light-hearted. 'And there's a message you don't get every day . . . And I'm here with Belle, and I'm waiting for you. I want to see you very much. So where are you right now?' She could feel herself reaching for him, willing him to be nearly home. 'Call me please and let me know how close you are.'

She put down the phone and looked back at Belle and Belle grinned back at her.

'You're doing the right thing.'

'Belle.' Honey leaned closer towards her. 'Don't you see? I don't care what you think.'

Belle laughed. 'Yes, you do.'

Then her phone rang again and this time she saw that it was Edouard, and she fell back onto the sofa with relief and told him everything that had happened.

'Get the train to Gatwick,' he insisted. 'You'll have most chance of a flight from there. I'll come and find you, I'll be right behind you. Don't wait for me at the flat, I'll catch you up.'

'No, I want to stay. I'm not leaving you again.'

'But I'll be there too.'

'I won't catch a flight without you.'

'I'll be there.'

'You have to go,' said Belle, coming back into the room as soon as Honey put down the telephone.

'You were listening!'

'Just a little. Get a cab to Victoria. I'd call you one but I think you'll be quicker getting one off the street.'

'I'm saying thank you even though I think I'm still rather angry with you,' Honey said against her hair.

'I thought you didn't care. You're so lucky.' Belle pushed her away.

Belle grabbed her keys and they left the

house together, running out onto the empty road.

'This way,' Belle insisted. 'I know where to find one,' and she took Honey's hand and ran with her, turning left and right, until she brought her out onto a wide main road, and a black cab slid to a halt right beside them.

'Got cash?' Belle called as Honey jumped in. Then she waved her away.

On the journey to Victoria Honey managed to get hold of easyJet and then her knowledge from Can Falco became priceless. It was a Sunday afternoon, August, she could name the flight numbers and times in her head. There was the six o'clock from Gatwick with spare seats, which taking into account the hour difference would get her in to the airport at about nine. She should be back at Can Falco by ten. She booked it and, afterwards, having quickly called Nat to tell him what she'd decided to do, sat back in her seat and fell back to worrying again as the cab made its painfully slow way through the London traffic. She worried about whether to call Hughie and Tora to warn them that Beth was on her way, but what could she say? Beth hadn't said a word about who she was, and then Honey would have plunged in with the news herself.

And then she had to wonder whether she

was wrong to be charging straight back to Can Falco. How much was it about her wanting to take control, when in fact, wasn't she being presented with one occasion when she should be willing to step back? Perhaps Beth had a right to tell her own father who she was, without Honey's interference, and perhaps Hughie still had a right to hear it first hand from Beth and show them all that he could behave with a dignity she knew was there somewhere.

At Gatwick she joined the queue for easyJet's check-in, slipped through easily with hand luggage only, and then found herself on the other side with time on her hands and nothing to do but wait.

She made her way to a half-empty cafe, bought a plastic-looking cheese and tomato sandwich and a cup of coffee and sat down, took one sip of the coffee and realized she couldn't physically bear the sensation of anything passing her lips even though she'd eaten nothing all day.

'Hi,' said a voice.

It was Edouard, looking so dear and so familiar, the old trusty flight bag slung around his shoulder.

She jumped up and straight into his arms, hugging him close.

'So what's been going on in your life today?'

'Oh,' she cried with pleasure and relief, 'just a bit too much.'

He laid down his passport on the table in front of her, his boarding pass slipped inside.

'You're not coming on this plane?' She laughed. 'Are you? With Masterplan falling down around your ears and you having just flown home from Paris? Tell me. Are you getting on this plane with me now and coming back to Ibiza?'

'I surely am.' He bent and kissed her lips, held her face in his hands and kissed her again.

'Belle told me,' she said, pushing him away so she could tell him, 'how desperate it's been for you, how hard it's been to pull out of the Santa Medea project without Paul Dix crucifying you.'

'I had to stop him building it without me. That was what was so difficult to arrange. I knew I had to find him something else . . . ' He grinned at her. 'But you have to admit, Bee, Santa Medea would have made a fantastic site. No wonder he wouldn't let it go.'

'Absolutely right.' She laughed. 'Of course it would have done. When he showed me the plans it was the first thing I thought too. Nowhere could beat it.'

'Then I went there, the morning after Es

Palmador, early morning, before I came to find you. I parked the jeep and walked down through the cliffs to the beach, and then I sat on the sand and of course I knew it couldn't happen. And then I thought how I loved you and how I mustn't leave Ibiza without telling you. And then I did just that.'

'Oh,' she cried in surprise. 'I think that's the nicest thing I've ever heard.' She waited. 'So? You could tell me now.'

He laughed. 'I love you, I love you. I love you.'

'And I love you, love you too. I always did.' She stroked his face. 'I always will.' She kissed him then rested her head against his shoulder. 'So then what happened? What did you do next?'

He hugged her tightly as he spoke. 'Next I had to find Paul a new site, very, very quickly. And not just any site, it had to be one that we didn't mind him having and one he would want to have, which is where Pineapple Beach comes into play.'

'But how? Paul couldn't possibly think Pineapple Beach is a fair swap for Santa Medea? It's the grottiest place on earth, and even if he tore it down, the whole area around it is a wreck.'

'Which means there are grants to help him pull it around. It was obvious that's what he should do, the problem was convincing him. But he's going to do it, Bee. He's going to redevelop the whole sordid, sleazy area, miles of it. He's pulling down the Pineapple Beach and putting up Pure in its place, not with quite such a sea view, but as he said, people have always had trouble when they try to build on sand. He's ripping down whole streets of hotels.' He laughed. 'Can you imagine anyone else doing it quite so thoroughly as Paul? Don't you think it's a spectacular solution? Take one seedy bloke with too much money, point him towards the dodgiest, dirtiest spot we can find for him and let him clean it up. Give it five years and that part of San Antonio will be like Notting Hill.'

'But how did you steer him away from Santa Medea?'

'He still needed me. He needed me to make the Santa Medea project work and when I wouldn't he tried to make life hard. First he pushed, bullied, called up my backers and my other clients, dropped hints to City editors, tried his hardest to make me crack. And definitely there were times when I thought he might win, not that he'd persuade me but that he'd pull Masterplan under as he tried. It was only in Paris that I knew he wasn't going to pull it off.'

'He came around to your house to see me. He seemed very confident of you, but he was threatening too, and angry when I wouldn't cooperate.'

'On Saturday morning — yesterday, it was only yesterday — I went to him with the ideas for the Pineapple Beach project. And ultimately he realized he had to change tack, that he couldn't have Santa Medea and that he needed me to help make it happen somewhere else. In the end he knew he had far less of a choice. But you were his last attempt, his last way to change my mind.'

'He barely tried. I think I said *no* and that was it. He was out through the door. A couple of lies about you but he didn't even hang around long enough to see if they'd had any impact. Perhaps even then he was starting to see that things were going very wrong.'

18

Ibiza

Their plane was full of partygoers heading straight for the clubs. Honey, secure beside him, fell asleep on Edouard's shoulder before the plane took off and woke again as they began their descent, to find his coat and his arm around her, while the other arm wrote notes in a big black leather book which he snapped shut as soon as he saw that she was awake.

'Hello.'

She took his hand, thinking this was the first time in ages that she'd woken without an instant lurch of worry.

He brought his face down close to hers and kissed her gently on the lips. 'When we arrive I'm going to put you in a cab and then I'll go back to El Figo and I'll come and find you in the morning. This evening is about you and Beth and your father, much as I'd like to be there. But then, first thing in the morning I'll be back, and I'm not leaving your side again.'

Gratefully she shifted beneath his arm and

he looked back at her steadily, then bent his head and gently kissed her again, so softly, so deliciously, and it seemed he thought so too because he lifted his coat over their heads and kissed her again as the landing lights were dimmed and the reverse throttles roared, and he carried on kissing her all the way down to the ground.

She was sped out from the airport, the roads thankfully clear until they hit the heavy traffic around Ibiza town that slowed her taxi down to a crawl. She gritted her teeth as they crept along, even though she knew she'd be too late to stop anything now. What she was expecting to see and hear she didn't know. Shouts? Screams and cries? The sight of Beth weeping, devastated, her father out of control, Tora chanting furiously, blocking out the sound.

When her taxi finally drew up outside Can Falco her first reaction was relief that the hotel was still standing, as calm and white and reassuringly immaculate as it always had been. Then the front door opened and Claudio came striding out, at first looking confused because of course he knew just which guests to be expecting and he certainly wasn't expecting her.

'Honey, why are you back?' he cried out in surprise. 'You've only been gone for two days.

You are home too soon.'

'Is she here?' she asked urgently.

He picked up her case, looking decidedly shifty. 'How did you know? I thought perhaps, Belle said she wouldn't tell you.'

'Claudio!' Despite her fear of what she was about to find once she got inside she had to smile. 'Who did you think I was talking about?'

'She's staying in my room. She's not taking a guest bedroom, so we didn't think you would mind.'

She laughed and walked ahead of him, pushing open the front door.

'Honey!' Nancy rose to greet her as she appeared in the hall on the other side. She'd been sitting on a chair beside Claudio's desk. 'Please don't mind! Remember you kind of set us up, so you really can't.' She was laughing as she said it, but was so self-conscious too, walking towards Honey in a new, very floating, very Ibicenco kaftan, the sun already evident on her skin, everything glowing about her. 'Claudio would have told you, but he hadn't a chance and we didn't want to interrupt your time in England.'

Honey took her hands and kissed her cheeks enthusiastically. 'You know I think it's perfect.' As she said it she was looking towards the doorway towards the bar. It was just past midnight, it would be astonishing if Hughie wasn't sitting somewhere there.

'Claudio, let me see the book,' she said, turning back to him. 'I was talking about another girl. I'm looking for someone who may have checked in. A girl, on her own, she might have arrived tonight.'

'I know exactly the one!' Claudio declared. 'Elizabeth Paget. She has taken the single room. She rang earlier on today and she was very lucky because we had just had a cancellation. She arrived a couple of hours ago. I think she is even sitting with your father now, in the bar. Do you want to join them? Would you like me to take your bag to your house while you go and say hello?'

And even as Claudio was speaking, Honey could see Beth sitting in the bar, facing the door. She was at a little table, with her father sitting opposite her. If she looked up now she would catch Honey's eye, but she didn't look up. She was speaking rapidly, concentrating hard, eyes clearly fixed on Hughie.

'Remember your friend Lucinda?' Nancy came up and slipped her arm through Honey's. 'Remember how after we'd bought the belts she invited us to a party? Do you remember?' Honey could hear Nancy talking but she wasn't listening to a word she said. 'Well, the party was last night. Even though you hadn't mentioned it again, I took my courage in my hands and I came back for it. I stood up Paul and I bought a ticket in the airport and I flew over. I've never done anything like that before in my life. But there's something about this place that makes you so spontaneous. And then I got here and you'd gone. It never occurred to me that you might not be here. But oh, Honey, Claudio was. And the party . . . we went together, and there was an island in the middle of her swimming pool with a man playing the piano. And so many of your friends were there, Maggie and Troy, Claire and Tony, Inca and Nash, Victoria and Hilly, they were all so kind I wanted to stay here for ever. And you know your mother looked after the hotel while we went. And she was marvellous at it, everybody loved her . . . '

'Nancy, wait a moment,' Honey said. She walked away, towards the doorway, keeping close to the wall.

Hughie and Beth were sitting opposite each other at a table, with half a bottle of red wine and two half-full glasses in front of them. Hughie with a bandage on his head that had slipped over one eye — or had he pulled it down deliberately? And as she watched, he said something and Beth immediately laughed, a proper, delighted, open-mouthed laugh that immediately had Hughie roaring with laughter too, clearly very chuffed to be so entertaining.

She watched Beth pick up her glass, swirl around the wine expertly and then swallow a mouthful. Then she put down her glass and said something to him and in return he promptly downed the rest of his glass and clapped both hands down on his knees delightedly.

Honey looked at their two heads, close together, their two pairs of hands on the table between them, and then, as she watched, Hughie lifted one hand and rested it gently on Beth's shoulder and, seeing that, Honey had to hang on to herself not to burst into tears, because how come he could laugh so easily with Beth but never with her? And why, despite all the time and the attention and the love, did she never merit such an affectionate touch?

As to whether Beth had told Hughie who she was, she didn't know, and there was now just one way to find out.

Honey moved forwards into the room, then hesitantly towards their table.

Beth saw her first and Honey saw the look of fear upon her face before her father turned in curiosity and then exclaimed 'Honey!' loud enough to be heard above the noise of the bar.

In response the bar went quiet and then immediately surged loud with sound again as the room seemed to repeat after him, *Honey!* Familiar faces, affectionate voices calling out, *We missed you. Thank God you're back. The place has collapsed, look at us, no food, nothing to drink!* Any other time she'd have loved such a welcome, this time she took it all in only dimly, while all the time her gaze was fixed on Beth, who was staring back at her, and slowly shaking her head.

'This is Elizabeth and she is quite the most marvellous girl,' Hughie declared, looking back at Beth enthusiastically. He brought Honey quickly up to speed. 'She's staying just one night. She's got a sister on the island — she hopes she's going to see her tomorrow. The sister's coming here in the morning.'

'But then perhaps she might surprise you and arrive tonight,' said Honey tightly, looking at Beth.

'I doubt it darling,' said Hughie. 'It's getting rather late.' He rubbed his hands together gleefully. 'Whatever, in the meantime. I've promised to look after Beth.' Belatedly something then occurred to him and he frowned. 'But why are *you* here, Honeybee? Surely you shouldn't be back yet.' He leaned in and kissed her cheek. 'Welcome home.' Then he added in a whisper, 'And of

343

course I'm on tenterhooks wondering what happened in England.'

'So why are you here?' he repeated more loudly, smiling and including Beth in the question. 'Honey's been on a weekend away,' he explained to Beth, 'seems to have ended rather sooner than expected. I know, let me get you a drink and then you can tell me properly.'

He rose to his feet, adjusted his bandage and set off for the bar, and as soon as he was gone Honey dragged a chair from a nearby table and sat down opposite Beth.

'What the hell do you think you are doing?' She wanted to slap Beth.

Beth looked back at her unflinchingly. 'I haven't told him.'

'But you're going to? I presume that's why you're here? And yes, I would if I was you, or you might find he starts flirting even more than he is already.'

'Don't say that.'

'It's true.'

'You should be pleased we've been getting on so well.'

'You have a right to be here, a right to tell Hughie exactly what you want to tell him, you even had a right to leave Lingcott without telling anyone where you were going.' Honey glanced quickly to the bar, desperate to finish before her father returned. 'But what you can't do is pretend you're not looking to provoke a reaction because of course you are, you *know* you are ... And here I am, provoked.' She again looked to the bar but thankfully Hughie had been caught in a conversation. 'You knew by leaving like you did that everybody would wonder. You must have known you'd get me on the next flight back. What I don't understand, if you don't feel the need to punish me, is why you had to put me through today!'

At that Beth looked stricken, appalled. 'But of course I don't want to punish you.' She shook her head. 'It was the last thing I wanted to do. Of course it's not like that.' She glanced over to Hughie then back to Honey, pleading with her to understand. 'I don't want to punish him either. I wanted him to know who I am but I don't even dare tell him. He's such a wonderful man.' She shook suddenly, her hands trembling violently on the table in front of her. 'I don't know what to do. I don't want to upset him but I know I will. But you tell him, Honey, if you think it's right. I'll leave it to you to decide. Please,' she pleaded. 'None of this was meant to hurt you. I just couldn't stand the thought of waiting any more. I felt as if I'd been stalled, over and over again and that I had to take charge of my life, stop letting everybody else make the important decisions on my behalf. He's my father, Honey, and he could have died too, here on Ibiza, before I'd had a chance to tell him who I was, before I'd had a chance to meet him.'

Honey was still not quite ready to let her off the hook. 'You should have told me where you were going. Why you needed to run away. Can you imagine how it was when we couldn't find you, how worried everybody was?'

And for the first time Honey saw something in Beth's stare that admitted, of course she'd known a little of what she was doing to her family. She stuck out her jaw. 'Yes, I suppose I was proving something to them. I thought why not let them worry. I was sick of being so predictable, following everybody else's lead, *don't try to find him.*' She nodded to the bar. '*Don't try to find you.* Nat and Julia always had an opinion and so I waited. I've been waiting to meet you and Hughie for the last four bloody years! And they've always stopped me, always told me later would be better. And then you walk into the house, and you're wonderful, everything I could possibly have hoped you'd be. But still everything goes on exactly the same. We'd come to this monumental turning point and nobody was turning, everything was exactly the same.'

'You hardly gave us a chance.' Honey had to laugh at Beth's nerve, her lack of logic. 'Remember, I'd only just met you. I'd only been at Lingcott one day!'

'I know.' Beth had the grace to look contrite. 'It wasn't a question of time. It was a question of attitude. And yes it was selfish of me because I knew I'd scare you and I knew it would make you run back here. But you know what.' She laughed, looking embarrassed. 'When I did it, I didn't care. So what if I did spoil your trip to England, you'd already done the most important bit, you'd come to find us, all I was doing was hastening your return.'

'You think? Actually it was all more complicated than that.'

Then Hughie left the bar and they had to stop speaking. The two of them watched him make his way back to their table. He passed Honey a vodka and tonic, and then placed another bottle of red wine into Beth's hands.

'Ribera del Duero, 1997. See what you make of it.'

'Corkscrew please,' she said and stuck out her hand.

'Girl after my own heart.' He handed her one with a smile then sat heavily back down in his chair, and turned to Honey.

'Not even a long weekend? Was it so hard to stay away?' He was joking for Beth's benefit but she could see the question in his eyes. *What went wrong?* But of course he couldn't ask.

'I'll tell you what,' he went on. 'We've been having rather a hoot while you've been away.' Honey waited, looking back at him, seeing the traces of his two black eyes still there in the bags beneath his eyes. 'Can you believe Tora and I even did the washing-up after lunch today? Granted we broke a few plates and Tora ended up twisting her ankle, floor got rather bloody slippery . . . but the truth is, we did a very good job. We *marched* to the kitchens. We said, '*Paloma we insist you take the afternoon off.*' We shooed her out and we took control. And then,' he went on with great satisfaction, 'then I got Claudio to show me how to clean the pool with that marvellous sucking thing.' He turned to Beth, 'Finally got a chance to have a go,' then he boomed with sudden laughter. 'When the cat's away, that's what they say . . . But you know what?' He turned back to Honey and started to guffaw with laughter, 'I think I hoovered up somebody's specs.'

'Great,' she said.

'Not that anybody complained.' He beamed

back at her, then clearly decided he'd been getting it wrong. 'Not that we didn't miss you, darling,' he said in a rush. 'Did you have a good time? Did you have an *interesting* time?'

'How much have you given him to drink tonight?' Honey asked Beth, wondering whether this wasn't perhaps the moment to tell him. Whenever she did it, it would be the same monumental shock, and at least tonight, now, he had the two of them there together. They were planning on telling him the truth, no secrets, and in his own roundabout way that's what he was asking, so what was the point in holding anything back?

The point was it was very difficult to find the right words. It was, without a doubt, the hardest thing she'd ever had to do.

'Dad,' she said, in a voice that caught his attention.

'What's wrong?' he demanded immediately. He hastily took an almighty swig of wine and grabbed hold of one of Honey's hands. 'What is it?' he asked in alarm, and then he threw a glance to Beth, who smiled a wobbly smile back at him and at that something fearful passed across his face. Honey waited until she was sure he'd finished the mouthful of wine and then she took Beth's hand with her other hand.

'This is Rachel's daughter.'

At that Hughie inhaled deeply and held his breath and the grip on her hand tightened. Honey looked to Beth, sitting now so still and so upright, staring straight at her father.

'But more than that, Dad. Beth is your daughter too.'

His eyes darted swiftly to Beth then back to Honey, where they locked on, and he stared at her imploringly. She didn't say anything, just held his gaze until eventually he broke the stare and slowly turned to Beth.

'Perhaps I should have written first?' She smiled at him weakly.

'We met each other yesterday, I didn't know before.' Honey knew that Hughie wouldn't be hearing a word she said, but hoped that the sound of her voice might just ground him, help him, while he tried to take it in. His hand was still gripping tightly on to hers. He'd still not said a word. 'Yesterday, I can't believe I've only known her a day. It feels like years.' She glanced at Beth as she said it, tightened the grip on her hand. 'Beth's known about you all her life, Dad. She's known about me too, and our life here, and Can Falco. She's been brought up in England. She's got a brother and a sister and a stepfather called Nick.'

'But what about Rachel?' Hughie asked in a broken whisper. 'Does she? Does she forgive this horrible wretch of a man for leaving you both? I didn't know,' he said pleadingly to Beth. 'You have to believe that I didn't know.'

'Of course she forgives you,' Beth told him. 'Never ever did she think you hadn't made the right decision for both of you.'

Hughie nodded. 'That's very generous of you to say so.' Then he put his head in his hands and started to cry. 'No, I'm telling a lie and I can't do that any more. I feel that I've been lying all my life and I have to stop now.' He looked up and held Beth's kind, questioning gaze, then turned to Honey, who threw everything she had back into her stare, willing him to stop, shut up, to understand that a lie isn't a lie if it's never said. 'I . . . ' he stumbled, then glanced to Honey again, while Beth waited, sitting very still. 'If I'd been kinder . . . if I'd taken more trouble over Rachel, if I'd been more in tune with her, I might have realized that she was carrying our child, you, our baby girl.'

He'd realized, he'd stopped himself in time, even if it had been Honey who'd made the decision for him that Beth shouldn't know, that there was no benefit and only harm for her to learn now that Hughie had knowingly left her behind; that he had known all along that Beth was out there somewhere, that some part of him, deep inside had been waiting for this day, but that he'd never gone to look himself.

'I want to speak to your mother,' he told Beth, and looked at his watch. 'Now that I've met you it can't wait any longer. It's two o'clock in the morning. Do you think she'd mind if I woke her up?'

Honey closed her eyes, swallowed, wondering how she was going to be able to do it, this third revelation.

'You can't do that,' she began.

'Rachel is dead.' Beth said it for her. 'My mother is dead. She died eight years ago.'

'She's dead?' Hughie started weeping properly now. 'She's dead. I can never say sorry?'

'Don't think like that,' Beth tried to comfort him. Two days, two bombshells to deliver. Beth had had to give an awful lot of herself away and she'd done it brilliantly well. 'She forgave you a long time ago,' she told Hughie gently. 'She married my father, who loved her very much. She had a good life.'

'But she's died. Oh, God, oh God, she died.' He cried it out loudly, pulling his hands free of the two of them, attracting attention from the guests and friends standing at the bar. 'Rachel has died,' he told them all standing up, wringing his hands. 'None of you knew her, but I'm telling you even so. Rachel has died.'

The fact that there'd been another even more dramatic aspect to the revelations had been momentarily forgotten, but that was Hughie through and through, not that Beth was to know it. 'She's died,' he cried again. 'Oh God, she's died.'

From the throng of people standing speechless at the bar came a dear, familiar face. It was Maggie, marching purposefully towards Hughie, and gathering him up in her arms.

'Darling girls,' she told Honey and Beth, patting Hughie soothingly on the back. 'I'll take him home and put him to bed. Honey, why don't you find your mother?' Honey nodded, speechless. 'Of course it's all the most terrible shock. And getting him pissed doesn't help either.' Maggie rolled her eyes at Beth, while Hughie stayed sobbing against her chest. 'I watched you two all evening, knocking back the bottles. I knew exactly who you were and I thought, she's getting him pissed, doesn't she realize? She's about to tell him this monumental news and she has got him completely blotto? No wonder it's all ended in tears.'

'How did you know who I was?' Beth asked timidly.

'Spitting image of him, you are, my darling.' She looked at Beth kindly. 'I'm very pleased to meet you.'

With Maggie helping them and Troy bringing up the rear, they shepherded Hughie out of the bar, then through the hall of the hotel and out into the gardens, following the pathways to his cottage. Inside there were still lights on and as they approached the door, it opened to reveal Tora waiting to greet them, dressed in a bejewelled bikini and a shimmering gold housecoat, busily mashing herbs with a pestle and mortar, producing a noxious stench of fennel and bergamot.

'Good evening, Honey,' she said calmly at the sight of her daughter, missing Hughie's distraught manner altogether. 'My darling, I had no idea I'd miss you so.' She kissed the top of her head then stroked her cheeks. 'Why are you home so soon?' She looked into Honey's troubled face and shook her head. 'Naughty girl, you were meant to stay away. Did you not think we could survive without you?' Belatedly she took in her husband shuffling on past her through another doorway, Maggie supporting him. When he disappeared into the bedroom and shut the door she turned back to Honey, and only then noticed Beth.

'Beth's come from England,' said Honey.

'Oh yes?' Immediately she was suspicious. 'Is that why Hughie's crying?'

And the way that she asked made Honey suddenly certain that she knew the truth, understood who Beth was.

'He's crying because she's his daughter,' Maggie said from the doorway and Tora spun around, stared at her imperiously for a long moment and then swivelled her attention back to Beth, who in return cowered in trepidation at the force of her stare.

But there was no need to be afraid.

'So, you're not a girlfriend,' Tora breathed. 'You are his daughter.'

She stretched out a slim hand and shook Beth's. And Beth wasn't to know that Tora had never shaken hands with anybody in the whole of Honey's life; and that if ever there was a sign of her discomfort, that was probably as obvious as it was going to get.

'I'm sure I'm a terrible shock. I've been so worried what you might think,' Beth started to confess shyly, trying to hold herself straight. 'All day, I've been wondering desperately how to tell you.'

And simply by uttering those words, *terrible, worried, desperately,* Honey saw her transform in Tora's mind, no longer the potential threat, no longer even the stepchild, but simply someone in need, and therefore potentially the new disciple. Raw, uncertain, hurt, vulnerable, Beth was perfect.

Gracefully Tora stepped forwards and took Beth's hands, held them out in front of her, then threaded her fingers through Beth's and said, 'I am so charmed to meet you.'

'Oh,' Beth stuttered. 'That's very kind.'

And because Tora was so ethereally beautiful, so charismatic, so certain of what she was doing, Honey saw that Beth was falling instantly under her spell.

In her wonderful husky voice, still holding on to Beth's hands, Tora whispered.

'As gentle as the rain at the window,
As soft as the whisper of the trees,
As joyful as the sun,
As it breaks a new dawn . . .
You shall dance little angel on the breeze.'

Completely transfixed, Beth stared back at her. 'That's beautiful,' she breathed, and with thankfulness and delight Tora stepped forwards and folded Beth against her. 'And so are you, my dear, so are you. Welcome to Can Falco.' Then she looked up at Honey and said in a far more businesslike voice, 'Did you catch the six-fifteen tonight?'

'Yes we both did.'

'Tora, she's your stepdaughter,' Hughie bellowed from the doorway, making everybody start. 'React like a normal human being, please!'

Tora turned and a look of mild disdain crossed her face at the sight of him.

'But, Hughie dear, I think she's delightful.'

'Oh, Tora!' he groaned.

Now she seemed genuinely confused. 'How would you like me to be? I don't understand.'

'What don't you understand? That I left another woman for you? Left her pregnant? Is it not the most terrible shock that I have a child?'

'A terrible shock? No.' Tora looked back at him with a kindly smile, now falling completely into her earth mother role. 'For in this world we are *all* one family and through our new love for Beth we shall feel her joy. We shall comfort and protect her and through our love we shall set her free. We shall let her spirit fly.' She looked carefully at Beth as she spoke and despite Honey's own certainty that her mother always spoke the first words that entered her head, whatever they might be, still she couldn't deny that this time Tora's choices had been rather good ones.

'In this world we are all one family,' Tora repeated, then walked over to Hughie and kissed his cheek affectionately. 'Aren't we, darling? I welcome the chance to know Beth. I am happy that she is here.'

'Either you are amazing or you are completely nuts,' said Hughie, coming forwards and kissing her back. 'Thirty years and I still haven't worked out which it is.'

Tenderly Tora pushed his bandage further up his forehead. 'You worry too much.' She pulled on his arm. 'Now come to bed. Leave them until the morning. You need to sleep.'

'It's a bit of both, I think,' Maggie told Beth as Tora and Hughie disappeared into their bedroom. 'Tora's an exquisite mix of the nutty and the sane. You'll see.'

Beth looked after them rather longingly as the door shut quietly behind them.

'Come with me,' said Honey as Beth then started to sway on her feet. 'I'll take her to the cottage,' she told Maggie. 'Thank you,' she added. 'You sorted them out beautifully. We'll find you in the morning.'

So Honey took Beth by the hand and led her away and Maggie came out after them, muttering and laughing to herself, to pick up Troy, who was patiently waiting for her in the garden outside.

19

In the morning Honey brought Beth a cup of tea to her bedroom and gently called her name. She put the tea down beside her bed and went to the window opening the shutters and letting the bright Ibiza sun fall straight across Beth's face.

Predictably Beth stirred and sat up, rubbing her eyes.

'It's early but I thought you'd want to be awake.' She turned to look out of the window. 'You never know, something unexpected might happen today.'

At that Beth groaned and let herself fall back among the pillows, then she looked back at Honey and started to smile. 'Was it really all as mad and as wonderful as I remember?'

'Yes, it was.' Honey grinned at Beth. She felt so happy. Grab hold of the moment, she thought fleetingly, remember this time.

Beth took a deep, wobbly breath. 'You've forgiven me then? I promise I won't ever scare you again. I know I won't because even though I've just arrived here, and I can hardly explain how it felt to meet Hughie, I know already that something has settled inside me.

I feel this joy, this peace. It's hard to explain.'

'Talk to Tora about it.' Honey grinned. 'I'm sure she'll know just what you mean.' She got up off the bed. 'We should call Nat and Julia, let them know you're OK.'

'And Dad . . . Oh God,' Beth shook her head. 'I do feel very awful about running away from him.'

'I think he understood better than the rest of us did. Call him while I find you some clothes, then you can come back to the hotel and we can have breakfast. Find Tora and Hughie and see how they are this morning.'

While Beth called her father and dressed, Honey left her and went back to her own bedroom, opened her suitcase and methodically started sorting it out. One weekend, it was all she'd been away. Still less than a week had passed since her father had dived into the pool and blurted out Rachel's name, just ten days since she'd climbed the hills to El Figo and joined Edouard's party.

She came back into Beth's room with an armful of clothes. 'Sort through these, borrow anything you like. I should go over to reception to see Claudio. Come for breakfast when you're ready.' She blew her a kiss.

'Honey,' said Claudio when he saw her. His eyes were twinkling and bright, a smile refusing to disappear even though he was trying to look serious. 'I knew you wouldn't mind.'

'You are such a devilishly fast mover.'

He leaned forwards, shaking his head. 'It was Nancy, not me. I was '*No, no. Go away from me.*' ' He shushed his hands theatrically, 'I kept telling her, '*Honey wouldn't approve, we're not meant to have a relationship with the guests,*' but she was having none of it. 'I'm not a guest,' she kept telling me. 'I've never slept a night here in my life.' Anyway,' he smiled happily, 'she has now. She's asleep in my bed.' He laughed. 'My lovely Nancy is asleep in my bed and I am very happy about it and nothing you can do will change my mind.'

'I don't want to,' she told him. 'I said so last night. I think it's brilliant. You know I do.'

'She would like to stay. Decide what she wants to do. Perhaps she might find a job, somewhere nearby. Perhaps you might like the two of us to run Can Falco together, give you some proper time away? You know what Ibiza does to people, how it grabs hold of them and they never leave?' He nodded. 'I think that must be happening to Nancy. And Tora — ' His eyes widened, 'Tora loves her. Nancy's been to every one of her classes. Apart from the Barely Yoga. Nancy says she must wait for you before she does that class

361

again, but she's doing all the others, can you believe it?'

'Never,' Honey insisted. 'Everything else you've told me sounds absolutely believable, but don't tell me Nancy will ever do another Barely Yoga class.'

She could hear a car making its way up the drive towards Can Falco and she spun around.

'Claudio,' she said quickly, ' . . . even though I'm back, and of course I'll be around to help you out tonight, would you mind if I kept today free?'

'Honey!' he exclaimed, outraged. 'I would mind if you didn't. Please, you must take four days off, even if you don't leave the island at all.'

'Four days?'

'I mean *any* number of days, as many as you want. Four was just the first number that came into my head. Because you see Honey, how I can cope when you're not here? You see that Can Falco is not a smouldering ruin, it's still standing, even without you here to prop it up?'

'Yes, it's great to see.' Just how great he wasn't yet to know.

Now the car was pulling up outside Can Falco and immediately she left Claudio and ran towards the door thinking that it had to be Edouard, even though logically she knew that it couldn't be — he had an old jeep that certainly didn't sound like that.

It was a taxi, pulling up in a cloud of dust, the doors opening even before it had come to a halt and she stopped shocked to a standstill to see it was Julia and Nat who were climbing out.

'We had to come!' Julia cried. As soon as she was free of the car she started running towards Honey. 'When we heard where she was and what she'd done. We caught the first flight this morning. Are we too late? What's happened?'

'She's fine. She's here. Everything's good, everybody knows everything, and we've all survived!'

Then Nat came around from the other side of the taxi, didn't need to say anything, just enveloped her in a huge hug. 'Thank God, you found her.'

'Thank God Honey hasn't killed her, you mean,' Julia corrected him.

'No. I haven't killed her. You must come and see her,' Honey told them, laughing. 'She's in my cottage, she's still in bed.' A bemused Claudio had come out to take their bags and Honey turned back to him, still laughing. 'I'm not sure they're moving in, Claudio. I don't know if we have any room.' She looked to Nat and Julia. 'Are you staying?' she asked them.

'Do you want to stay?'

Claudio shook his head to Honey. 'We are completely full.'

She grinned at them broadly. 'If you want to you can have my cottage, move in with Beth and catch up on all her news. I have somewhere else I can go to. Go and find Beth,' she said again. 'Let Claudio show you the way.'

And so Honey stayed at reception, where she could hear Edouard's car when it finally arrived. But then she found she couldn't do that either; couldn't stand to be inside, and so she wandered out and stood, leaning against the whitewashed wall, until finally she heard the sound of an engine, saw the dust building on the track below.

When finally his jeep pulled to a halt on the gravel outside she ran to greet him, didn't stop as he got out of the car, just ran straight into his arms.

'Thank you for bringing me back,' she told him. 'Did I say that last night?'

'No.' He laughed.

'Did I say anything at all? There were so many things I wanted to say.'

He dropped his head and kissed her and she closed her eyes and kissed him back. 'Like what?'

'Like take me away, now, without telling

anybody where we are going, just take me away.'

'You realize we've still got a date to go on?'

'Santa Medea?'

'Of course.'

She turned briefly back to Can Falco. Through the windows she could see Nat and Julia making their way down the pathways towards her cottage. She knew that any moment Beth would open the door to them. She knew that back in Angel's Wings, Hughie and Tora were waking up to a new day, and she saw — finally — that they would and could all get on just fine without her; all of them apart from Edouard, and that the only place she needed and wanted to be was with him.

She ran around to the side of his jeep and jumped in. He started the engine, turned the car and then they were out on the road, twisting down to the coast, the wind in her hair.

They flew along the cliff road and then began to climb again, up through the pine forests and then down again the other side until the road narrowed and became nothing more than a bouncing, stone-covered track.

'You remember where it is?' she asked him.

'Of course I do. I told you I came here on my own, like I said I would.'

'I'm sorry.' She looked at him shamefaced. 'How could I ever have doubted you?'

'Oh, you were right to doubt.' He grinned, the wind blowing his hair back from his face, and he looked completely, wonderfully carefree. 'I deserved every doubt.'

'But Belle told me you were never so keen on Pure as you made out.'

'A grotty club in San Antonio is being demolished to make way for it. I've been very keen on Pure. And I spoke to Paul again this morning. He's delighted, I've saved him a fortune.'

'Oh great that we've made life so easy for him!' She laughed. 'At least he lost Nancy.' She took his hand. 'Do you think we can lose that tacky pink glass from the front door of your house?'

'But then I won't be able to look through it to see when you're coming.'

'Then I'll stay with you, safe inside, and you'll know just where I am. How about it? I do need somewhere to stay for the next few nights. Would you mind?'

'Stay for ever.' He looked back at her. 'Not just in El Figo but all over the world. Come with me, let's run away and explore.'

'I want to build a hotel on the Perfume River.'

He laughed. 'Then we'll do it.'

He tucked the jeep up against the side of the track and turned off the engine, then lifted their picnic from the back seat and led her by the hand, carefully, slowly, down a sand-covered path to where the ground opened out onto a little clearing and the cliffs dropped away below to the sea. This was where the cliff jumpers came, she'd told Belle, the daredevil ones who liked to leap forty or fifty feet down into the sea. As teenagers she and Edouard used to come by dinghy, to sit in the water and watch them.

Sheltered from the wind, he spread their blanket out on the sand.

'I stole it,' he admitted. 'You didn't notice, did you, how it never came back with you from Es Palmador? It's been on my bed ever since. But today I thought it should come for the picnic and give us something soft to lie on.'

In answer she came forwards, grabbed hold of him and kissed him hard on the mouth and in answer he dropped the picnic basket and crushed her into his arms, falling with her back to the ground, to pin her down on the rug and stare down into her face.

'Shall we do it?' he whispered and she looked back at him with bright eyes, understanding immediately.

'Do you dare?'

'I've always been too scared.'

'Not with me.'

'No, not with you. Let's do it.'

'Will we die?' she asked, stepping out of her shoes, while still tightly gripping his hand.

'I don't think so.' He had to let go of her to pull off his T-shirt.

'Kiss me again in case we do,' she told him, laughing and terrified at the same time. 'It would be such a bad ending otherwise.'

They kissed hurriedly, laughing with fear, finding it unbearable to let each other go and yet at the same time knowing that to jump would be their perfect ending and their perfect beginning, daring each other on.

'Shall we do it?' Edouard asked again.

'Yes.'

'Shall we run, or shall we go to the edge and look first?'

'We must run.'

'Ok. We must run.'

'Kiss me again.'

He kissed her again, clashing his teeth against hers and she kissed him back, scratching her fingers down his back, tangling his hair in her hands. And then they broke free from each other once more, and this time they ran, hands held fast, and with a shout of exultation leaped off the cliff and high out above the sea.

We do hope that you have enjoyed reading this large print book.

Did you know that all of our titles are available for purchase?

We publish a wide range of high quality large print books including:
Romances, Mysteries, Classics
General Fiction
Non Fiction and Westerns

Special interest titles available in large print are:
The Little Oxford Dictionary
Music Book
Song Book
Hymn Book
Service Book

Also available from us courtesy of Oxford University Press:
Young Readers' Dictionary
(large print edition)
Young Readers' Thesaurus
(large print edition)

For further information or a free brochure, please contact us at:
Ulverscroft Large Print Books Ltd.,
The Green, Bradgate Road, Anstey,
Leicester, LE7 7FU, England.
Tel: (00 44) 0116 236 4325
Fax: (00 44) 0116 234 0205

LUCY BLUE, WHERE ARE YOU?

Louise Harwood

Lucy Blue is not the sort of girl to pick up a stranger in a snow-bound airport and she's certainly not the sort to then leap into bed with him in a motorway motel . . . Yet this is a strange, once-in-a-lifetime day, and in any case nobody will know and they'll never meet again . . . But actions can catch up with you and secrets have a way of being told, and a spectacular gesture means that this time Lucy just can't walk away.

CALLING ON LILY

Louise Harwood

What do you do if your best friend is about to marry the wrong girl? Buy the matching bathrobes and keep your mouth shut? Or kidnap the groom on his stag night and hold him in a remote cottage in the Welsh borders until the wedding day has safely passed? Hal's friends know what they want to do, but they haven't reckoned on being overheard by Lily — who has already witnessed the devastation of her sister's wedding day, and is going to do anything she can to save this one — and Kirsty, Lily's friend, initially more interested in pulling the groom, but swift to take up the challenge.

THE LIFE OF REILLY

Paul Burke

Sean Reilly seems to have his life sorted: gorgeous wife, beautiful house and lucrative career as a voice-over artist. But he craves the sort of romance and affection that he no longer receives from his wife. Why is it, he wonders, that once married, women want men to change? Whereas men hate it when women change. Lucy Ross, 'caught single' after breaking up with her long-term boyfriend, is also looking for romance when she meets Sean. She doesn't want him to change; she wants him the way he is. So could the life of Reilly be sorted after all?